PLANTS VS. ZOMBIES™

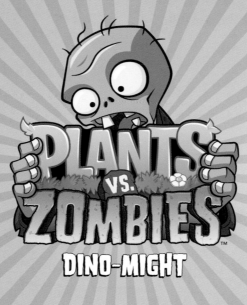

DINO-MIGHT

Written by **PAUL TOBIN**
Art by **RON CHAN**
Colors by **HEATHER BRECKEL**
Letters by **STEVE DUTRO**
Cover by **RON CHAN**
Bonus Story Art by **PHILIP MURPHY**

DARK HORSE BOOKS

PLANTS VS. ZOMBIES™

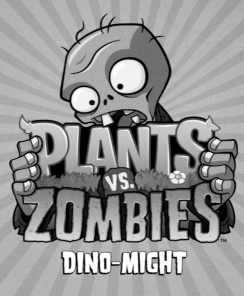

DINO-MIGHT

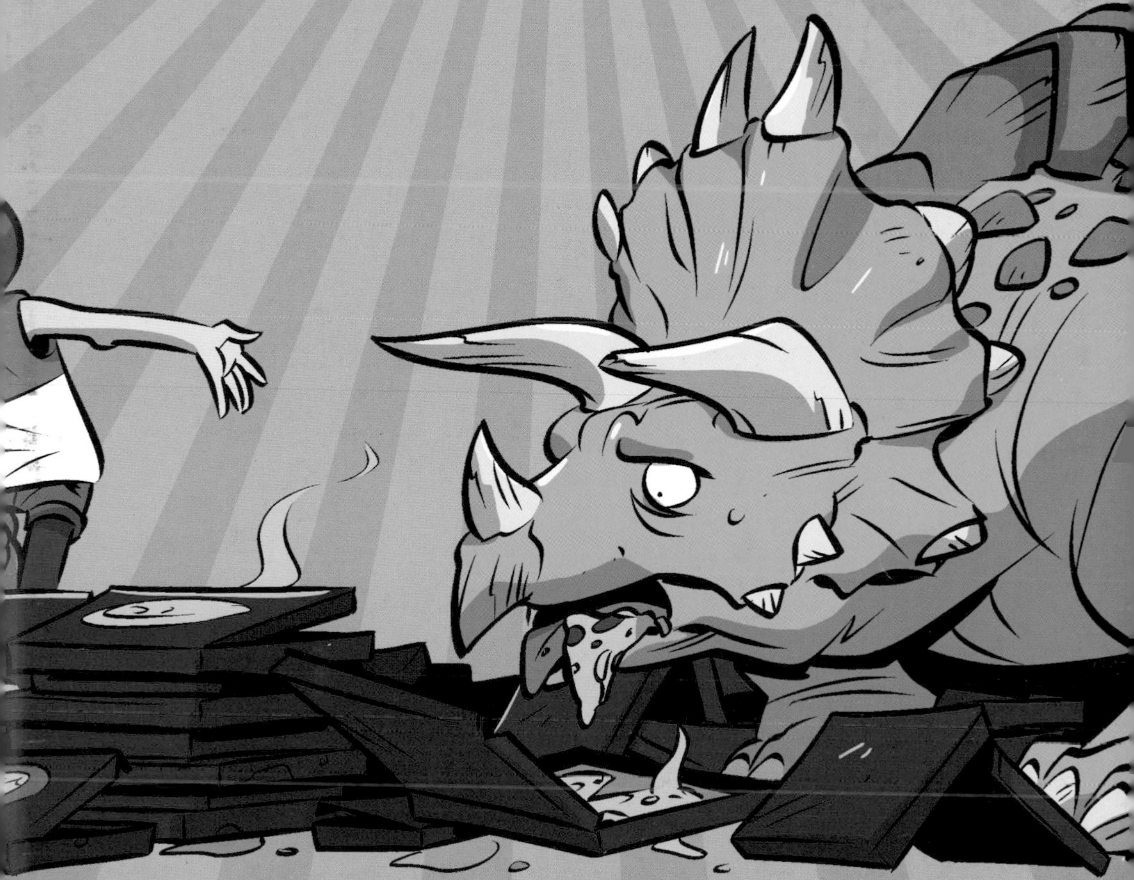

Publisher **MIKE RICHARDSON**
Senior Editor **PHILIP R. SIMON**
Associate Editor **MEGAN WALKER**
Designer **BRENNAN THOME**
Digital Art Technician **CHRISTIANNE GILLENARDO-GOUDREAU**

Special thanks to Alexandria Land, A.J. Rathbun, Kristen Star, and everyone at PopCap Games.

First Edition: February 2019
ISBN 978-1-50670-838-6

10 9 8 7 6 5 4 3
Printed in China

DarkHorse.com
PopCap.com

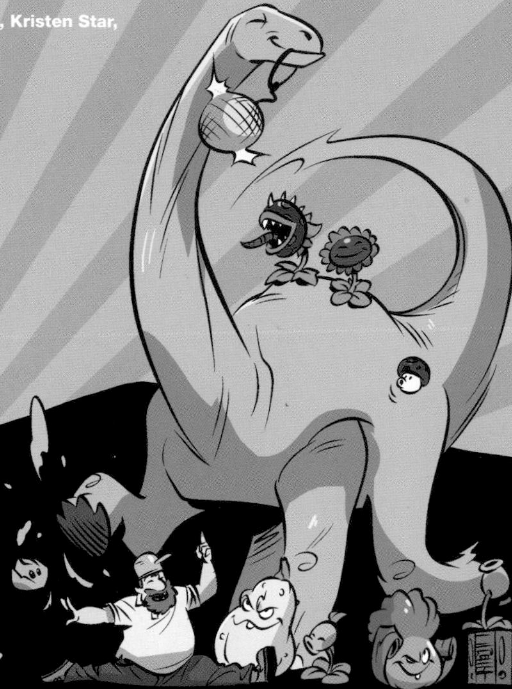

No plants, dogs, cats, hammock sloths, rabbits, or dinosaurs were harmed in the making of this graphic novel. However, one zombie did get into a scuffle with a dinosaur over the last Pop Smart and didn't win, so he ended up very hungry. Also, the editors learned that dinosaurs dont take too kindly to constructive criticism and won't be trying that again.

PLANTS vs. ZOMBIES: DINO-MIGHT | Published by Dark Horse Books, a division of Dark Horse Comics LLC, 10956 SE Main Street, Milwaukie, OR 97222 | To find a comics shop in your area, visit comicshoplocator.com |

Library of Congress Cataloging-in-Publication Data

Names: Tobin, Paul, 1965- writer. | Chan, Ron, artist. | Breckel, Heather, colourist. | Dutro, Steve, letterer. | Murphy, Phil, 1986- artist.
Title: Plants vs. zombies. Dino-might / written by Paul Tobin ; art by Ron Chan ; colors by Heather Breckel ; letters by Steve Dutro ; cover by Ron Chan ; bonus story art by Philip Murphy.
Other titles: Plants versus zombies. Dino-might | Dino-might
Description: First edition. | Milwaukie, OR : Dark Horse Books, February 2019. | Series: Plants vs. Zombies ; 12 | Summary: "When Zomboss sets his sights on destroying the yards in town, it is up to the daring duo, along with Crazy Dave and his band of plants, to thwart his plans and claim victory once again!"-- Provided by publisher.
Identifiers: LCCN 2018032933 | ISBN 9781506708386
Subjects: LCSH: Graphic novels. | CYAC: Graphic novels. | Humorous stories. | Zombies--Fiction. | Plants--Fiction.
Classification: LCC PZ7.7.T62 Pho 2019 | DDC 741.5/973--dc23
LC record available at https://lccn.loc.gov/2018032933

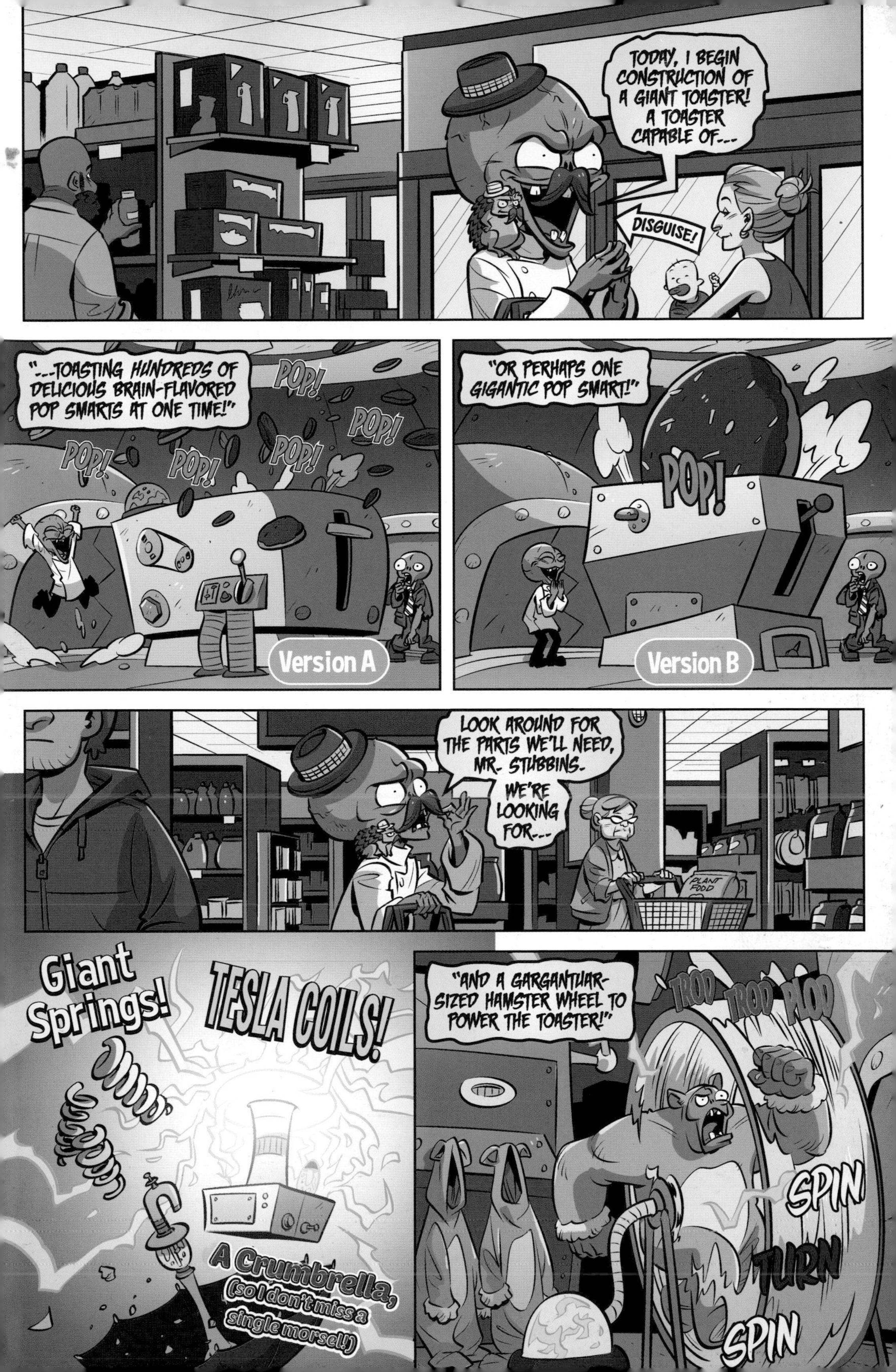
TODAY, I BEGIN CONSTRUCTION OF A GIANT TOASTER! A TOASTER CAPABLE OF...
DISGUISE!
"...TOASTING HUNDREDS OF DELICIOUS BRAIN-FLAVORED POP SMARTS AT ONE TIME!"
POP!
POP!
POP!
POP!
Version A
"OR PERHAPS ONE GIGANTIC POP SMART!"
POP!
Version B
LOOK AROUND FOR THE PARTS WE'LL NEED, MR. STUBBINS.
WE'RE LOOKING FOR...
PLANT FOOD
Giant Springs!
TESLA COILS!
A Crumbrella, (so I don't miss a single morsel!)
"AND A GARGANTUAR-SIZED HAMSTER WHEEL TO POWER THE TOASTER!"
TROD TROD PLOD
SPIN
TURN
SPIN

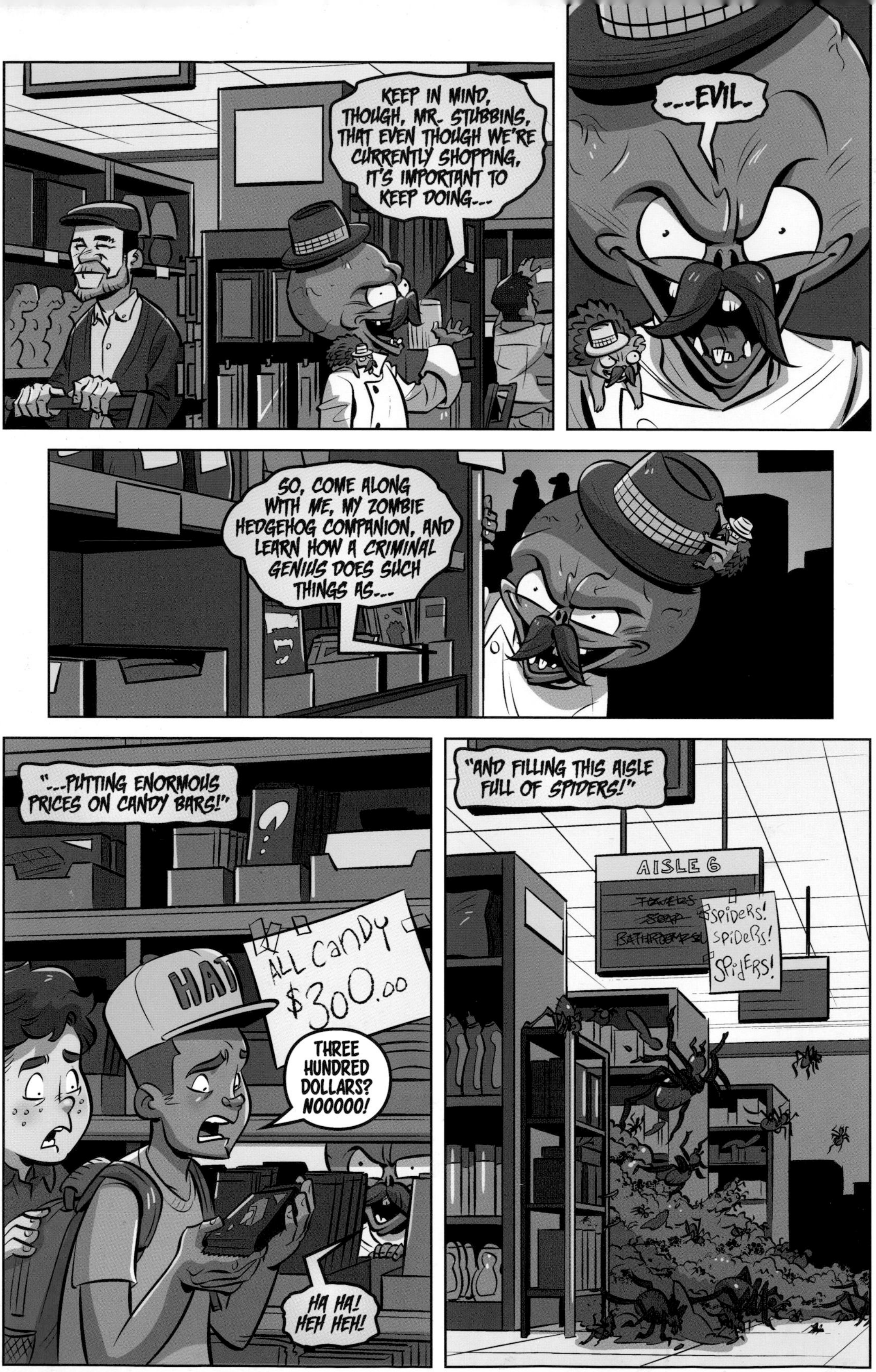
KEEP IN MIND, THOUGH, MR. STUBBINS, THAT EVEN THOUGH WE'RE CURRENTLY SHOPPING, IT'S IMPORTANT TO KEEP DOING...
...EVIL.
SO, COME ALONG WITH ME, MY ZOMBIE HEDGEHOG COMPANION, AND LEARN HOW A CRIMINAL GENIUS DOES SUCH THINGS AS...
"...PUTTING ENORMOUS PRICES ON CANDY BARS!"
HAT
ALL CANDY $300.00
THREE HUNDRED DOLLARS? NOOOOO!
HA HA! HEH HEH!
"AND FILLING THIS AISLE FULL OF SPIDERS!"
AISLE 6
SPIDERS! SPIDERS! SPIDERS!

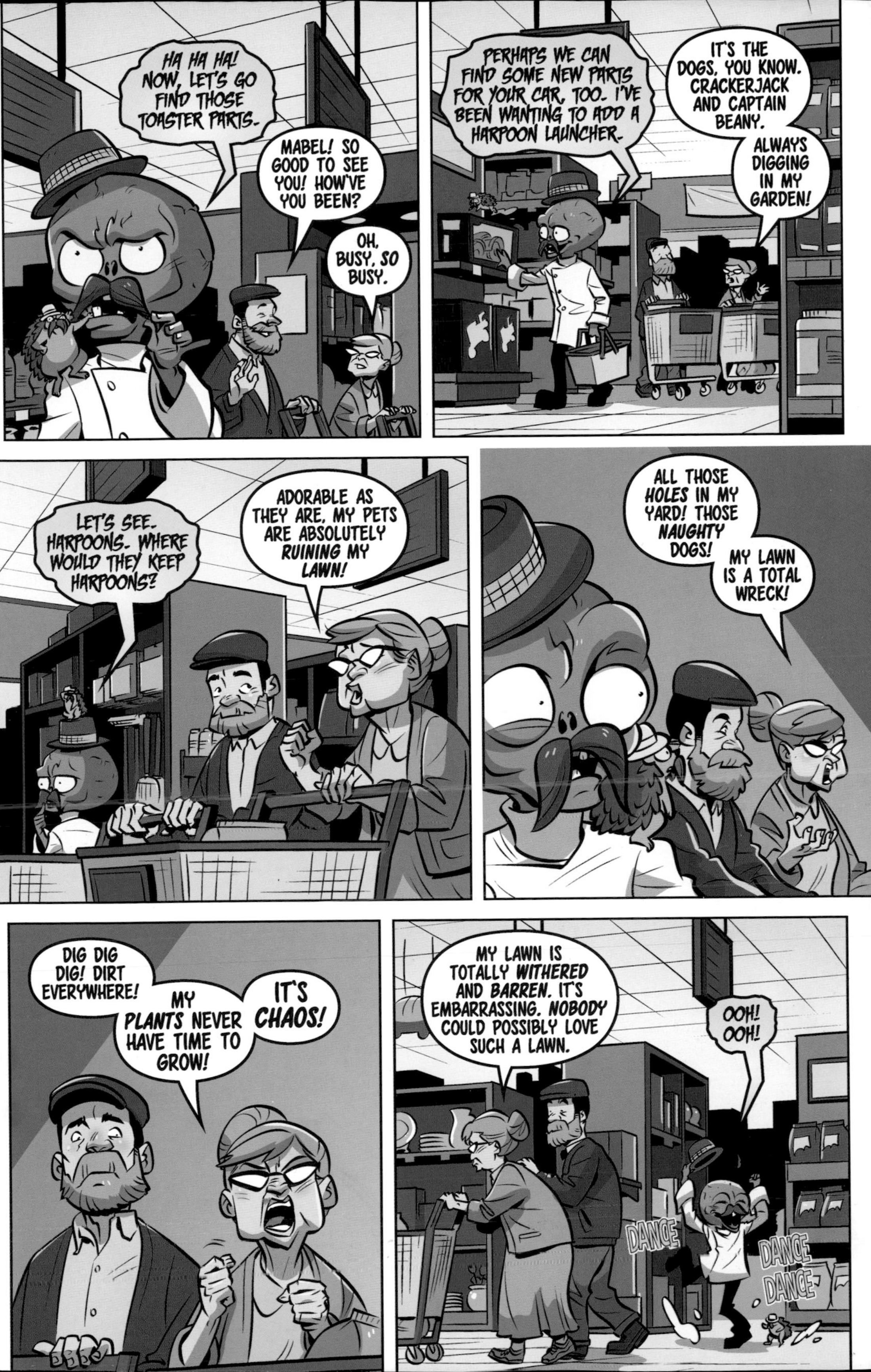

HA HA HA! NOW, LET'S GO FIND THOSE TOASTER PARTS.
MABEL! SO GOOD TO SEE YOU! HOW'VE YOU BEEN?
OH, BUSY, SO BUSY.
PERHAPS WE CAN FIND SOME NEW PARTS FOR YOUR CAR, TOO. I'VE BEEN WANTING TO ADD A HARPOON LAUNCHER.
IT'S THE DOGS, YOU KNOW. CRACKERJACK AND CAPTAIN BEANY.
ALWAYS DIGGING IN MY GARDEN!
LET'S SEE. HARPOONS. WHERE WOULD THEY KEEP HARPOONS?
ADORABLE AS THEY ARE, MY PETS ARE ABSOLUTELY RUINING MY LAWN!
ALL THOSE HOLES IN MY YARD! THOSE NAUGHTY DOGS!
MY LAWN IS A TOTAL WRECK!
DIG DIG DIG! DIRT EVERYWHERE!
MY PLANTS NEVER HAVE TIME TO GROW!
IT'S CHAOS!
MY LAWN IS TOTALLY WITHERED AND BARREN. IT'S EMBARRASSING. NOBODY COULD POSSIBLY LOVE SUCH A LAWN.
OOH! OOH!
DANCE
DANCE
DANCE

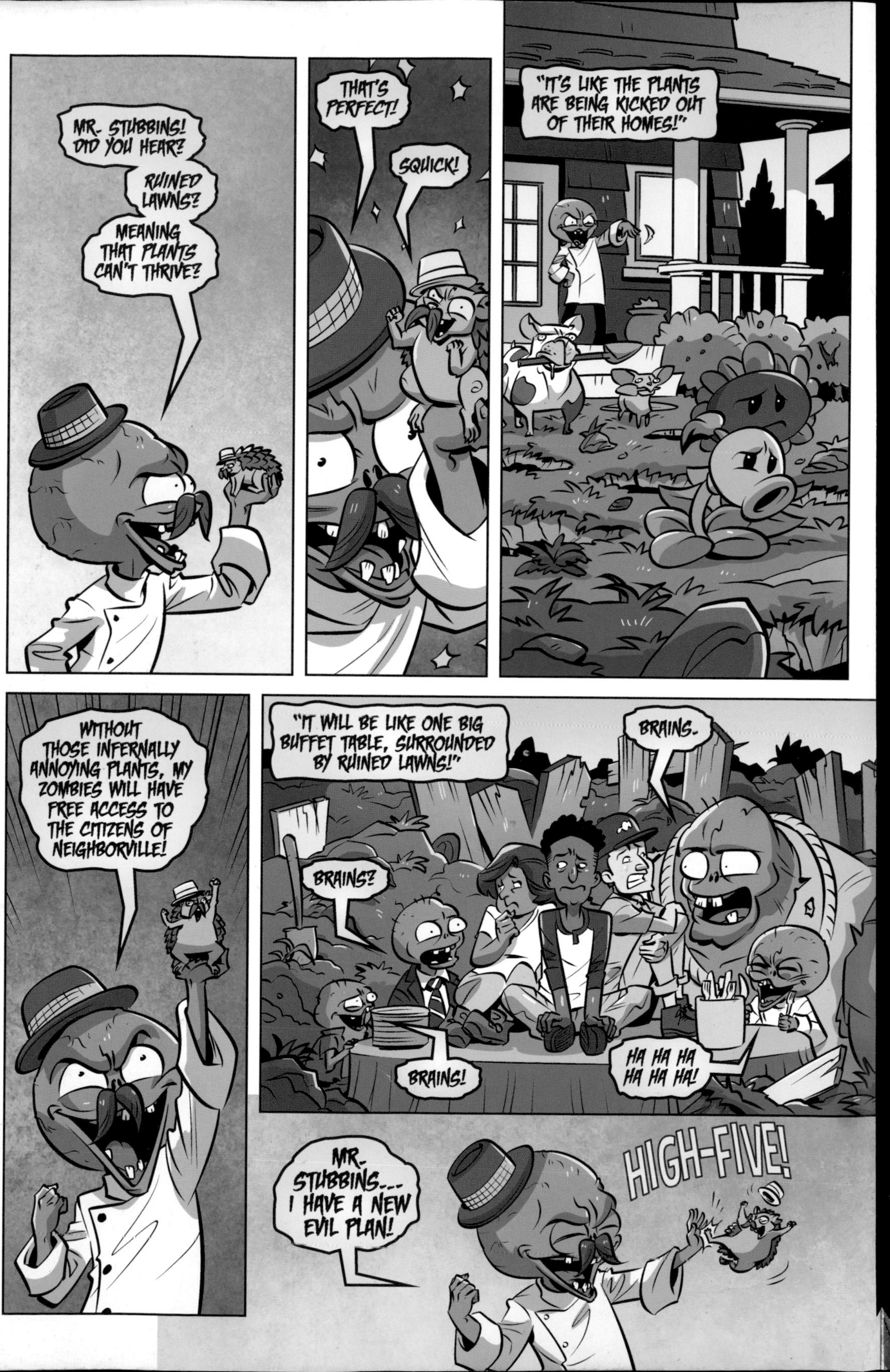
MR. STUBBINS! DID YOU HEAR?
RUINED LAWNS?
MEANING THAT PLANTS CAN'T THRIVE?
THAT'S PERFECT!
SQUICK!
"IT'S LIKE THE PLANTS ARE BEING KICKED OUT OF THEIR HOMES!"
WITHOUT THOSE INFERNALLY ANNOYING PLANTS, MY ZOMBIES WILL HAVE FREE ACCESS TO THE CITIZENS OF NEIGHBORVILLE!
"IT WILL BE LIKE ONE BIG BUFFET TABLE, SURROUNDED BY RUINED LAWNS!"
BRAINS.
BRAINS?
BRAINS!
HA HA HA HA HA HA!
MR. STUBBINS... I HAVE A NEW EVIL PLAN!
HIGH-FIVE!

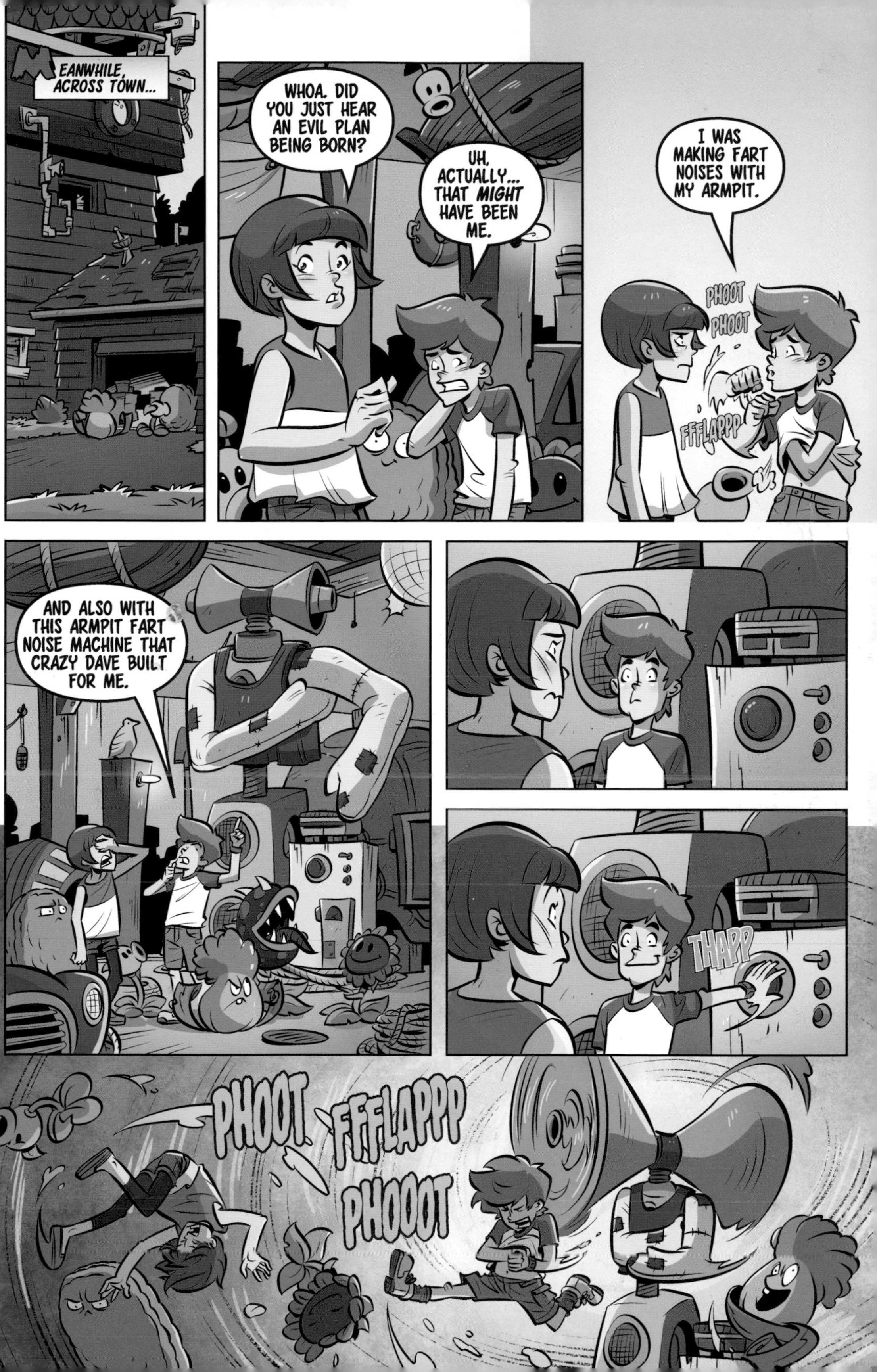
MEANWHILE, ACROSS TOWN...
WHOA. DID YOU JUST HEAR AN EVIL PLAN BEING BORN?
UH, ACTUALLY... THAT MIGHT HAVE BEEN ME.
I WAS MAKING FART NOISES WITH MY ARMPIT.
PHOOT
PHOOT
FFFLAPPP
AND ALSO WITH THIS ARMPIT FART NOISE MACHINE THAT CRAZY DAVE BUILT FOR ME.
THAPP
PHOOT
FFFLAPPP
PHOOOT

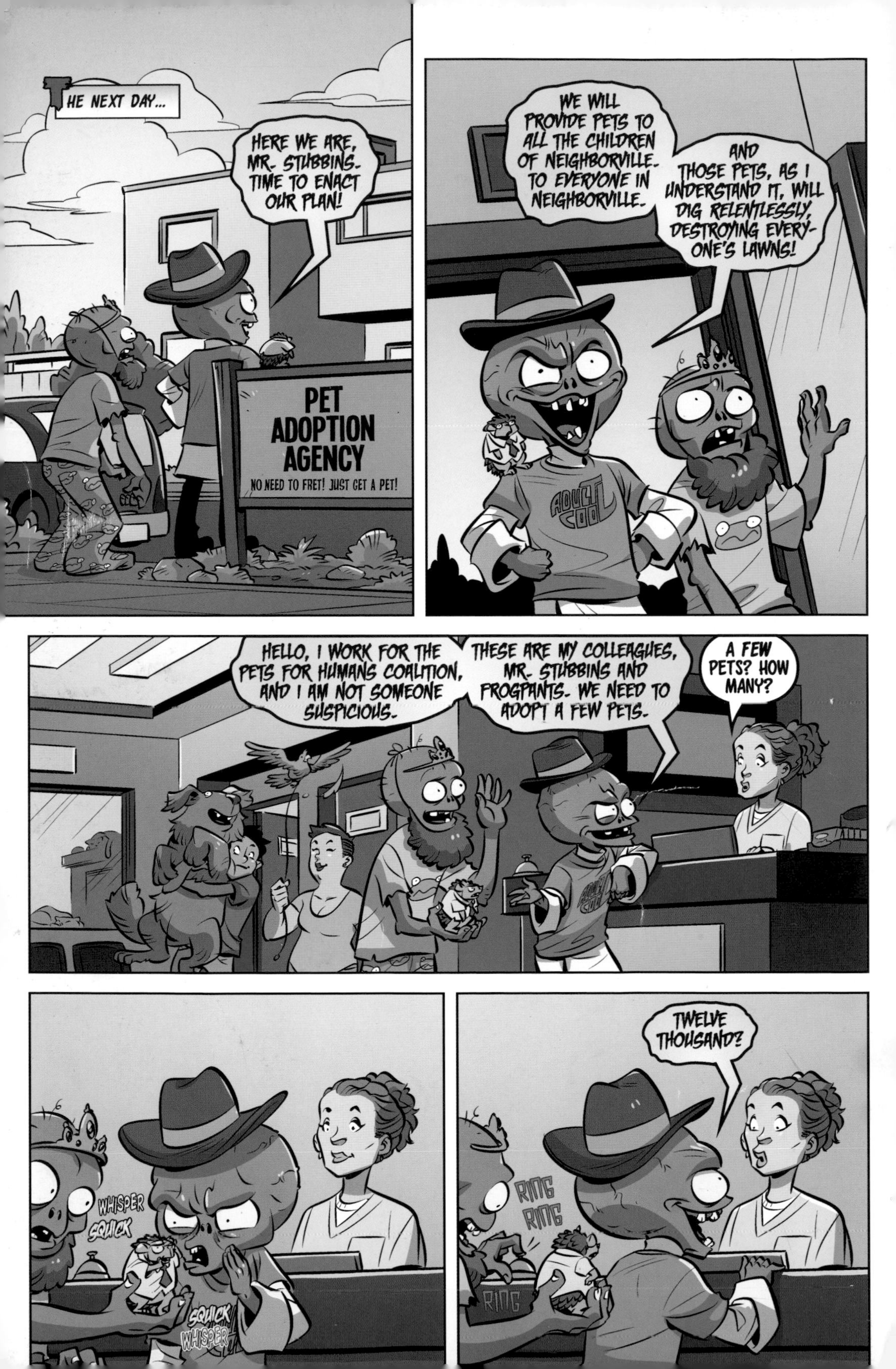
THE NEXT DAY...
HERE WE ARE, MR. STUBBINS. TIME TO ENACT OUR PLAN!
PET ADOPTION AGENCY
NO NEED TO FRET! JUST GET A PET!
WE WILL PROVIDE PETS TO ALL THE CHILDREN OF NEIGHBORVILLE. TO EVERYONE IN NEIGHBORVILLE.
AND THOSE PETS, AS I UNDERSTAND IT, WILL DIG RELENTLESSLY, DESTROYING EVERY-ONE'S LAWNS!
HELLO, I WORK FOR THE PETS FOR HUMANS COALITION, AND I AM NOT SOMEONE SUSPICIOUS.
THESE ARE MY COLLEAGUES, MR. STUBBINS AND FROGPANTS. WE NEED TO ADOPT A FEW PETS.
A FEW PETS? HOW MANY?
WHISPER
SQUICK
SQUICK
WHISPER
TWELVE THOUSAND?
RING
RING
RING

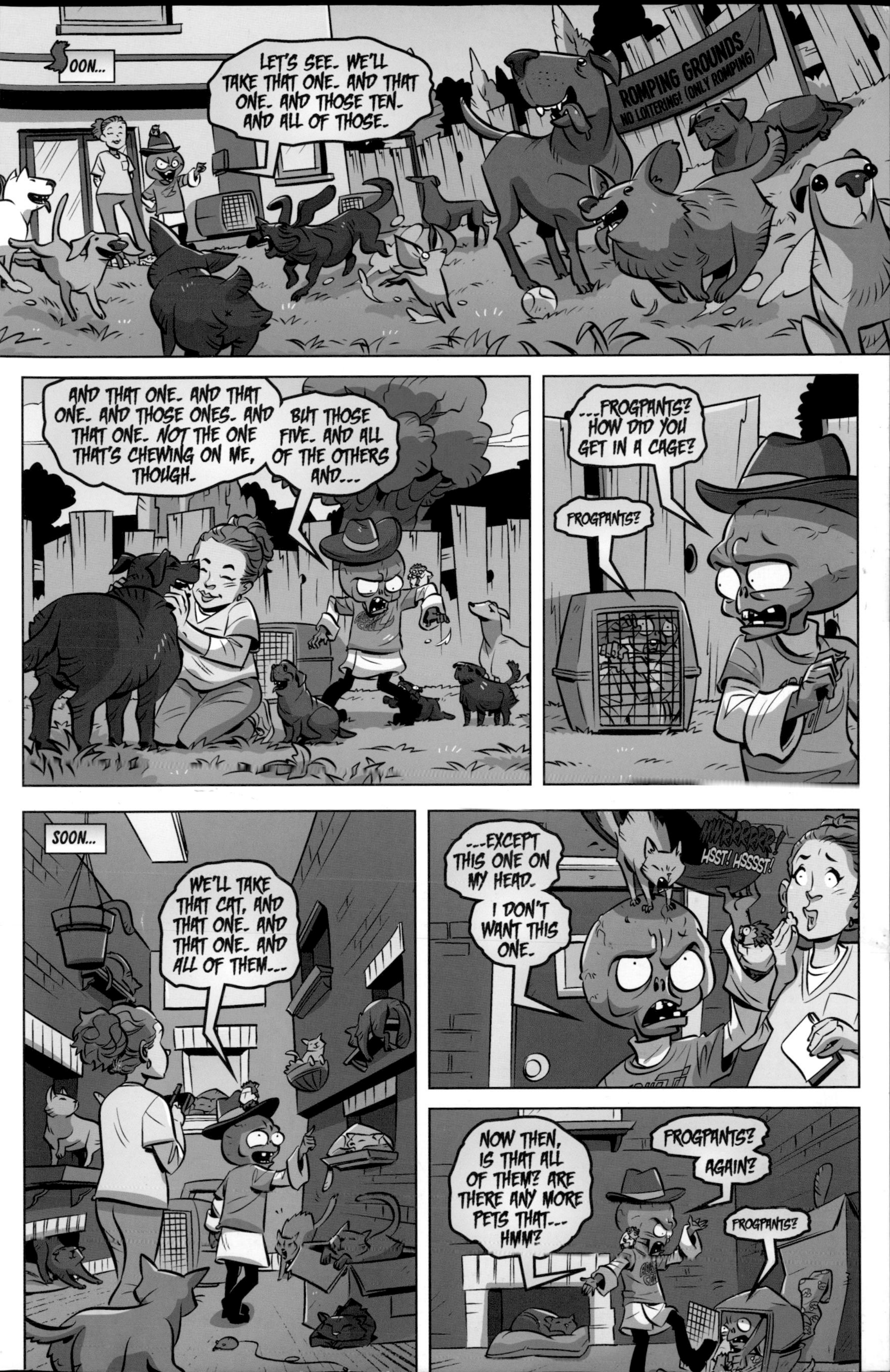
SOON...
LET'S SEE. WE'LL TAKE THAT ONE. AND THAT ONE. AND THOSE TEN. AND ALL OF THOSE.
ROMPING GROUNDS
NO LOITERING! (ONLY ROMPING)
AND THAT ONE. AND THAT ONE. AND THOSE ONES. AND THAT ONE. NOT THE ONE THAT'S CHEWING ON ME, THOUGH.
BUT THOSE FIVE. AND ALL OF THE OTHERS AND...
...FROGPANTS? HOW DID YOU GET IN A CAGE?
FROGPANTS?
SOON...
WE'LL TAKE THAT CAT, AND THAT ONE. AND THAT ONE. AND ALL OF THEM...
...EXCEPT THIS ONE ON MY HEAD.
I DON'T WANT THIS ONE.
HSST! HSSSST!
NOW THEN, IS THAT ALL OF THEM? ARE THERE ANY MORE PETS THAT... HMM?
FROGPANTS?
AGAIN?
FROGPANTS?

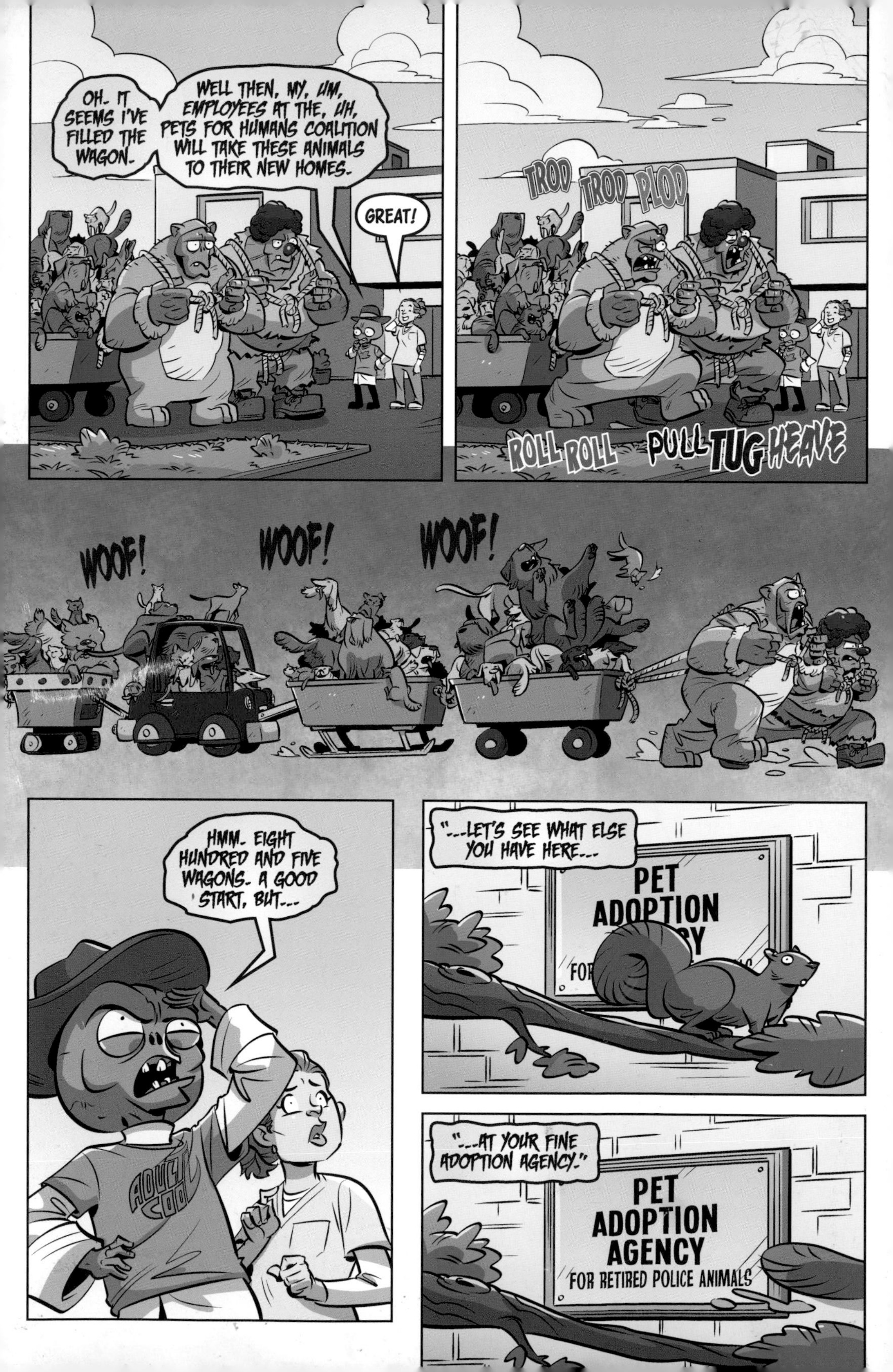

OH. IT SEEMS I'VE FILLED THE WAGON.
WELL THEN, MY, UM, EMPLOYEES AT THE, UH, PETS FOR HUMANS COALITION WILL TAKE THESE ANIMALS TO THEIR NEW HOMES.
GREAT!
TROD TROD PLOD
ROLL ROLL PULL TUG HEAVE
WOOF! WOOF! WOOF!
HMM. EIGHT HUNDRED AND FIVE WAGONS. A GOOD START, BUT...
"...LET'S SEE WHAT ELSE YOU HAVE HERE...
PET ADOPTION
"...AT YOUR FINE ADOPTION AGENCY."
PET ADOPTION AGENCY FOR RETIRED POLICE ANIMALS

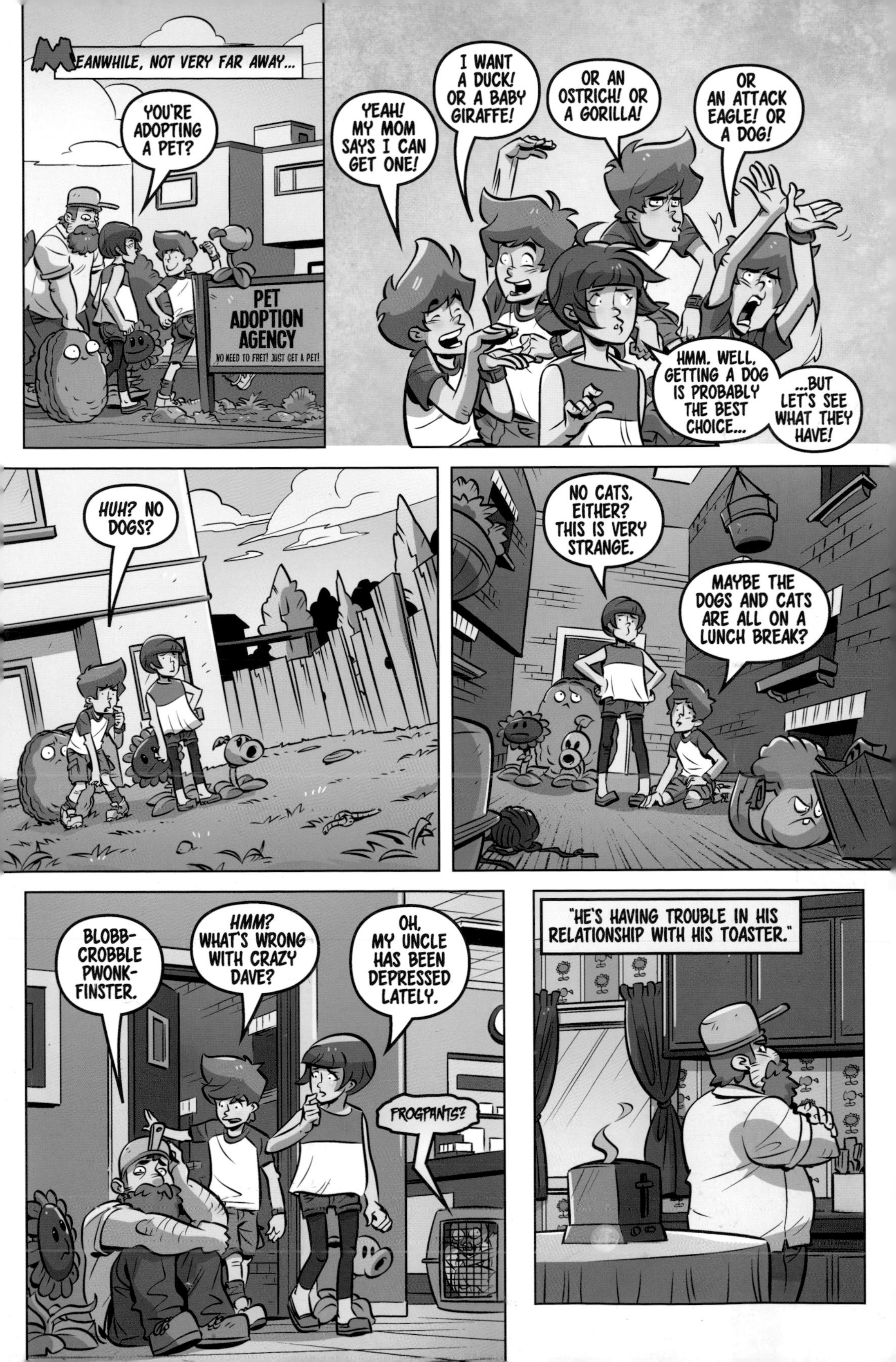
MEANWHILE, NOT VERY FAR AWAY...
YOU'RE ADOPTING A PET?
PET ADOPTION AGENCY
NO NEED TO FRET! JUST GET A PET!
YEAH! MY MOM SAYS I CAN GET ONE!
I WANT A DUCK! OR A BABY GIRAFFE!
OR AN OSTRICH! OR A GORILLA!
OR AN ATTACK EAGLE! OR A DOG!
HMM. WELL, GETTING A DOG IS PROBABLY THE BEST CHOICE...
...BUT LET'S SEE WHAT THEY HAVE!
HUH? NO DOGS?
NO CATS, EITHER? THIS IS VERY STRANGE.
MAYBE THE DOGS AND CATS ARE ALL ON A LUNCH BREAK?
BLOBB-CROBBLE PWONK-FINSTER.
HMM? WHAT'S WRONG WITH CRAZY DAVE?
OH, MY UNCLE HAS BEEN DEPRESSED LATELY.
FROGPANTS?
"HE'S HAVING TROUBLE IN HIS RELATIONSHIP WITH HIS TOASTER."

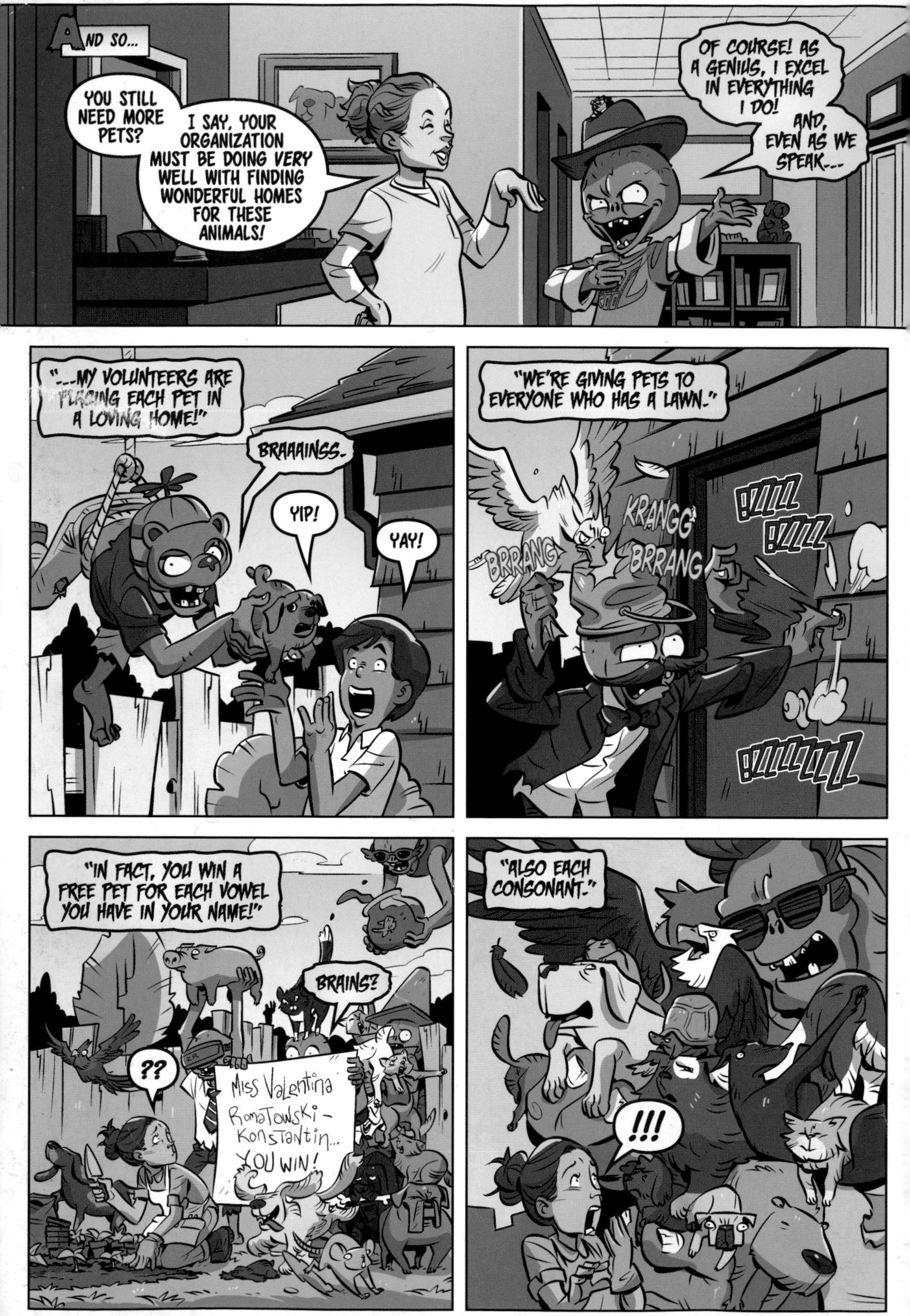
AND SO...
YOU STILL NEED MORE PETS?
I SAY, YOUR ORGANIZATION MUST BE DOING VERY WELL WITH FINDING WONDERFUL HOMES FOR THESE ANIMALS!
OF COURSE! AS A GENIUS, I EXCEL IN EVERYTHING I DO!
AND, EVEN AS WE SPEAK...
"...MY VOLUNTEERS ARE PLACING EACH PET IN A LOVING HOME!"
BRAAAINSS.
YIP!
YAY!
"WE'RE GIVING PETS TO EVERYONE WHO HAS A LAWN."
KRANGG
BRRANG
BRRANG
BZZZZ
BZZZZ
BZZZZZZZZ
"IN FACT, YOU WIN A FREE PET FOR EACH VOWEL YOU HAVE IN YOUR NAME!"
BRAINS?
??
Miss Valentina Romatowski-Konstantin... YOU WIN!
"ALSO EACH CONSONANT."
!!!

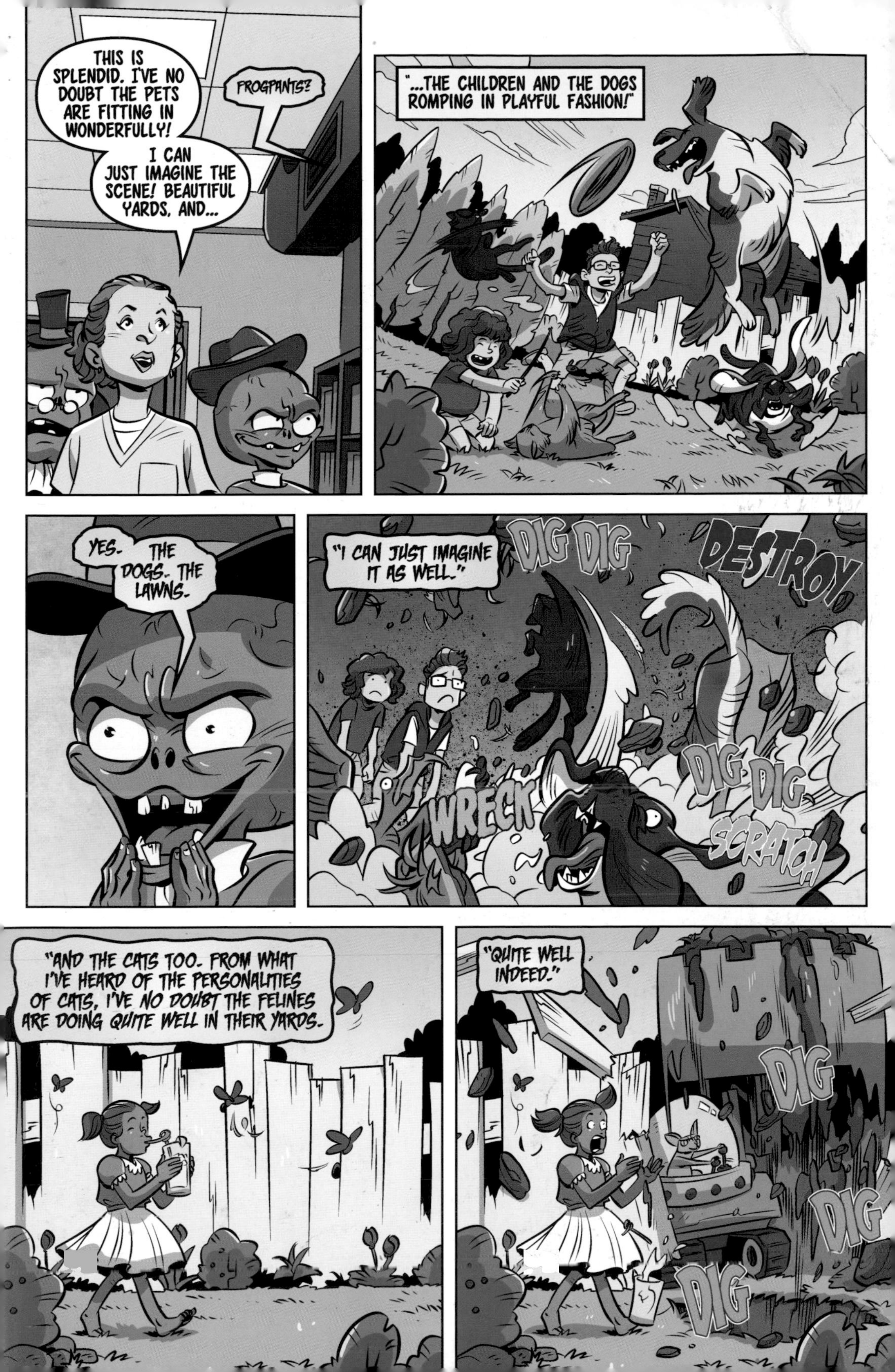
THIS IS SPLENDID. I'VE NO DOUBT THE PETS ARE FITTING IN WONDERFULLY!
I CAN JUST IMAGINE THE SCENE! BEAUTIFUL YARDS, AND...
FROGPANTS?
"...THE CHILDREN AND THE DOGS ROMPING IN PLAYFUL FASHION!"
YES.
THE DOGS. THE LAWNS.
"I CAN JUST IMAGINE IT AS WELL."
DIG DIG
DESTROY
WRECK
DIG DIG
SCRATCH
"AND THE CATS TOO. FROM WHAT I'VE HEARD OF THE PERSONALITIES OF CATS, I'VE NO DOUBT THE FELINES ARE DOING QUITE WELL IN THEIR YARDS.
"QUITE WELL INDEED."
DIG
DIG
DIG

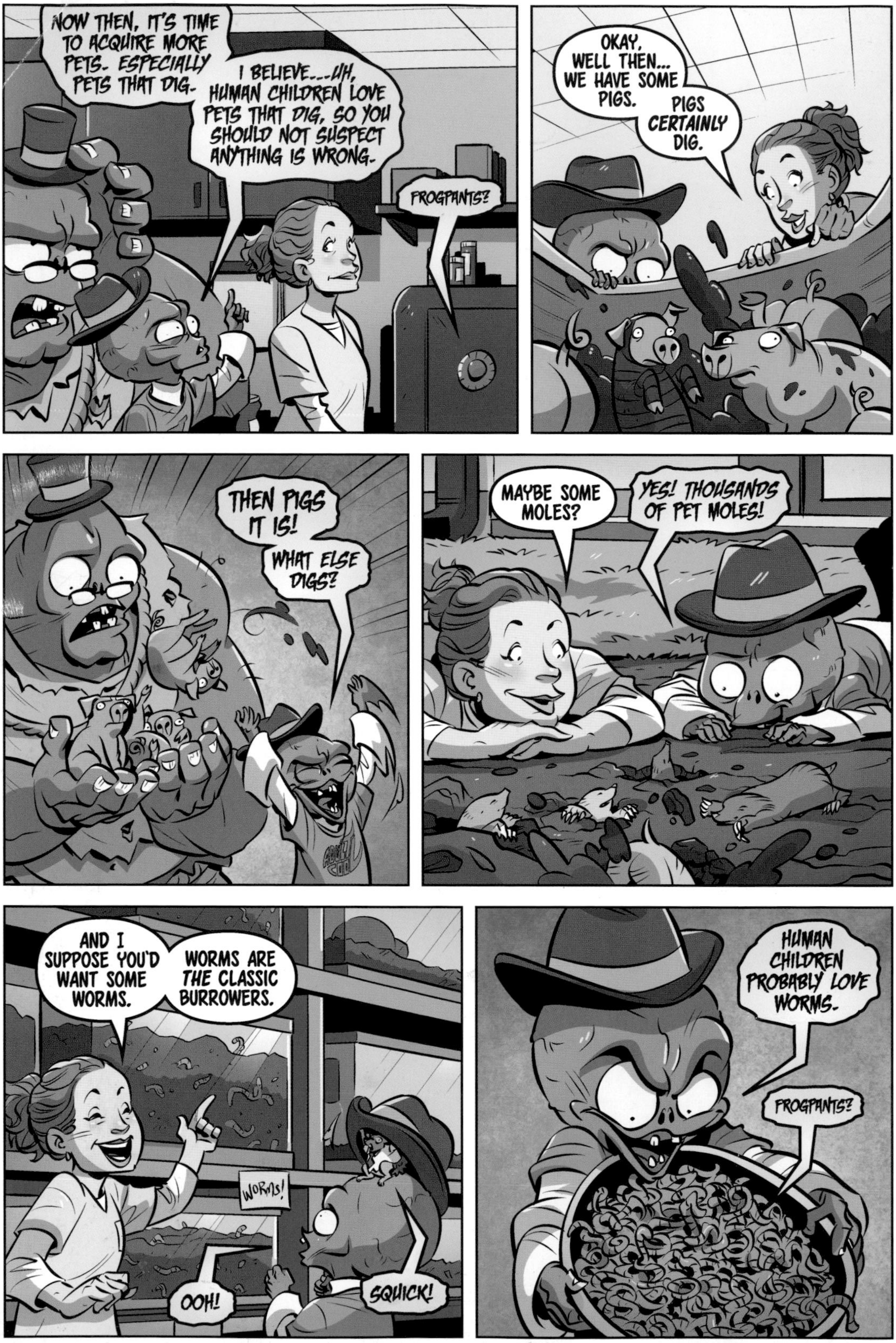
NOW THEN, IT'S TIME TO ACQUIRE MORE PETS. ESPECIALLY PETS THAT DIG.
I BELIEVE...UH, HUMAN CHILDREN LOVE PETS THAT DIG, SO YOU SHOULD NOT SUSPECT ANYTHING IS WRONG.
FROGPANTS?
OKAY, WELL THEN... WE HAVE SOME PIGS.
PIGS CERTAINLY DIG.
THEN PIGS IT IS!
WHAT ELSE DIGS?
MAYBE SOME MOLES?
YES! THOUSANDS OF PET MOLES!
AND I SUPPOSE YOU'D WANT SOME WORMS.
WORMS ARE THE CLASSIC BURROWERS.
WORMS!
OOH!
SQUICK!
HUMAN CHILDREN PROBABLY LOVE WORMS.
FROGPANTS?

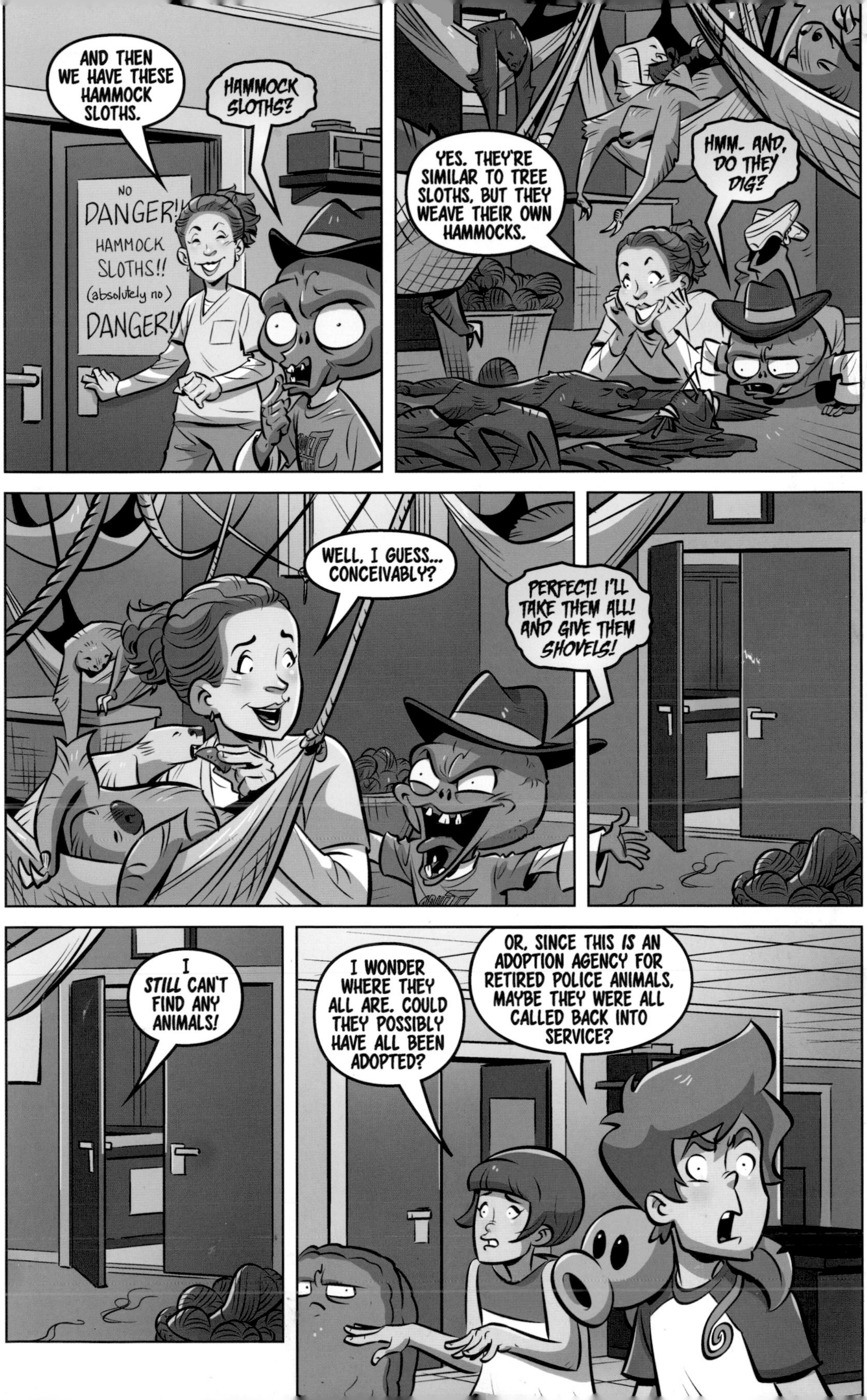

AND THEN WE HAVE THESE HAMMOCK SLOTHS.
HAMMOCK SLOTHS?
NO DANGER!! HAMMOCK SLOTHS!! (absolutely no) DANGER!!
YES. THEY'RE SIMILAR TO TREE SLOTHS, BUT THEY WEAVE THEIR OWN HAMMOCKS.
HMM. AND, DO THEY DIG?
WELL, I GUESS... CONCEIVABLY?
PERFECT! I'LL TAKE THEM ALL! AND GIVE THEM SHOVELS!
I STILL CAN'T FIND ANY ANIMALS!
I WONDER WHERE THEY ALL ARE. COULD THEY POSSIBLY HAVE ALL BEEN ADOPTED?
OR, SINCE THIS IS AN ADOPTION AGENCY FOR RETIRED POLICE ANIMALS, MAYBE THEY WERE ALL CALLED BACK INTO SERVICE?

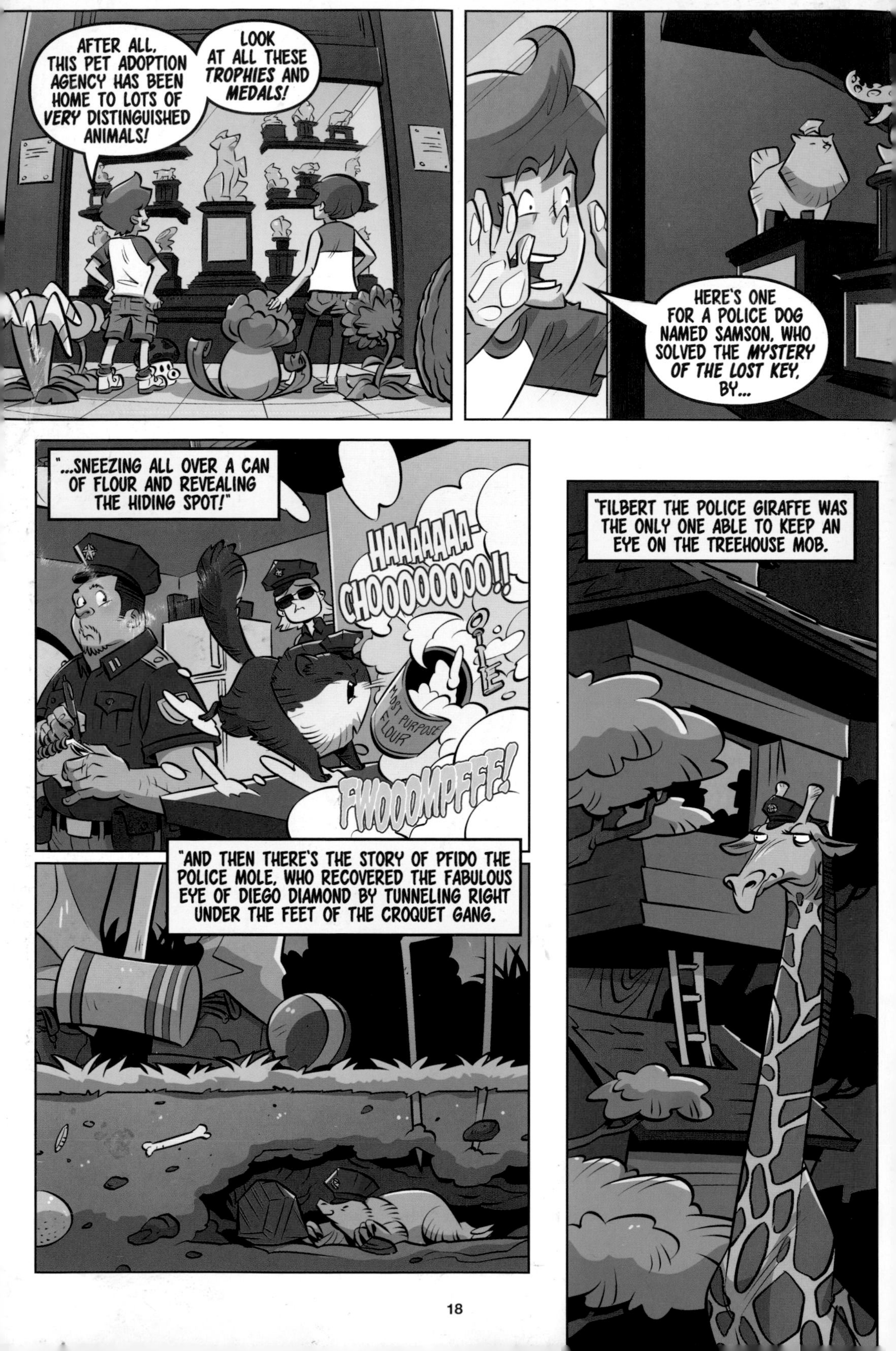
AFTER ALL, THIS PET ADOPTION AGENCY HAS BEEN HOME TO LOTS OF *VERY* DISTINGUISHED ANIMALS!
LOOK AT ALL THESE *TROPHIES* AND *MEDALS!*
HERE'S ONE FOR A POLICE DOG NAMED SAMSON, WHO SOLVED THE *MYSTERY OF THE LOST KEY,* BY...
"...SNEEZING ALL OVER A CAN OF FLOUR AND REVEALING THE HIDING SPOT!"
HAAAAAAA-CHOOOOOOOO!!
MOST PURPOSE FLOUR
FWOOOMPFFF!
"FILBERT THE POLICE GIRAFFE WAS THE ONLY ONE ABLE TO KEEP AN EYE ON THE TREEHOUSE MOB.
"AND THEN THERE'S THE STORY OF PFIDO THE POLICE MOLE, WHO RECOVERED THE FABULOUS EYE OF DIEGO DIAMOND BY TUNNELING RIGHT UNDER THE FEET OF THE CROQUET GANG.

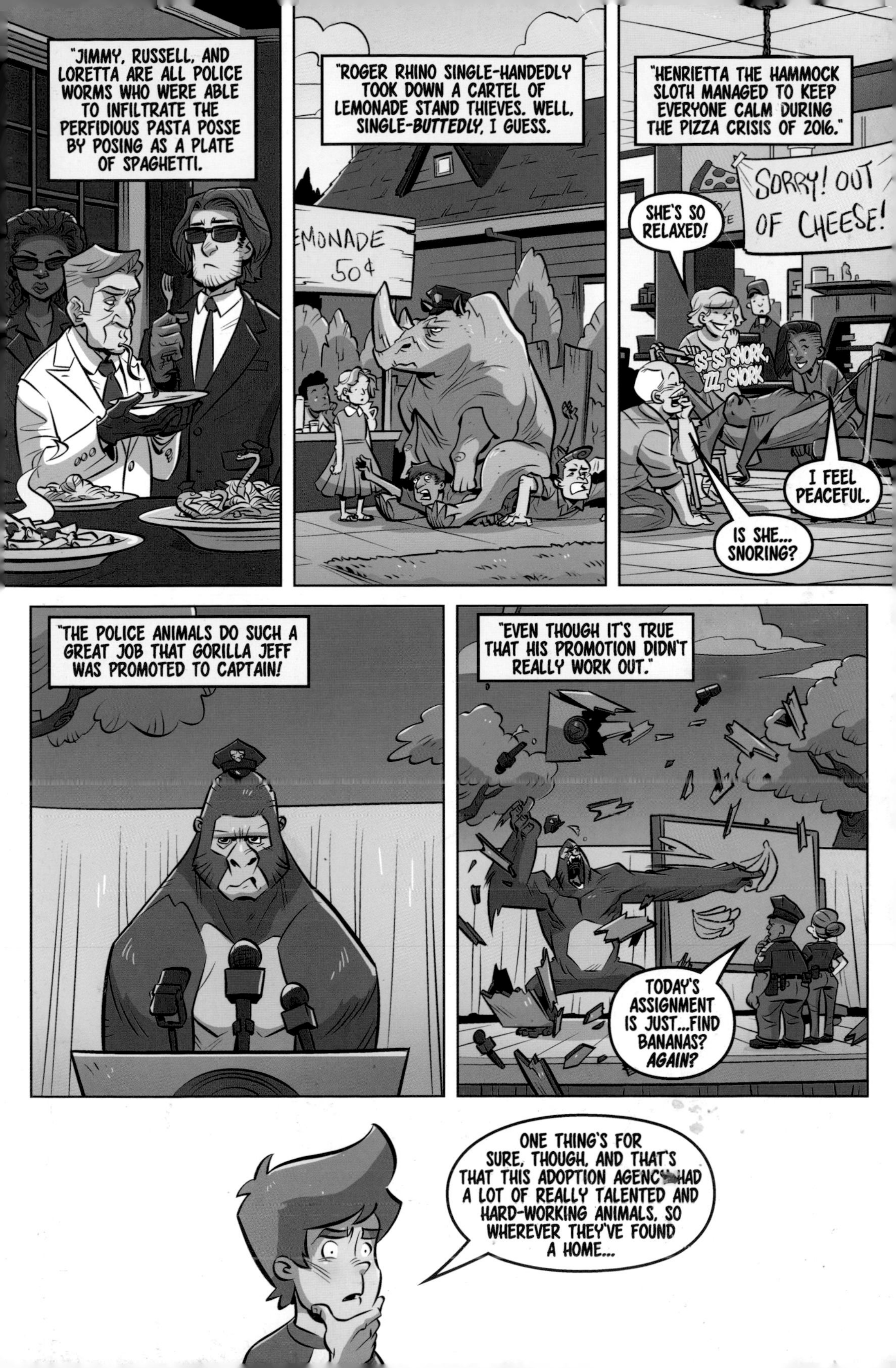
"JIMMY, RUSSELL, AND LORETTA ARE ALL POLICE WORMS WHO WERE ABLE TO INFILTRATE THE PERFIDIOUS PASTA POSSE BY POSING AS A PLATE OF SPAGHETTI.
"ROGER RHINO SINGLE-HANDEDLY TOOK DOWN A CARTEL OF LEMONADE STAND THIEVES. WELL, SINGLE-*BUTTEDLY*, I GUESS.
EMONADE 50¢
"HENRIETTA THE HAMMOCK SLOTH MANAGED TO KEEP EVERYONE CALM DURING THE PIZZA CRISIS OF 2016."
SORRY! OUT OF CHEESE!
SHE'S SO RELAXED!
SS-SS-SNORK, ZZZ, SNORK
I FEEL PEACEFUL.
IS SHE... SNORING?
"THE POLICE ANIMALS DO SUCH A GREAT JOB THAT GORILLA JEFF WAS PROMOTED TO CAPTAIN!
"EVEN THOUGH IT'S TRUE THAT HIS PROMOTION DIDN'T REALLY WORK OUT."
TODAY'S ASSIGNMENT IS JUST...FIND BANANAS? *AGAIN?*
ONE THING'S FOR SURE, THOUGH, AND THAT'S THAT THIS ADOPTION AGENCY HAD A LOT OF REALLY TALENTED AND HARD-WORKING ANIMALS, SO WHEREVER THEY'VE FOUND A HOME...

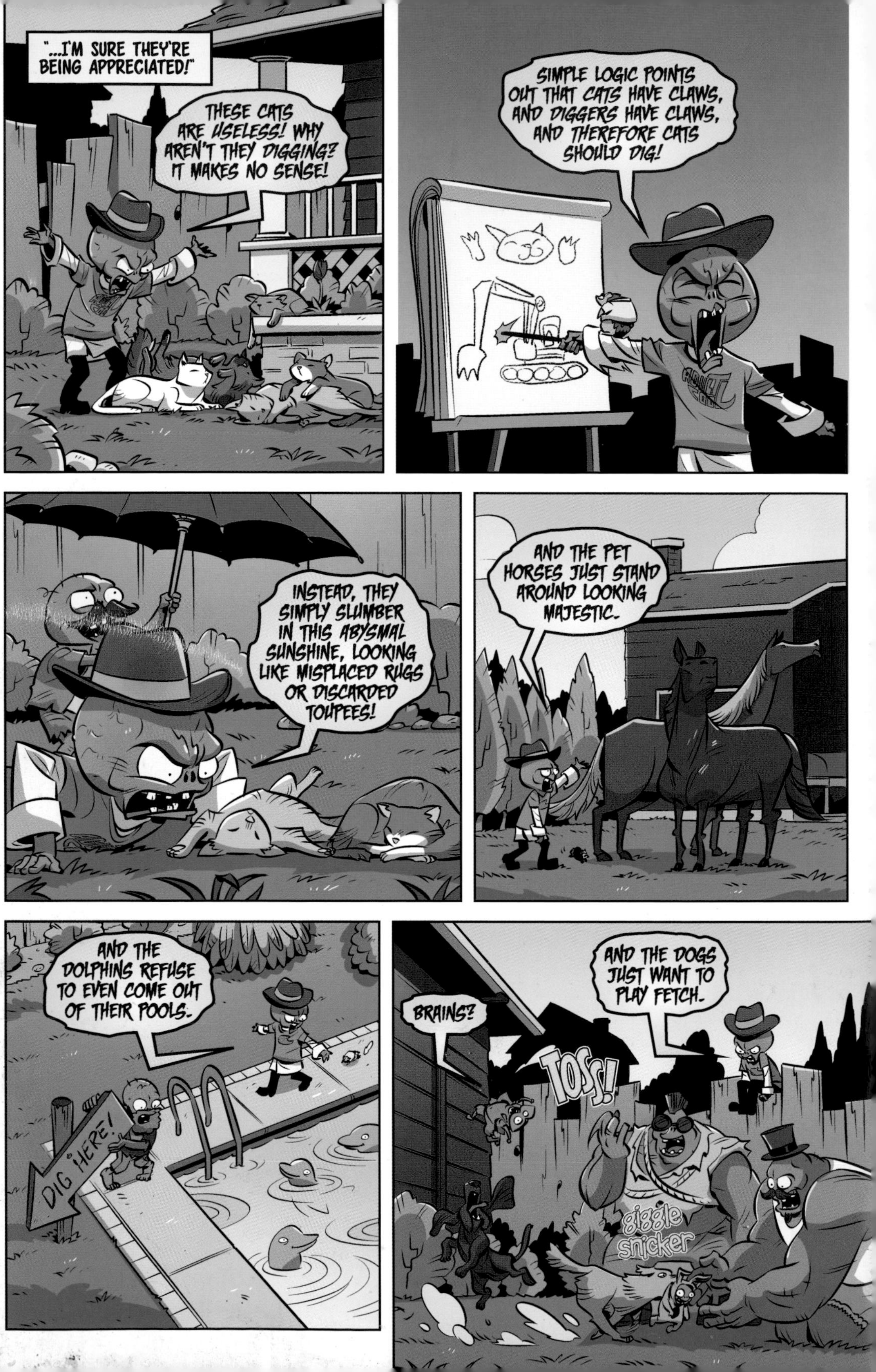
"...I'M SURE THEY'RE BEING APPRECIATED!"
THESE CATS ARE USELESS! WHY AREN'T THEY DIGGING? IT MAKES NO SENSE!
SIMPLE LOGIC POINTS OUT THAT CATS HAVE CLAWS, AND DIGGERS HAVE CLAWS, AND THEREFORE CATS SHOULD DIG!
INSTEAD, THEY SIMPLY SLUMBER IN THIS ABYSMAL SUNSHINE, LOOKING LIKE MISPLACED RUGS OR DISCARDED TOUPEES!
AND THE PET HORSES JUST STAND AROUND LOOKING MAJESTIC.
AND THE DOLPHINS REFUSE TO EVEN COME OUT OF THEIR POOLS.
DIG HERE!
BRAINS?
AND THE DOGS JUST WANT TO PLAY FETCH.
TOSS!
giggle
snicker

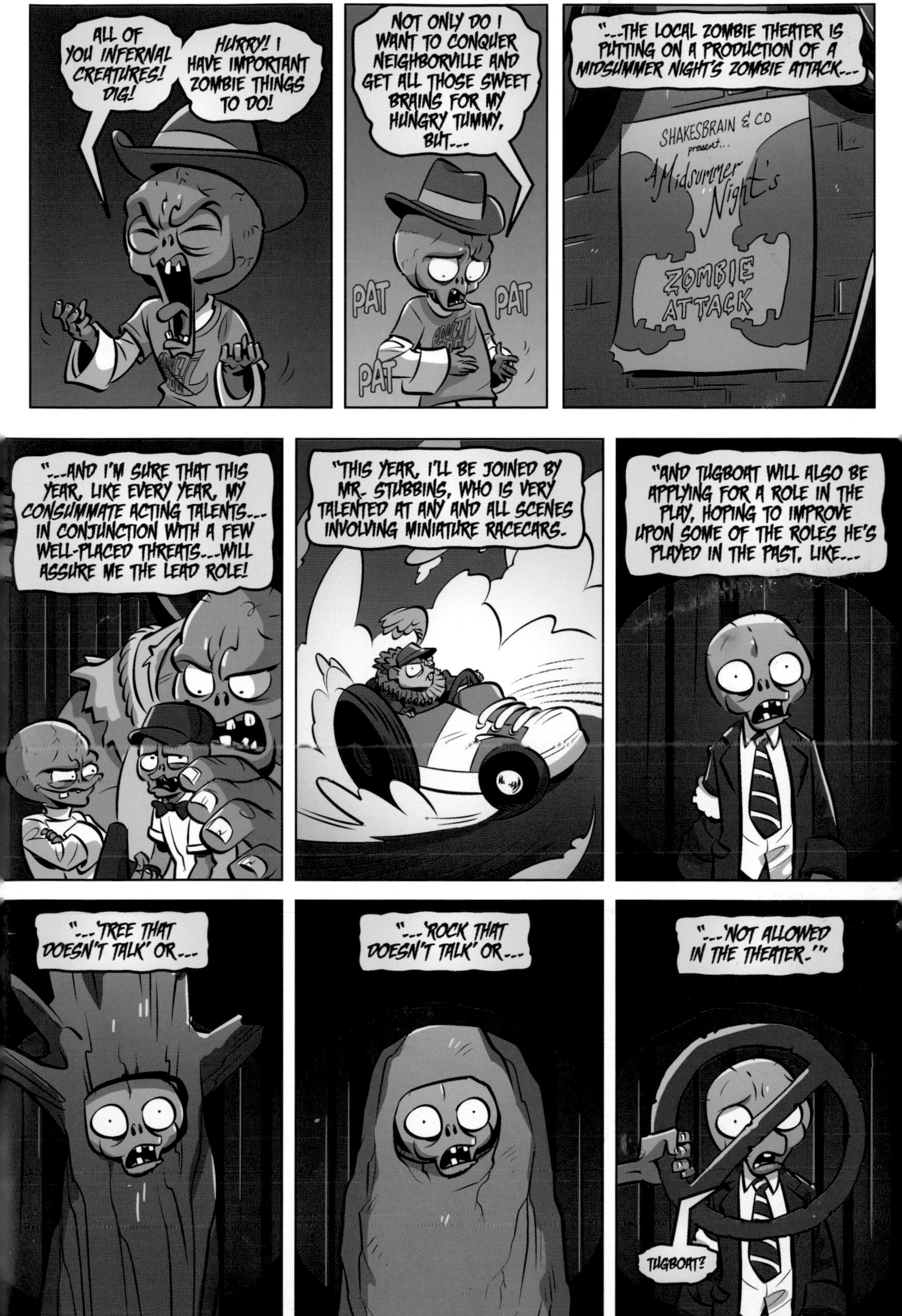
ALL OF YOU INFERNAL CREATURES! DIG!
HURRY! I HAVE IMPORTANT ZOMBIE THINGS TO DO!
NOT ONLY DO I WANT TO CONQUER NEIGHBORVILLE AND GET ALL THOSE SWEET BRAINS FOR MY HUNGRY TUMMY, BUT...
PAT
PAT
PAT
"...THE LOCAL ZOMBIE THEATER IS PUTTING ON A PRODUCTION OF A MIDSUMMER NIGHT'S ZOMBIE ATTACK...
SHAKESBRAIN & CO
present...
A Midsummer Night's
ZOMBIE ATTACK
"...AND I'M SURE THAT THIS YEAR, LIKE EVERY YEAR, MY CONSUMMATE ACTING TALENTS... IN CONJUNCTION WITH A FEW WELL-PLACED THREATS...WILL ASSURE ME THE LEAD ROLE!
"THIS YEAR, I'LL BE JOINED BY MR. STUBBINS, WHO IS VERY TALENTED AT ANY AND ALL SCENES INVOLVING MINIATURE RACECARS.
"AND TUGBOAT WILL ALSO BE APPLYING FOR A ROLE IN THE PLAY, HOPING TO IMPROVE UPON SOME OF THE ROLES HE'S PLAYED IN THE PAST, LIKE...
"...'TREE THAT DOESN'T TALK' OR...
"...'ROCK THAT DOESN'T TALK' OR...
"...'NOT ALLOWED IN THE THEATER.'"
TUGBOAT?

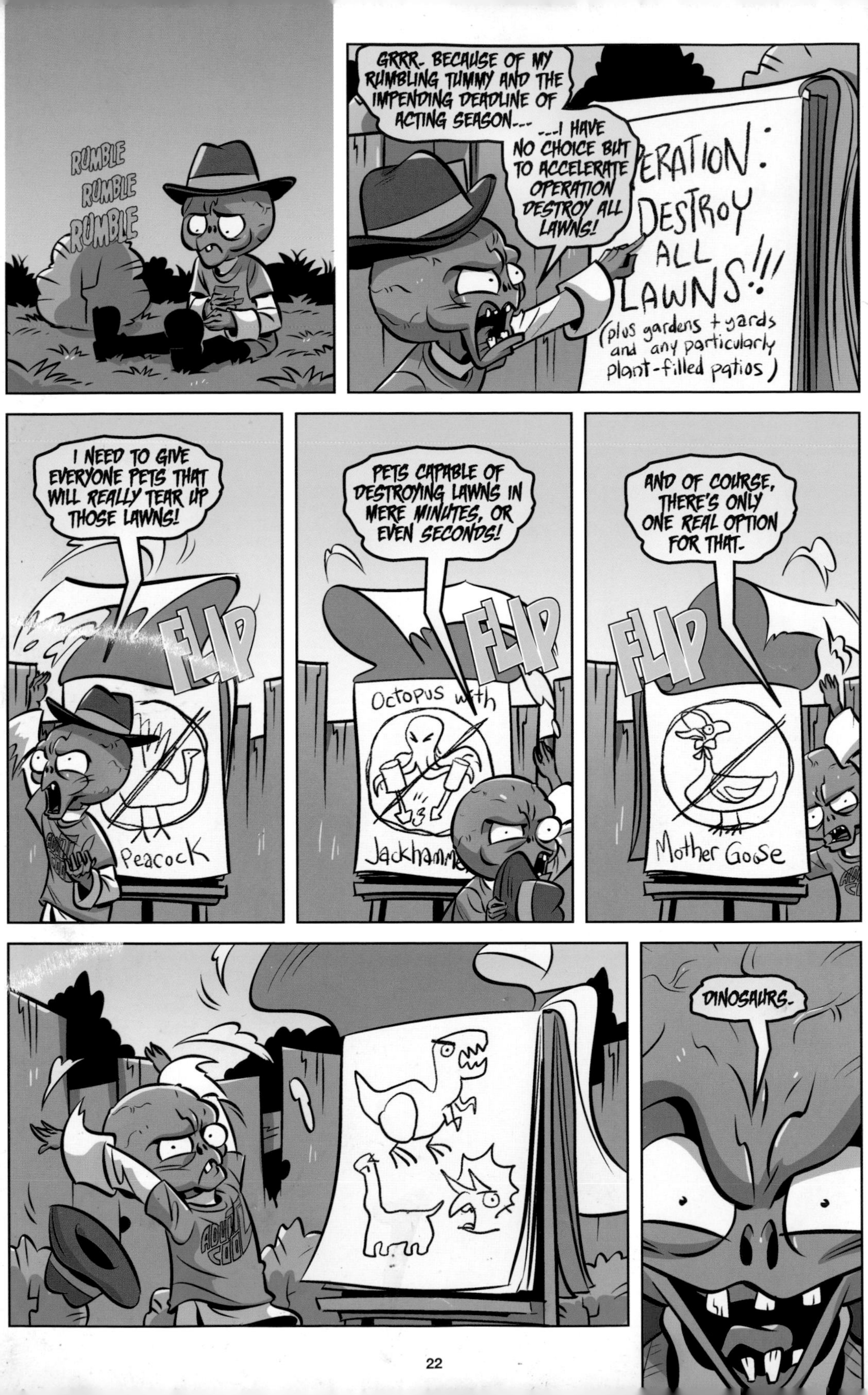
RUMBLE
RUMBLE
RUMBLE
GRRR. BECAUSE OF MY RUMBLING TUMMY AND THE IMPENDING DEADLINE OF ACTING SEASON...
...I HAVE NO CHOICE BUT TO ACCELERATE OPERATION DESTROY ALL LAWNS!
ERATION: DESTROY ALL LAWNS!!!
(plus gardens + yards and any particularly plant-filled patios)
I NEED TO GIVE EVERYONE PETS THAT WILL REALLY TEAR UP THOSE LAWNS!
FLIP
Peacock
PETS CAPABLE OF DESTROYING LAWNS IN MERE MINUTES, OR EVEN SECONDS!
FLIP
Octopus with
Jackhamme
AND OF COURSE, THERE'S ONLY ONE REAL OPTION FOR THAT.
FLIP
Mother Goose
DINOSAURS.

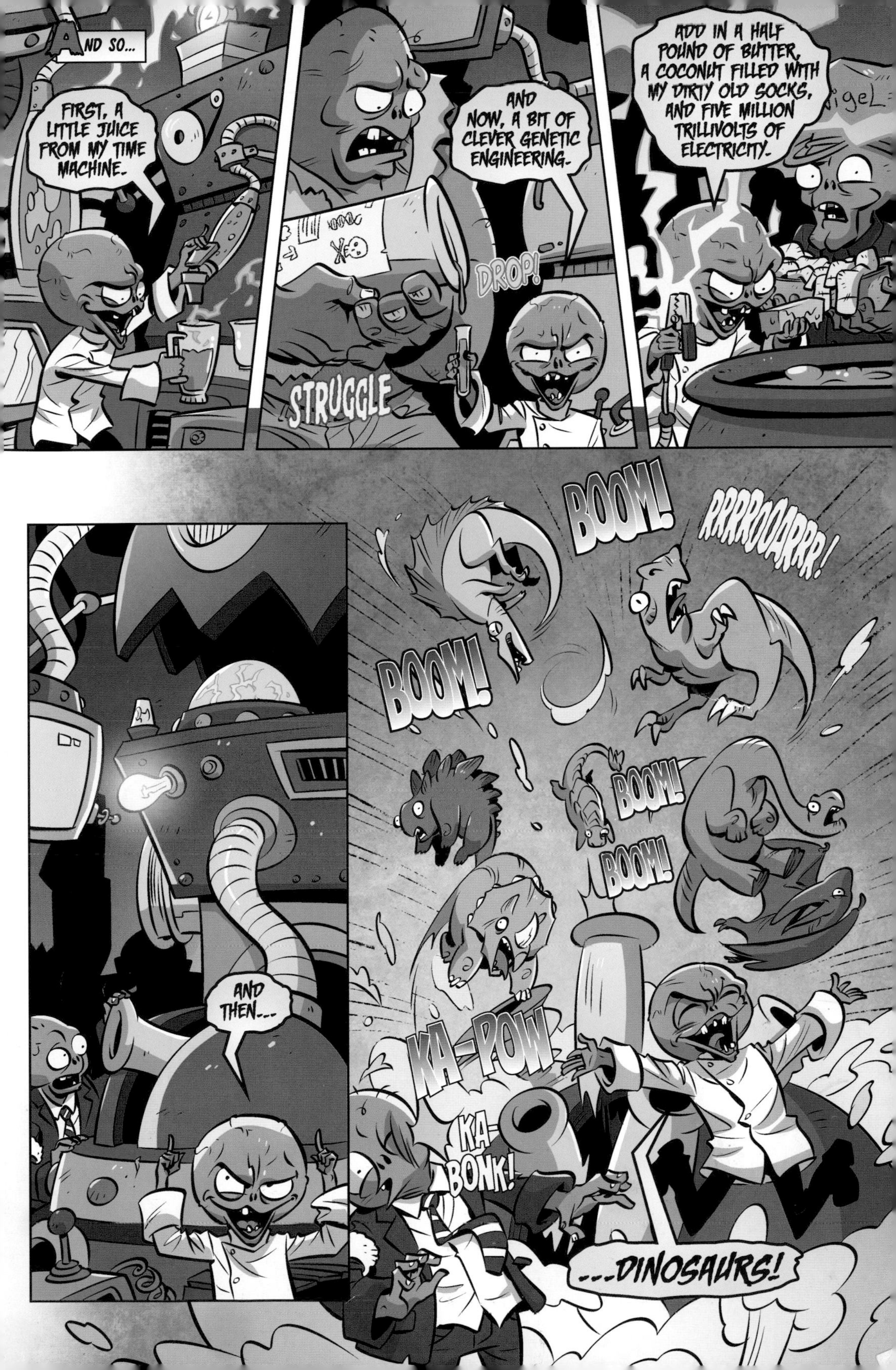
AND SO...
FIRST, A LITTLE JUICE FROM MY TIME MACHINE.
AND NOW, A BIT OF CLEVER GENETIC ENGINEERING.
DROP!
STRUGGLE
ADD IN A HALF POUND OF BUTTER, A COCONUT FILLED WITH MY DIRTY OLD SOCKS, AND FIVE MILLION TRILLIVOLTS OF ELECTRICITY.
AND THEN...
BOOM!
RRRROOARRR!
BOOM!
BOOM!
BOOM!
KA-POW
KA-BONK!
...DINOSAURS!

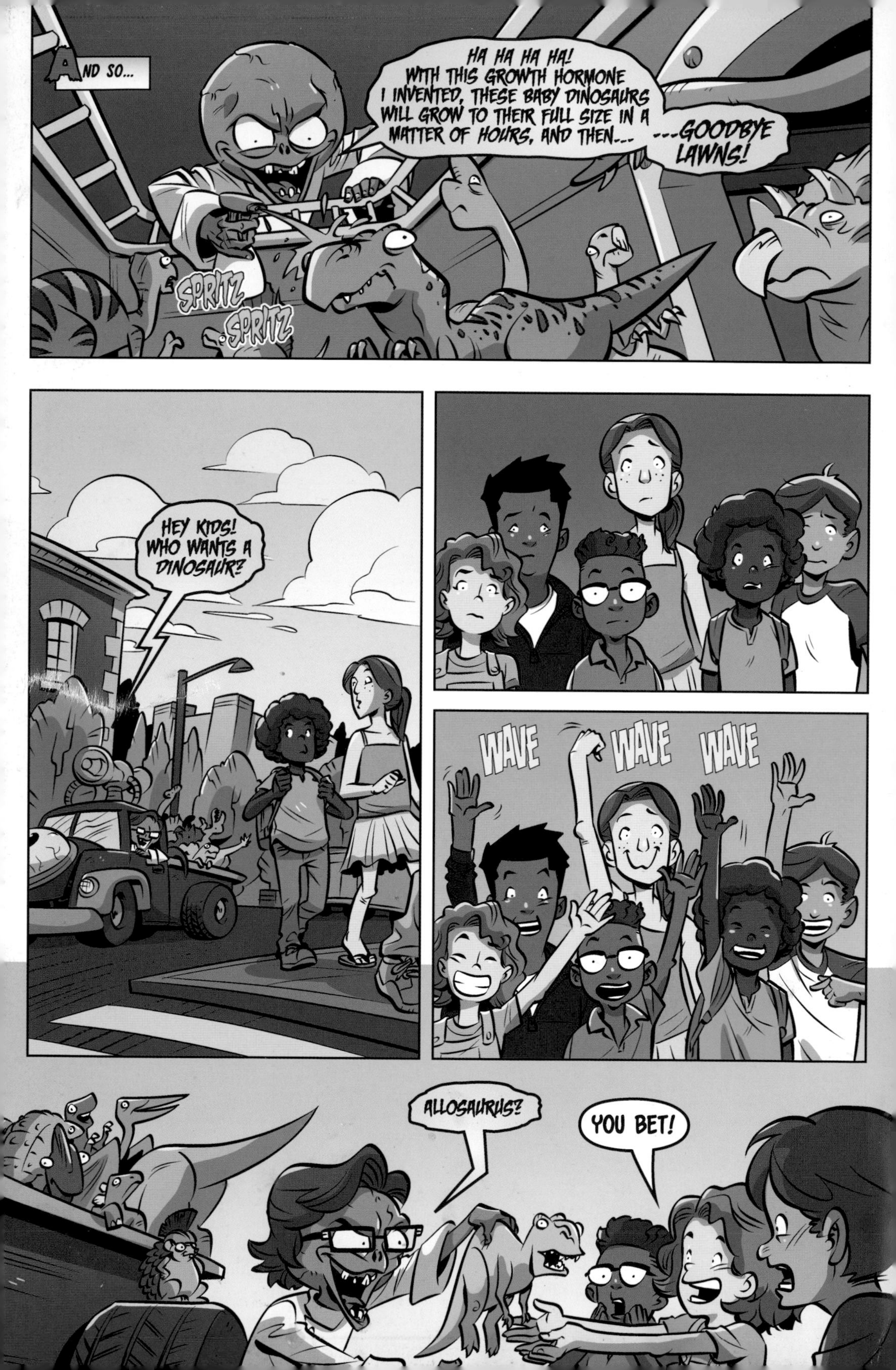
AND SO...
HA HA HA HA! WITH THIS GROWTH HORMONE I INVENTED, THESE BABY DINOSAURS WILL GROW TO THEIR FULL SIZE IN A MATTER OF HOURS, AND THEN...
...GOODBYE LAWNS!
SPRITZ
SPRITZ
HEY KIDS! WHO WANTS A DINOSAUR?
WAVE
WAVE
WAVE
ALLOSAURUS?
YOU BET!

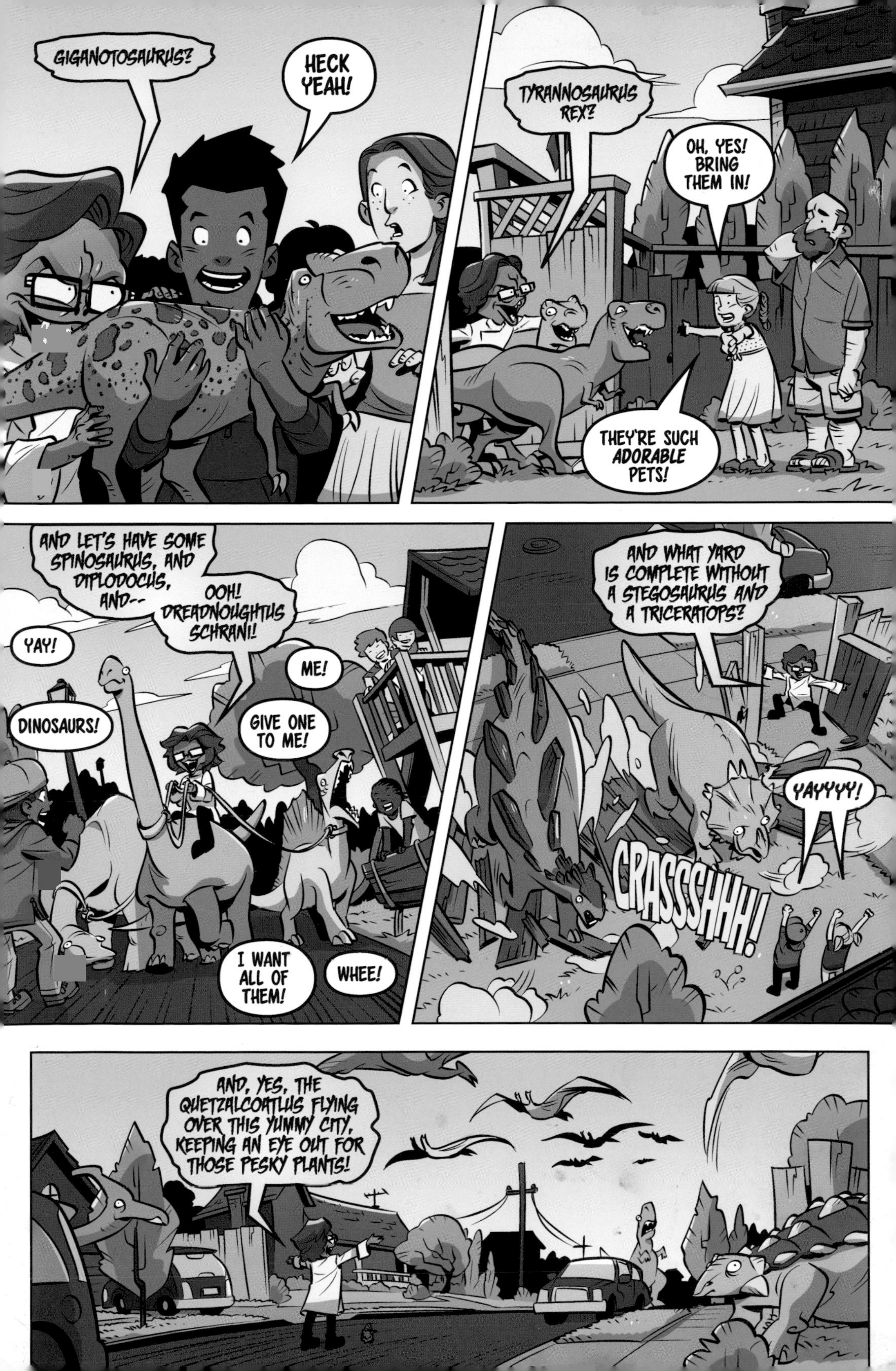
GIGANOTOSAURUS?
HECK YEAH!
TYRANNOSAURUS REX?
OH, YES! BRING THEM IN!
THEY'RE SUCH ADORABLE PETS!
AND LET'S HAVE SOME SPINOSAURUS, AND DIPLODOCUS, AND--
OOH! DREADNOUGHTUS SCHRANI!
YAY!
DINOSAURS!
ME!
GIVE ONE TO ME!
I WANT ALL OF THEM!
WHEE!
AND WHAT YARD IS COMPLETE WITHOUT A STEGOSAURUS AND A TRICERATOPS?
YAYYYY!
CRASSSHHH!
AND, YES, THE QUETZALCOATLUS FLYING OVER THIS YUMMY CITY, KEEPING AN EYE OUT FOR THOSE PESKY PLANTS!

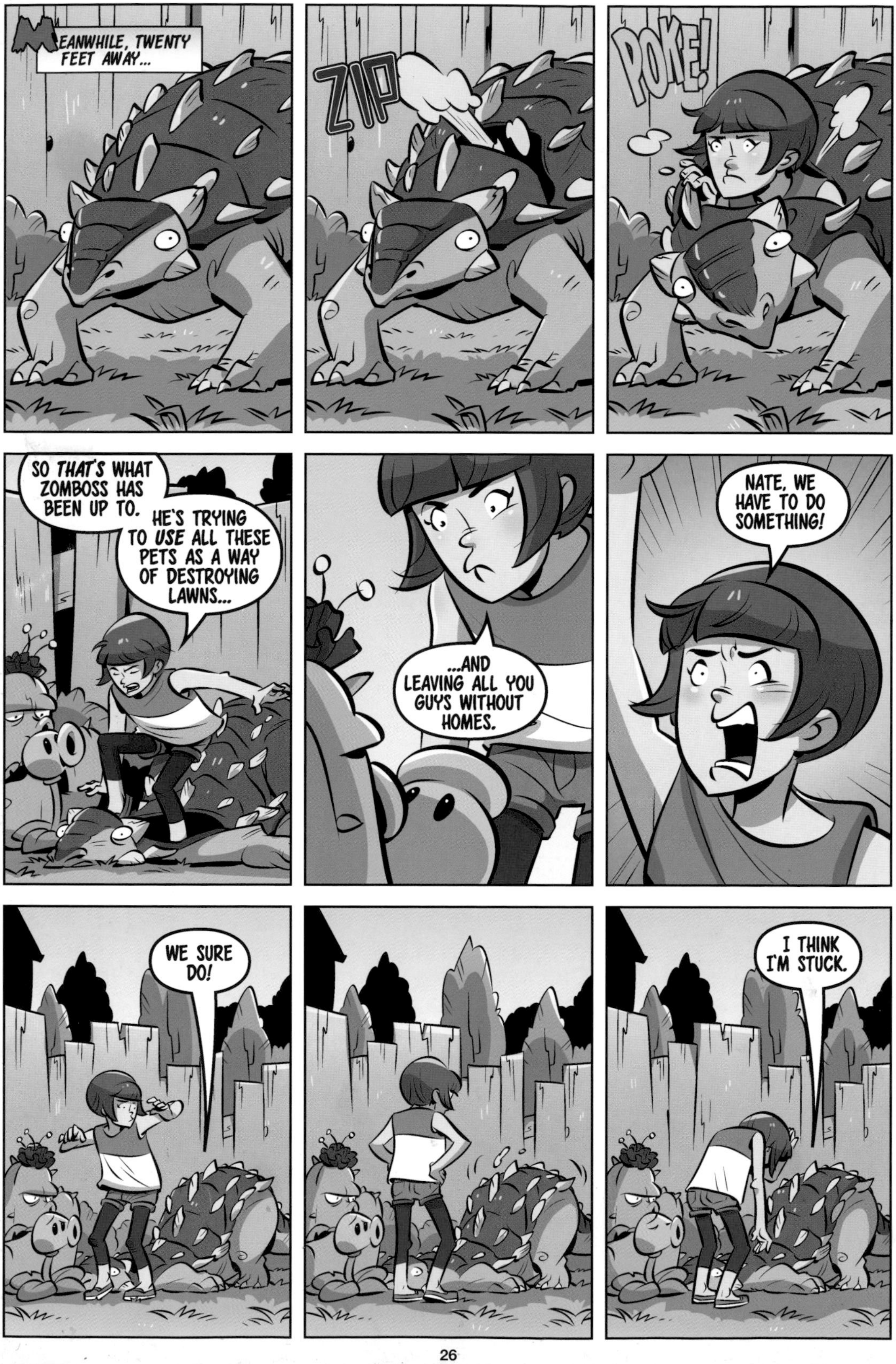
MEANWHILE, TWENTY FEET AWAY...
ZIP
POKE!
SO THAT'S WHAT ZOMBOSS HAS BEEN UP TO.
HE'S TRYING TO USE ALL THESE PETS AS A WAY OF DESTROYING LAWNS...
...AND LEAVING ALL YOU GUYS WITHOUT HOMES.
NATE, WE HAVE TO DO SOMETHING!
WE SURE DO!
I THINK I'M STUCK.

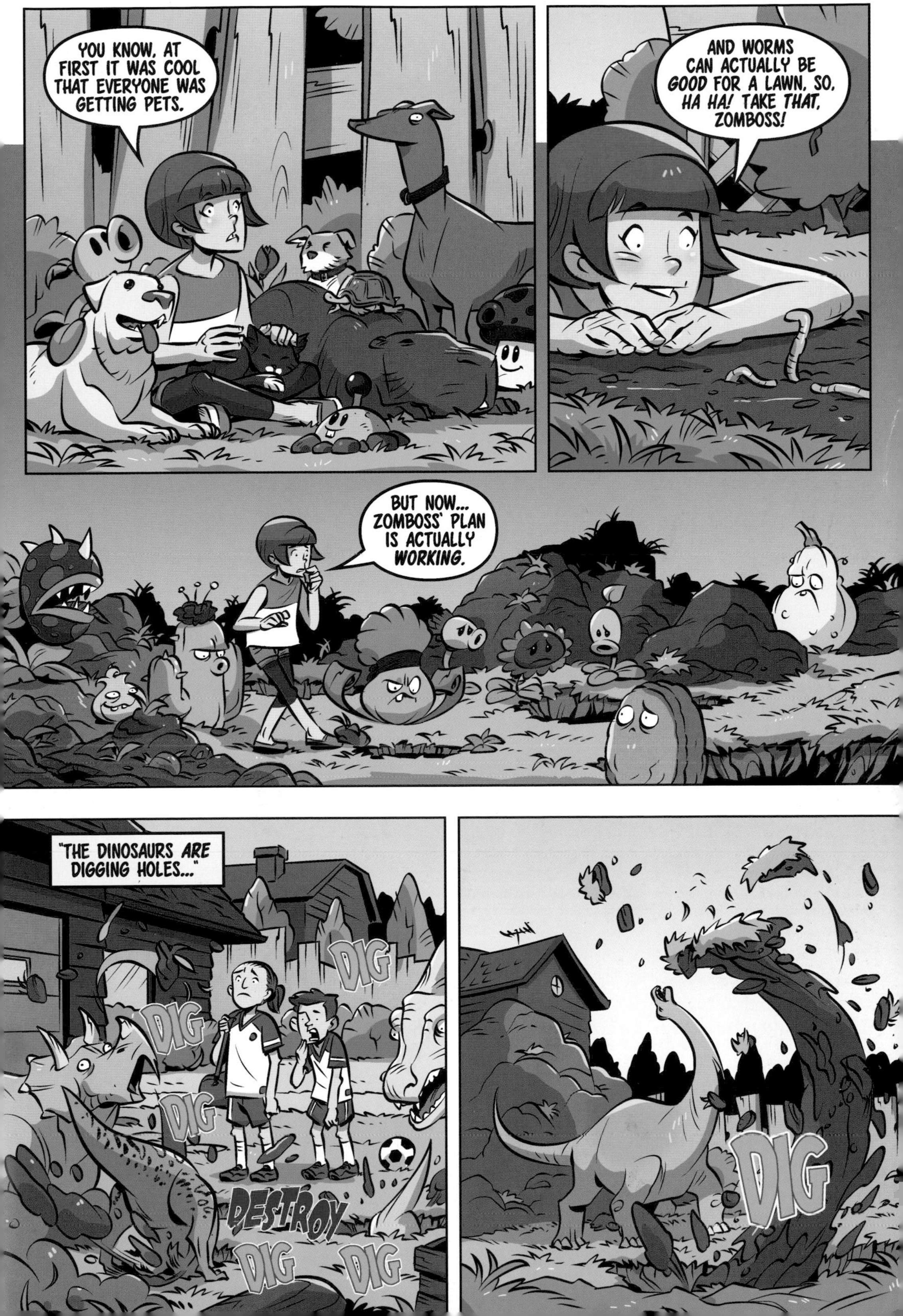
YOU KNOW, AT FIRST IT WAS COOL THAT EVERYONE WAS GETTING PETS.
AND WORMS CAN ACTUALLY BE GOOD FOR A LAWN, SO, HA HA! TAKE THAT, ZOMBOSS!
BUT NOW... ZOMBOSS' PLAN IS ACTUALLY WORKING.
"THE DINOSAURS ARE DIGGING HOLES..."
DIG
DIG
DIG
DESTROY
DIG
DIG
DIG

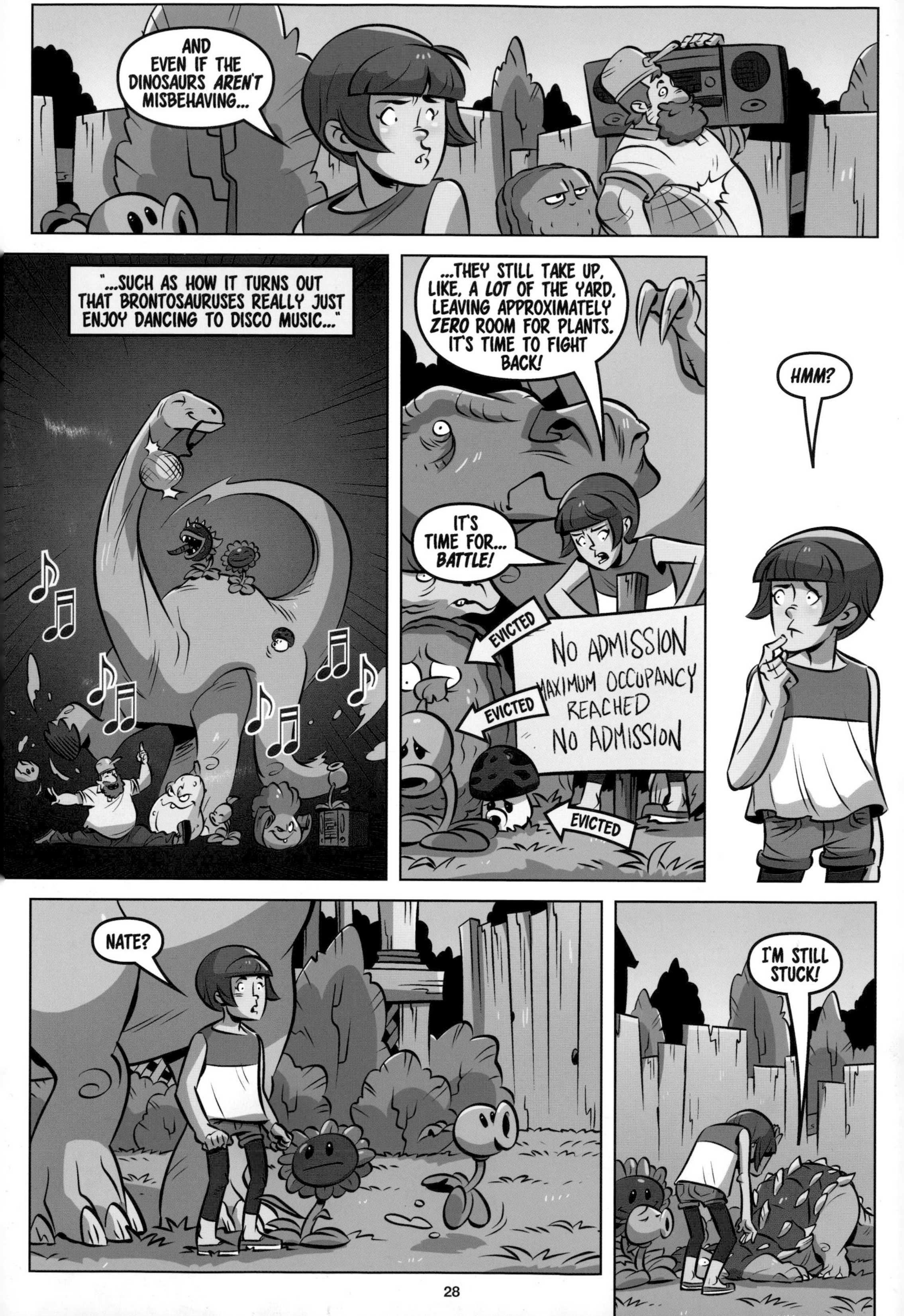
AND EVEN IF THE DINOSAURS *AREN'T* MISBEHAVING...
"...SUCH AS HOW IT TURNS OUT THAT BRONTOSAURUSES REALLY JUST ENJOY DANCING TO DISCO MUSIC..."
...THEY STILL TAKE UP, LIKE, A *LOT* OF THE YARD, LEAVING APPROXIMATELY *ZERO* ROOM FOR PLANTS. IT'S TIME TO FIGHT BACK!
IT'S TIME FOR... *BATTLE!*
EVICTED
NO ADMISSION
MAXIMUM OCCUPANCY REACHED
NO ADMISSION
EVICTED
EVICTED
HMM?
NATE?
I'M STILL STUCK!

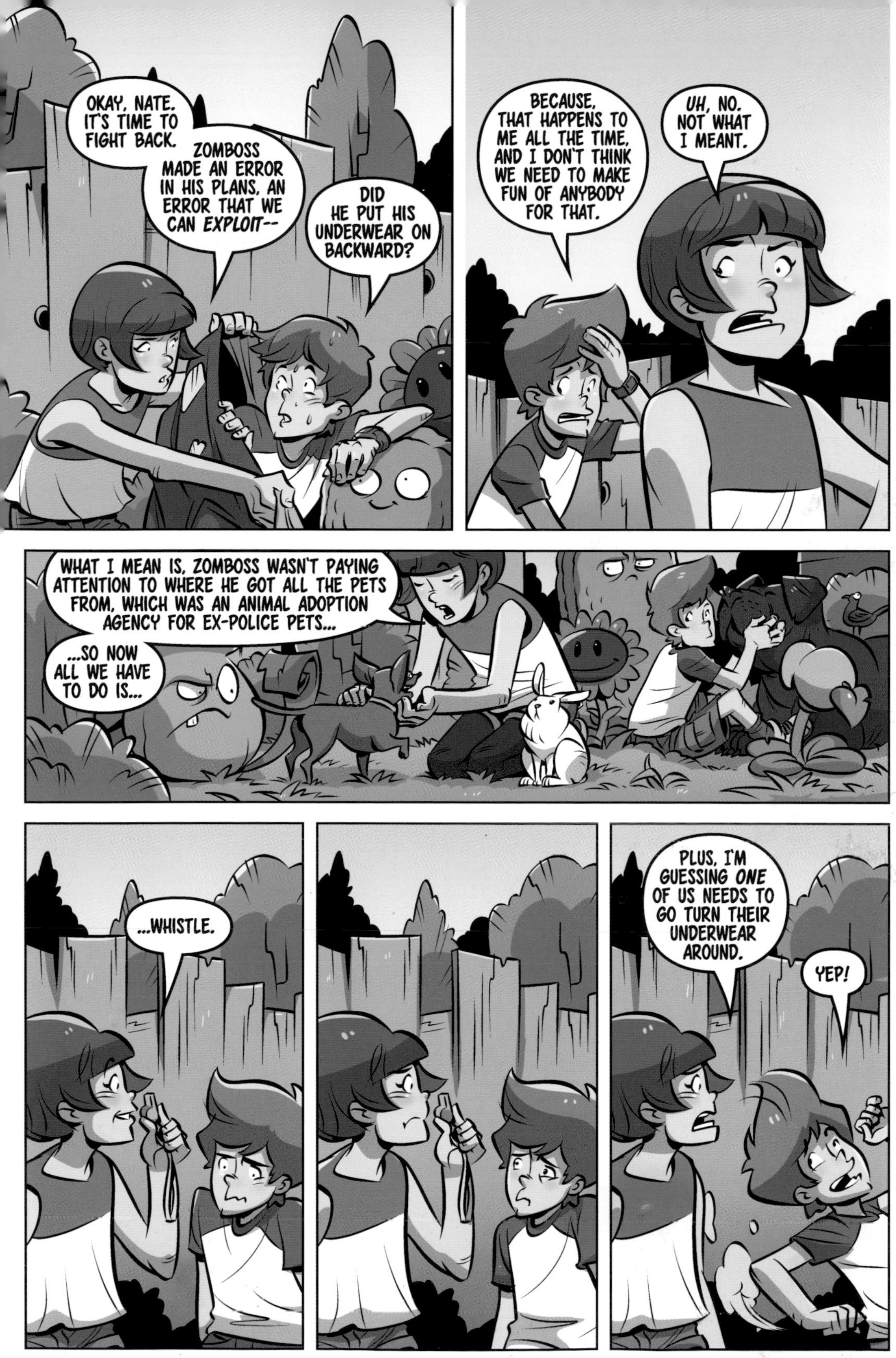
OKAY, NATE. IT'S TIME TO FIGHT BACK.
ZOMBOSS MADE AN ERROR IN HIS PLANS, AN ERROR THAT WE CAN *EXPLOIT*--
DID HE PUT HIS UNDERWEAR ON BACKWARD?
BECAUSE, THAT HAPPENS TO ME ALL THE TIME, AND I DON'T THINK WE NEED TO MAKE FUN OF ANYBODY FOR THAT.
UH, NO. NOT WHAT I MEANT.
WHAT I MEAN IS, ZOMBOSS WASN'T PAYING ATTENTION TO WHERE HE GOT ALL THE PETS FROM, WHICH WAS AN ANIMAL ADOPTION AGENCY FOR EX-POLICE PETS...
...SO NOW ALL WE HAVE TO DO IS...
...WHISTLE.
PLUS, I'M GUESSING *ONE* OF US NEEDS TO GO TURN THEIR UNDERWEAR AROUND.
YEP!

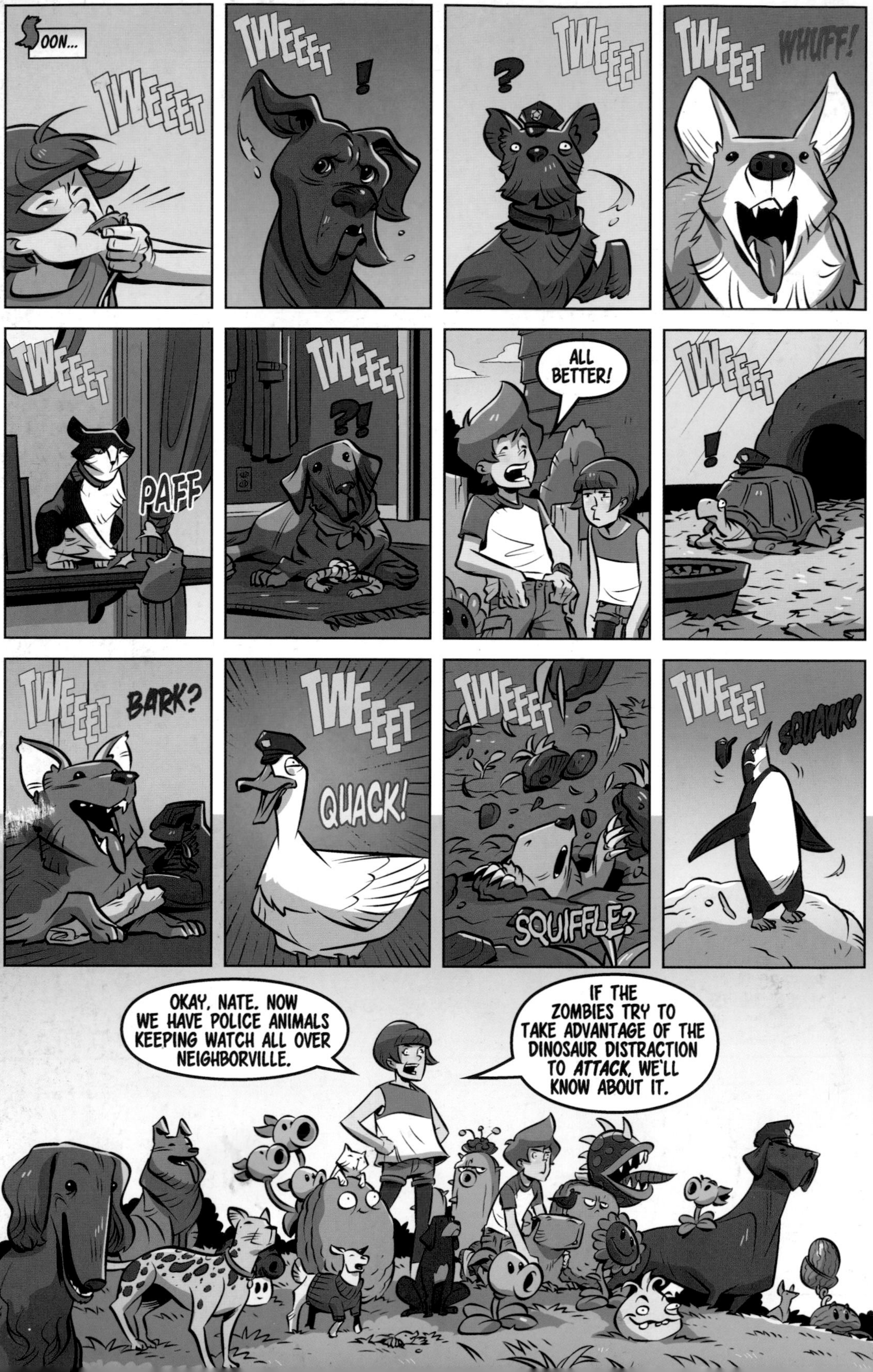
SOON...
TWEEEET
TWEEEET
!
?
TWEEEET
TWEEEET
WHUFF!
TWEEEET
PAFF
TWEEEET
?!
ALL BETTER!
TWEEEET
!
TWEEEET
BARK?
TWEEEET
QUACK!
TWEEEET
SQUIFFLE?
TWEEEET
SQUAWK!
OKAY, NATE. NOW WE HAVE POLICE ANIMALS KEEPING WATCH ALL OVER NEIGHBORVILLE.
IF THE ZOMBIES TRY TO TAKE ADVANTAGE OF THE DINOSAUR DISTRACTION TO ATTACK, WE'LL KNOW ABOUT IT.

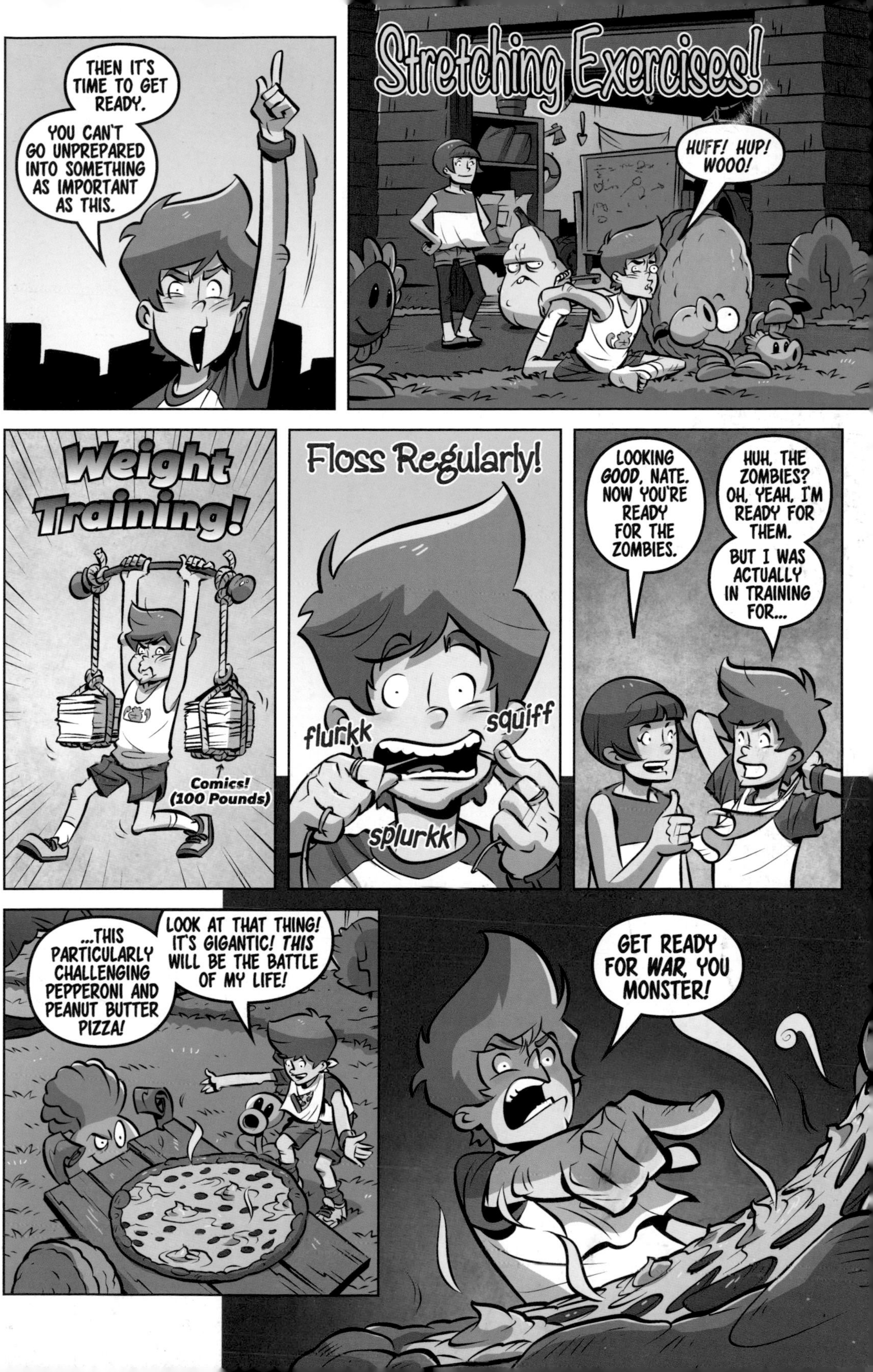
THEN IT'S TIME TO GET READY.
YOU CAN'T GO UNPREPARED INTO SOMETHING AS IMPORTANT AS THIS.
Stretching Exercises!
HUFF! HUP! WOOO!
Weight Training!
Comics! (100 Pounds)
Floss Regularly!
flurkk
squiff
splurkk
LOOKING GOOD, NATE. NOW YOU'RE READY FOR THE ZOMBIES.
HUH, THE ZOMBIES? OH, YEAH, I'M READY FOR THEM.
BUT I WAS ACTUALLY IN TRAINING FOR...
...THIS PARTICULARLY CHALLENGING PEPPERONI AND PEANUT BUTTER PIZZA!
LOOK AT THAT THING! IT'S GIGANTIC! THIS WILL BE THE BATTLE OF MY LIFE!
GET READY FOR WAR, YOU MONSTER!

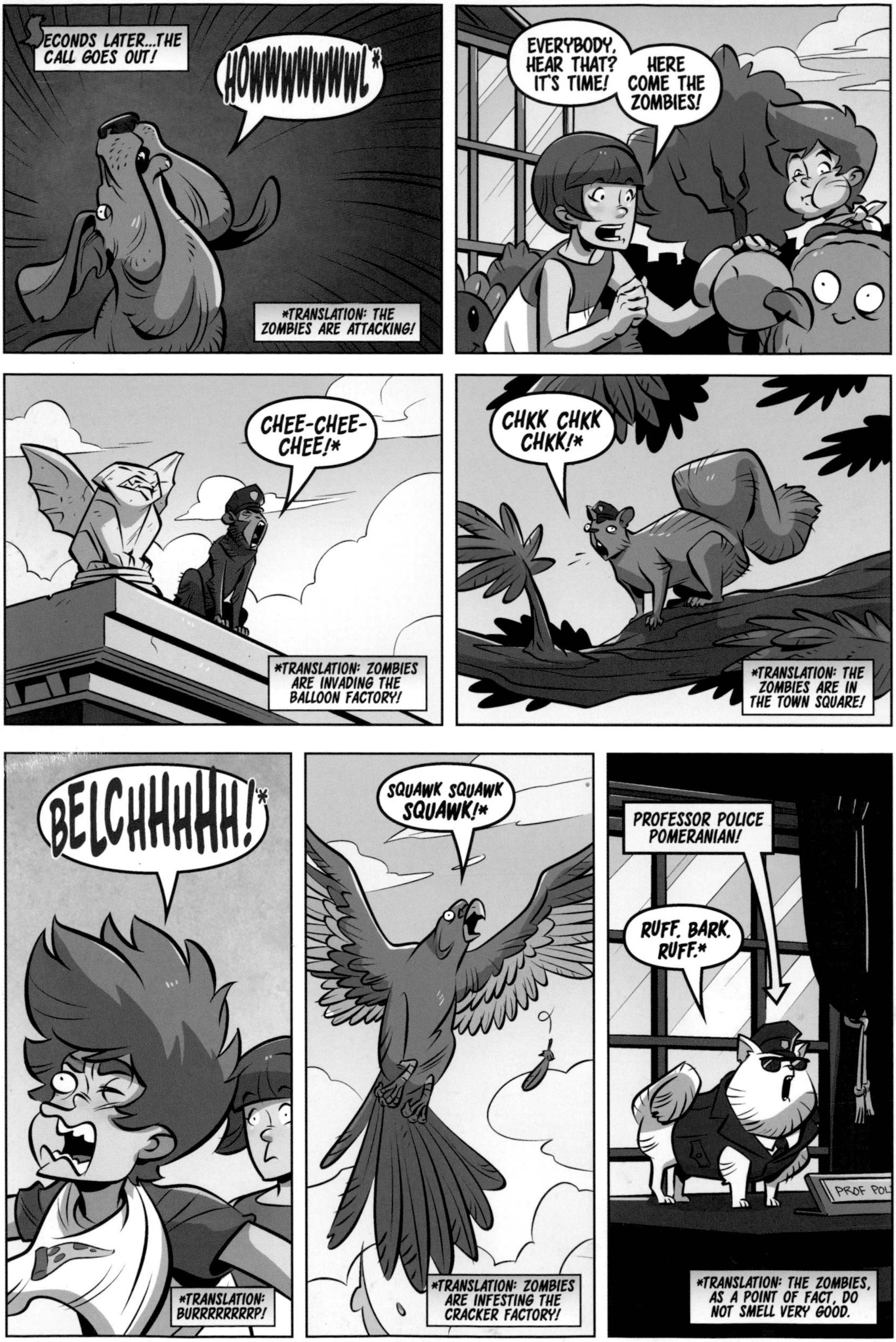
SECONDS LATER...THE CALL GOES OUT!
HOWWWWWWWL*
*TRANSLATION: THE ZOMBIES ARE ATTACKING!
EVERYBODY, HEAR THAT? IT'S TIME!
HERE COME THE ZOMBIES!
CHEE-CHEE-CHEE!*
*TRANSLATION: ZOMBIES ARE INVADING THE BALLOON FACTORY!
CHKK CHKK CHKK!*
*TRANSLATION: THE ZOMBIES ARE IN THE TOWN SQUARE!
BELCHHHHH!*
*TRANSLATION: BURRRRRRRRP!
SQUAWK SQUAWK SQUAWK!*
*TRANSLATION: ZOMBIES ARE INFESTING THE CRACKER FACTORY!
PROFESSOR POLICE POMERANIAN!
RUFF. BARK. RUFF.*
PROF POL
*TRANSLATION: THE ZOMBIES, AS A POINT OF FACT, DO NOT SMELL VERY GOOD.

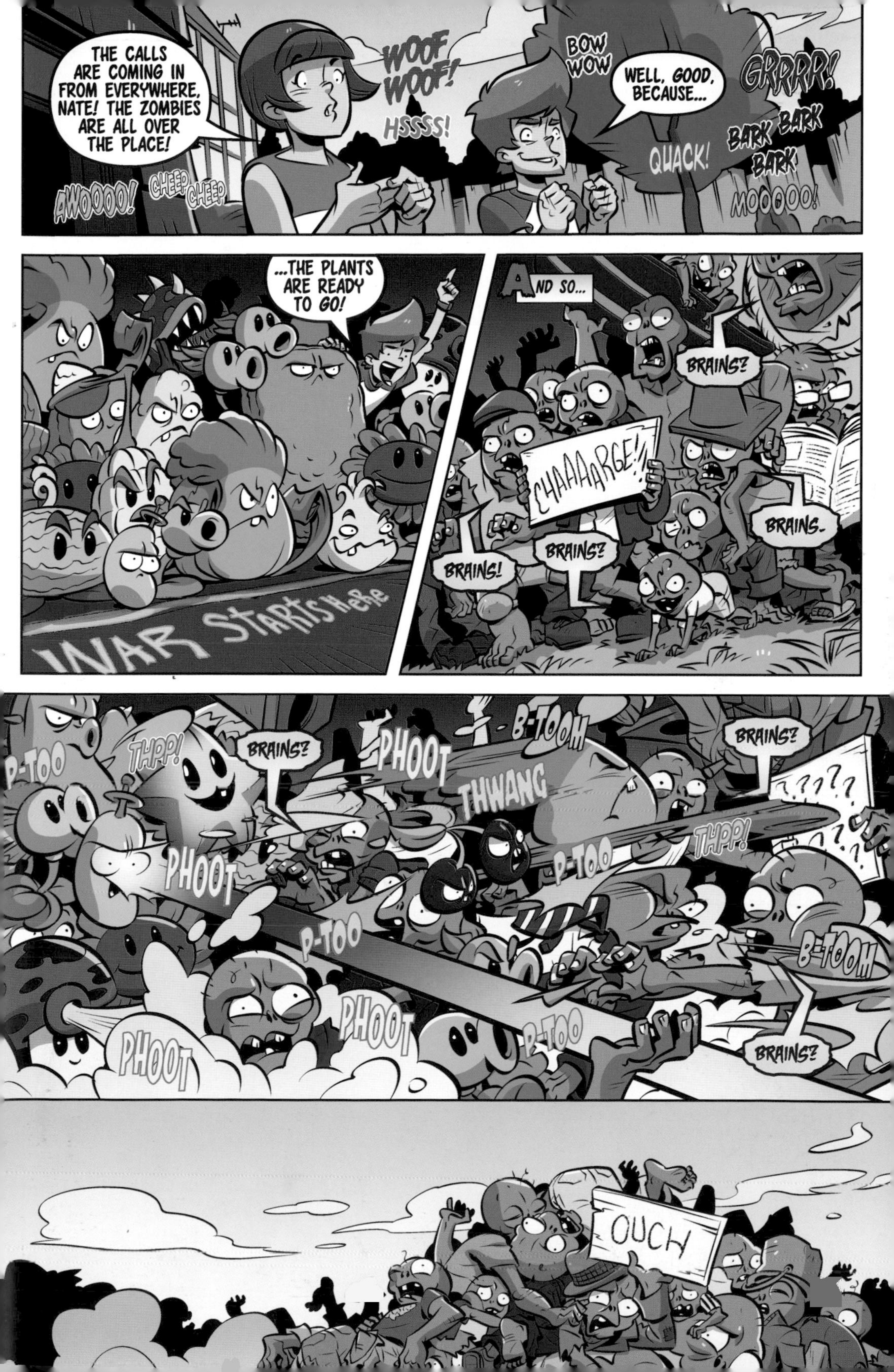

THE CALLS ARE COMING IN FROM EVERYWHERE, NATE! THE ZOMBIES ARE ALL OVER THE PLACE!
WOOF WOOF!
HSSSSS!
AWOOOO!
CHEEP CHEEP
BOW WOW
WELL, GOOD, BECAUSE...
GRRRR!
QUACK!
BARK BARK BARK
MOOOOO!
...THE PLANTS ARE READY TO GO!
WAR STARTS HERE
AND SO...
BRAINS?
CHAAAARGE!!
BRAINS.
BRAINS?
BRAINS!
P-TOO
THPP!
BRAINS?
PHOOT
B-TOOM
THWANG
BRAINS?
PHOOT
THPP!
P-TOO
P-TOO
B-TOOM
PHOOT
PHOOT
P-TOO
BRAINS?
OUCH

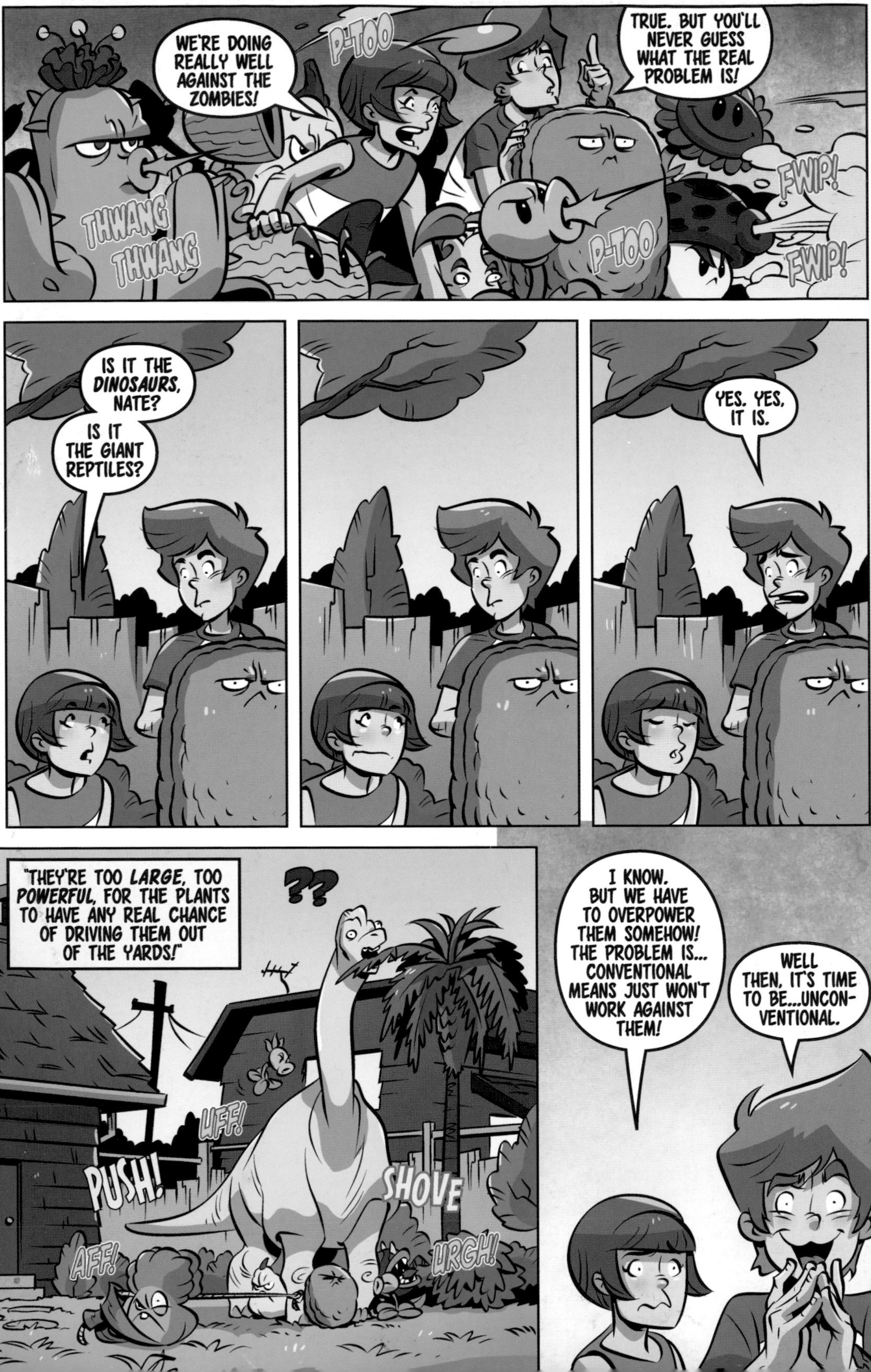
WE'RE DOING REALLY WELL AGAINST THE ZOMBIES!
P-TOO
TRUE. BUT YOU'LL NEVER GUESS WHAT THE REAL PROBLEM IS!
THWANG
THWANG
P-TOO
FWIP!
FWIP!
IS IT THE DINOSAURS, NATE?
IS IT THE GIANT REPTILES?
YES. YES, IT IS.
"THEY'RE TOO LARGE, TOO POWERFUL, FOR THE PLANTS TO HAVE ANY REAL CHANCE OF DRIVING THEM OUT OF THE YARDS!"
??
UFF!
PUSH!
SHOVE
AFF!
URGH!
I KNOW. BUT WE HAVE TO OVERPOWER THEM SOMEHOW! THE PROBLEM IS... CONVENTIONAL MEANS JUST WON'T WORK AGAINST THEM!
WELL THEN, IT'S TIME TO BE...UNCON-VENTIONAL.

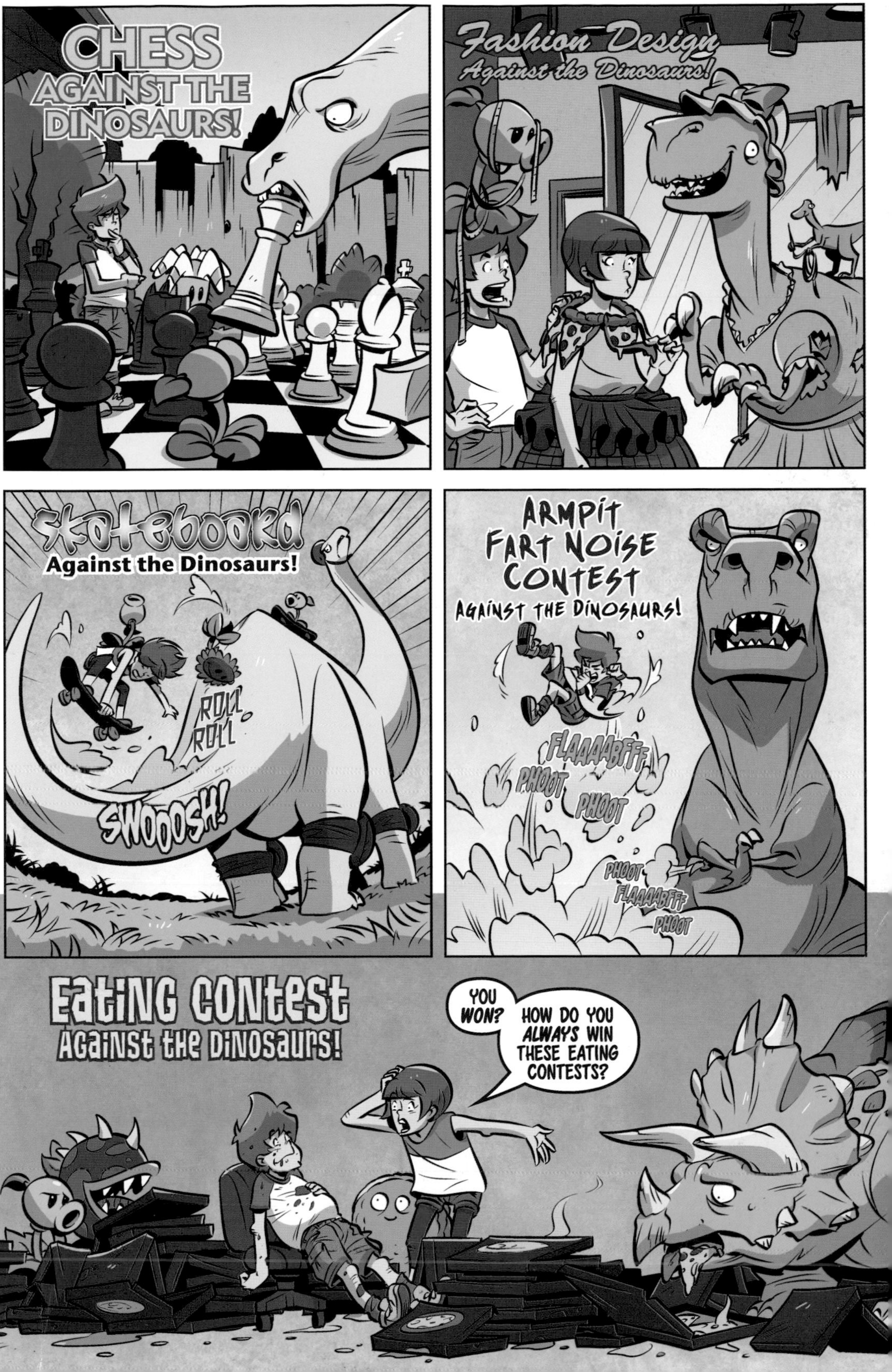
CHESS AGAINST THE DINOSAURS!
Fashion Design Against the Dinosaurs!
Skateboard Against the Dinosaurs!
ROLL ROLL
SWOOOSH!
ARMPIT FART NOISE CONTEST AGAINST THE DINOSAURS!
FLAAAABFFF
PHOOT
PHOOT
PHOOT
FLAAAABFFF
PHOOT
Eating Contest Against the Dinosaurs!
YOU WON?
HOW DO YOU ALWAYS WIN THESE EATING CONTESTS?

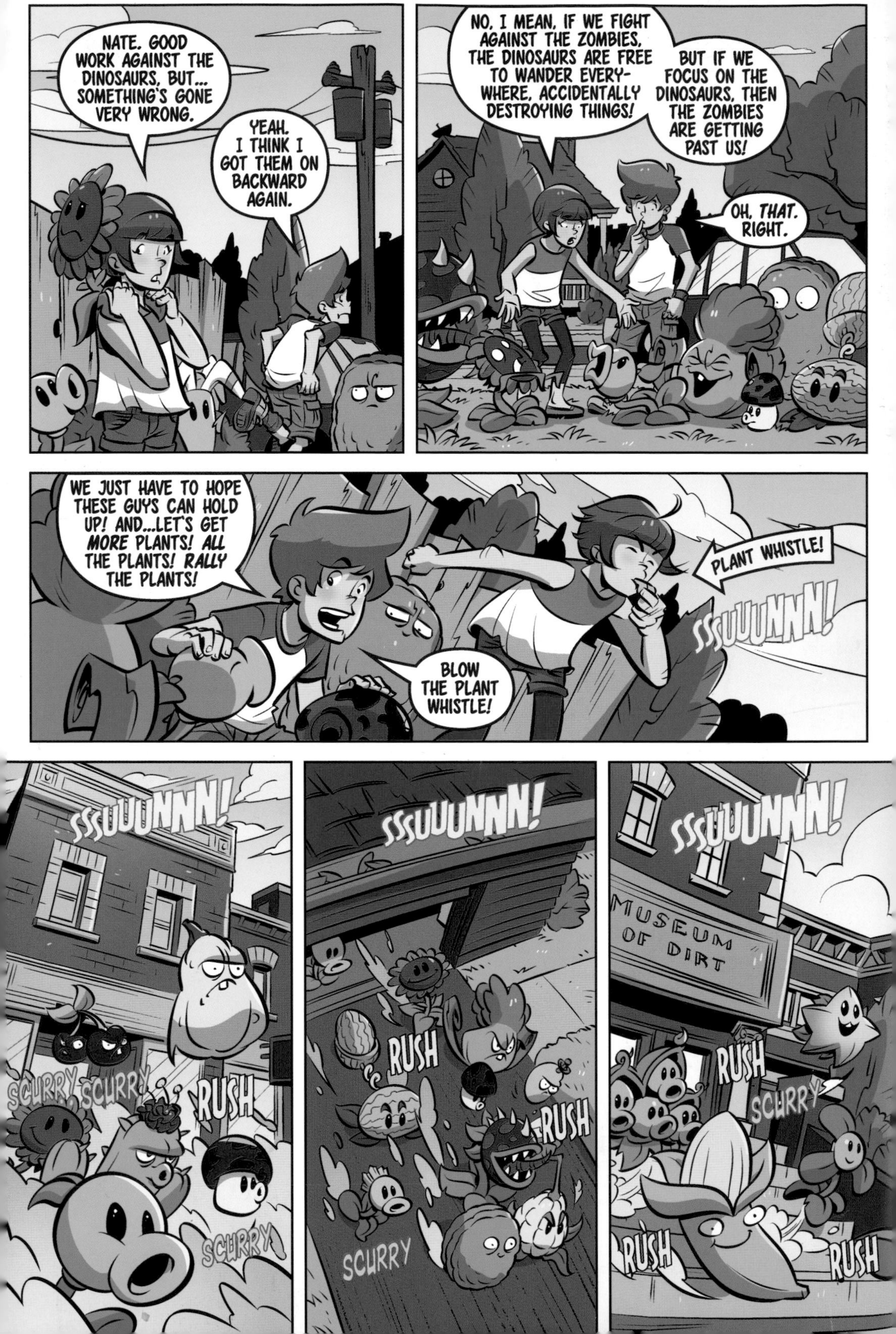
NATE. GOOD WORK AGAINST THE DINOSAURS, BUT... SOMETHING'S GONE VERY WRONG.
YEAH. I THINK I GOT THEM ON BACKWARD AGAIN.
NO, I MEAN, IF WE FIGHT AGAINST THE ZOMBIES, THE DINOSAURS ARE FREE TO WANDER EVERYWHERE, ACCIDENTALLY DESTROYING THINGS!
BUT IF WE FOCUS ON THE DINOSAURS, THEN THE ZOMBIES ARE GETTING PAST US!
OH, THAT. RIGHT.
WE JUST HAVE TO HOPE THESE GUYS CAN HOLD UP! AND...LET'S GET MORE PLANTS! ALL THE PLANTS! RALLY THE PLANTS!
BLOW THE PLANT WHISTLE!
PLANT WHISTLE!
SSSUUUNNN!
SSSUUUNNN!
SCURRY SCURRY
RUSH
SCURRY
SSSUUUNNN!
RUSH
RUSH
SCURRY
SSSUUUNNN!
MUSEUM OF DIRT
RUSH
SCURRY
RUSH
RUSH

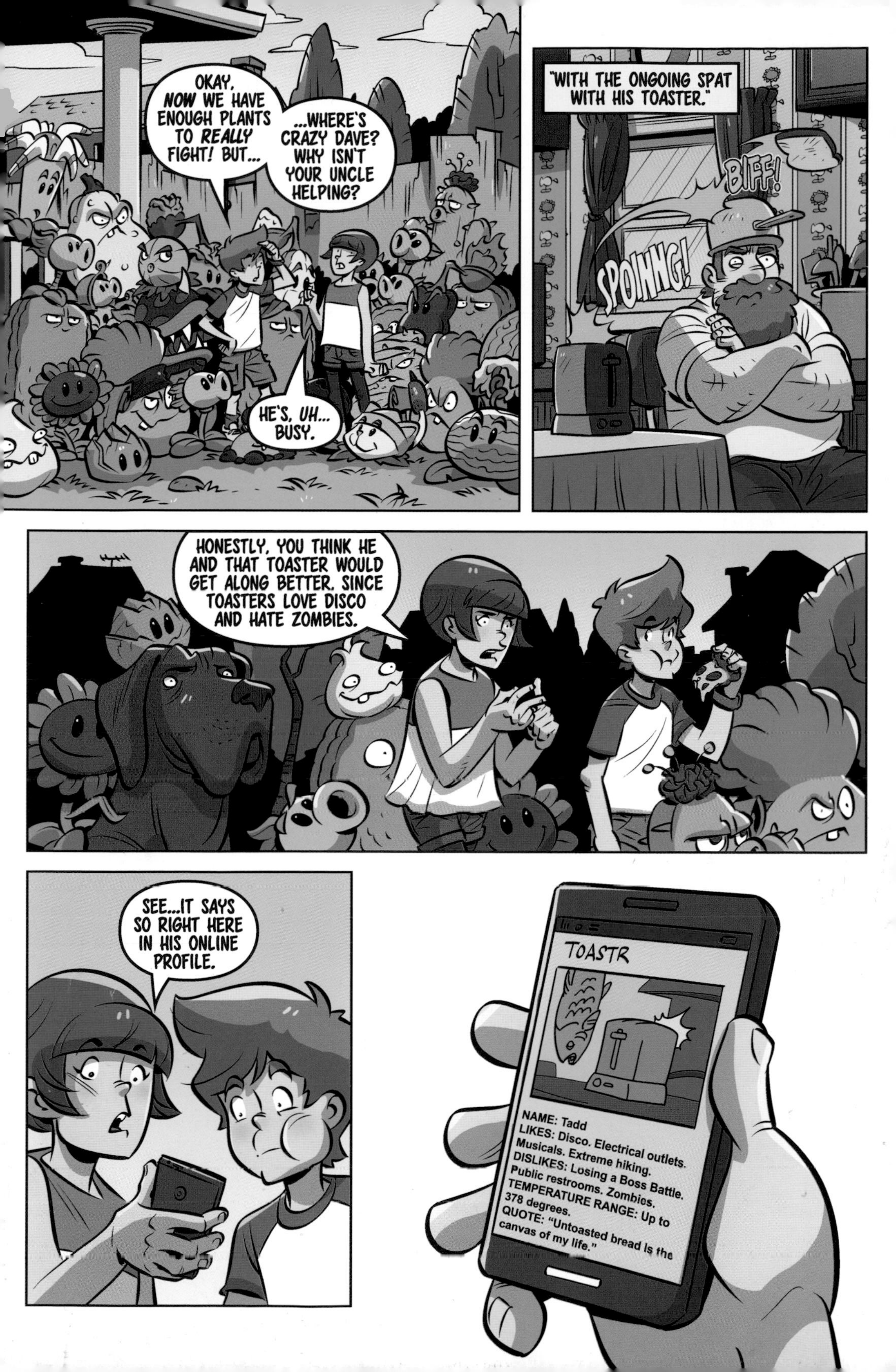
OKAY, NOW WE HAVE ENOUGH PLANTS TO REALLY FIGHT! BUT...
...WHERE'S CRAZY DAVE? WHY ISN'T YOUR UNCLE HELPING?
HE'S, UH... BUSY.
"WITH THE ONGOING SPAT WITH HIS TOASTER."
BIFF!
SPOINNG!
HONESTLY, YOU THINK HE AND THAT TOASTER WOULD GET ALONG BETTER, SINCE TOASTERS LOVE DISCO AND HATE ZOMBIES.
SEE...IT SAYS SO RIGHT HERE IN HIS ONLINE PROFILE.
TOASTR
NAME: Tadd
LIKES: Disco. Electrical outlets. Musicals. Extreme hiking.
DISLIKES: Losing a Boss Battle. Public restrooms. Zombies.
TEMPERATURE RANGE: Up to 378 degrees.
QUOTE: "Untoasted bread is the canvas of my life."

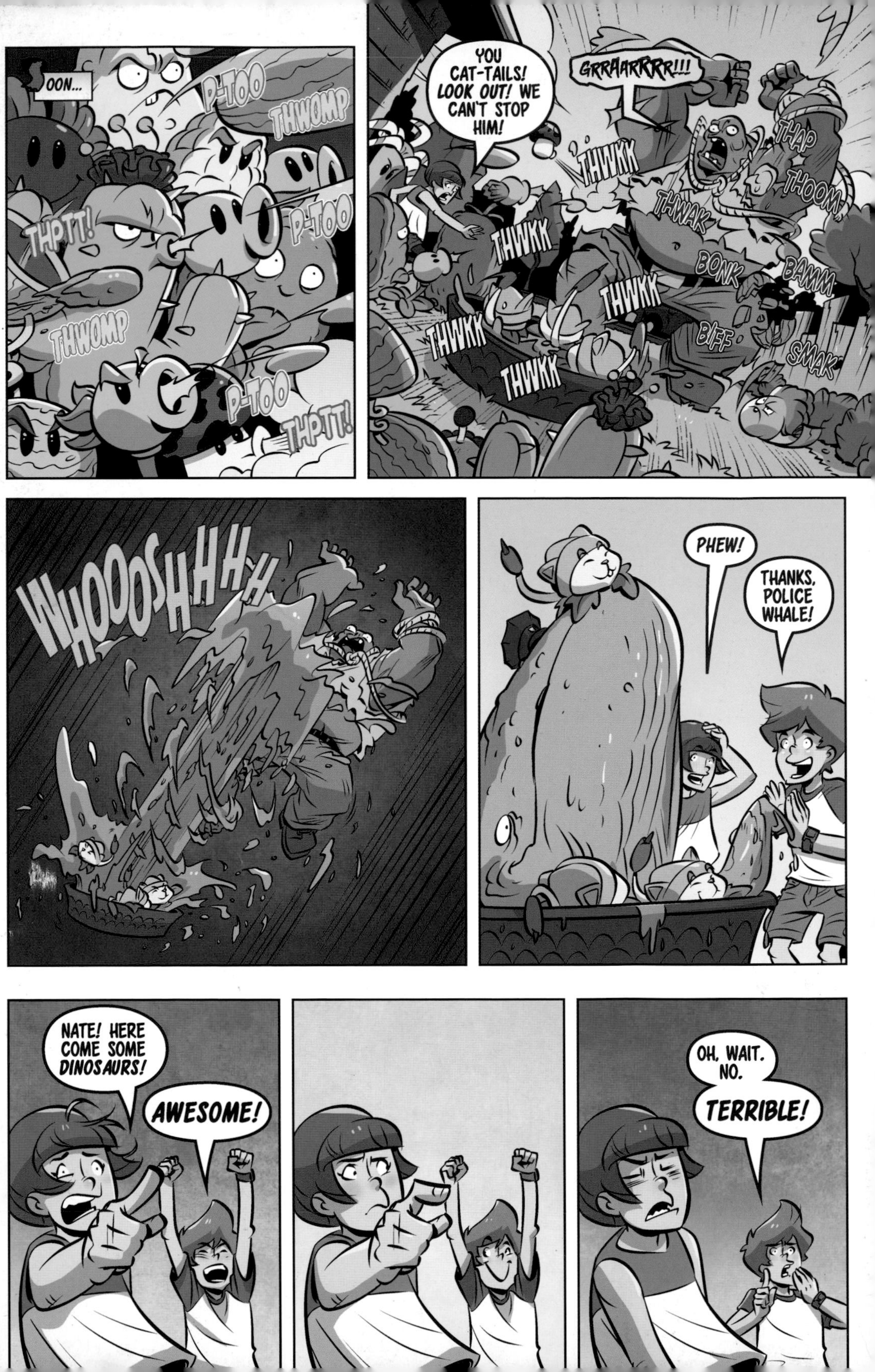
OON...
D-TOO
THWOMP
THPTT!
D-TOO
THWOMP
D-TOO
THPTT!
YOU CAT-TAILS! LOOK OUT! WE CAN'T STOP HIM!
GRRAARRRR!!!
THWKK
THAP
THOOM
THWAK
THWKK
BONK
BAMM
THWKK
BIFF
SMAK
THWKK
THWKK
WHOOOSHHHH
PHEW!
THANKS, POLICE WHALE!
NATE! HERE COME SOME DINOSAURS!
AWESOME!
OH, WAIT. NO.
TERRIBLE!

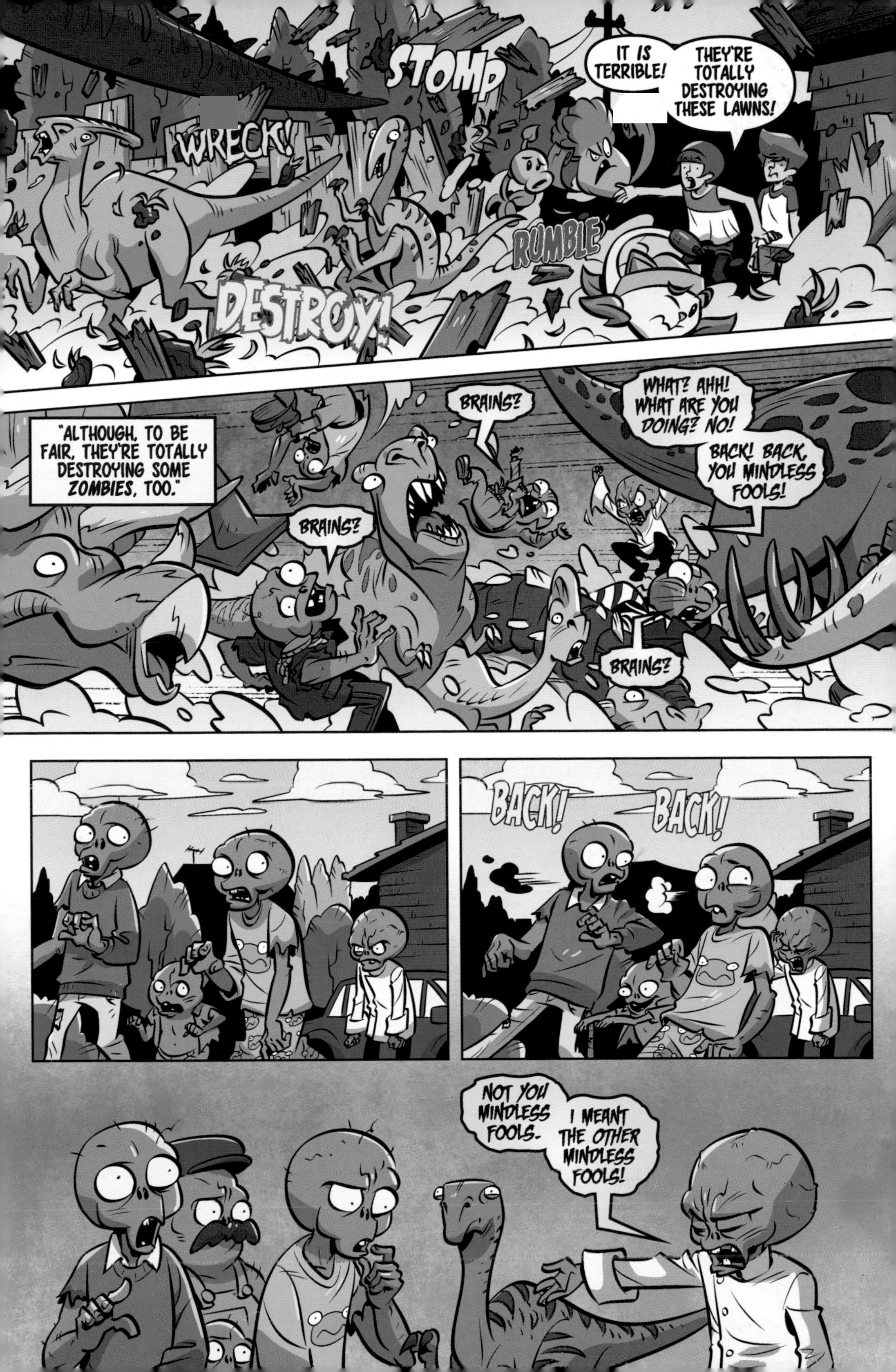
STOMP
WRECK!
IT IS TERRIBLE!
THEY'RE TOTALLY DESTROYING THESE LAWNS!
RUMBLE
DESTROY!
"ALTHOUGH, TO BE FAIR, THEY'RE TOTALLY DESTROYING SOME ZOMBIES, TOO."
BRAINS?
BRAINS?
WHAT? AHH! WHAT ARE YOU DOING? NO!
BACK! BACK, YOU MINDLESS FOOLS!
BRAINS?
BACK!
BACK!
NOT YOU MINDLESS FOOLS.
I MEANT THE OTHER MINDLESS FOOLS!

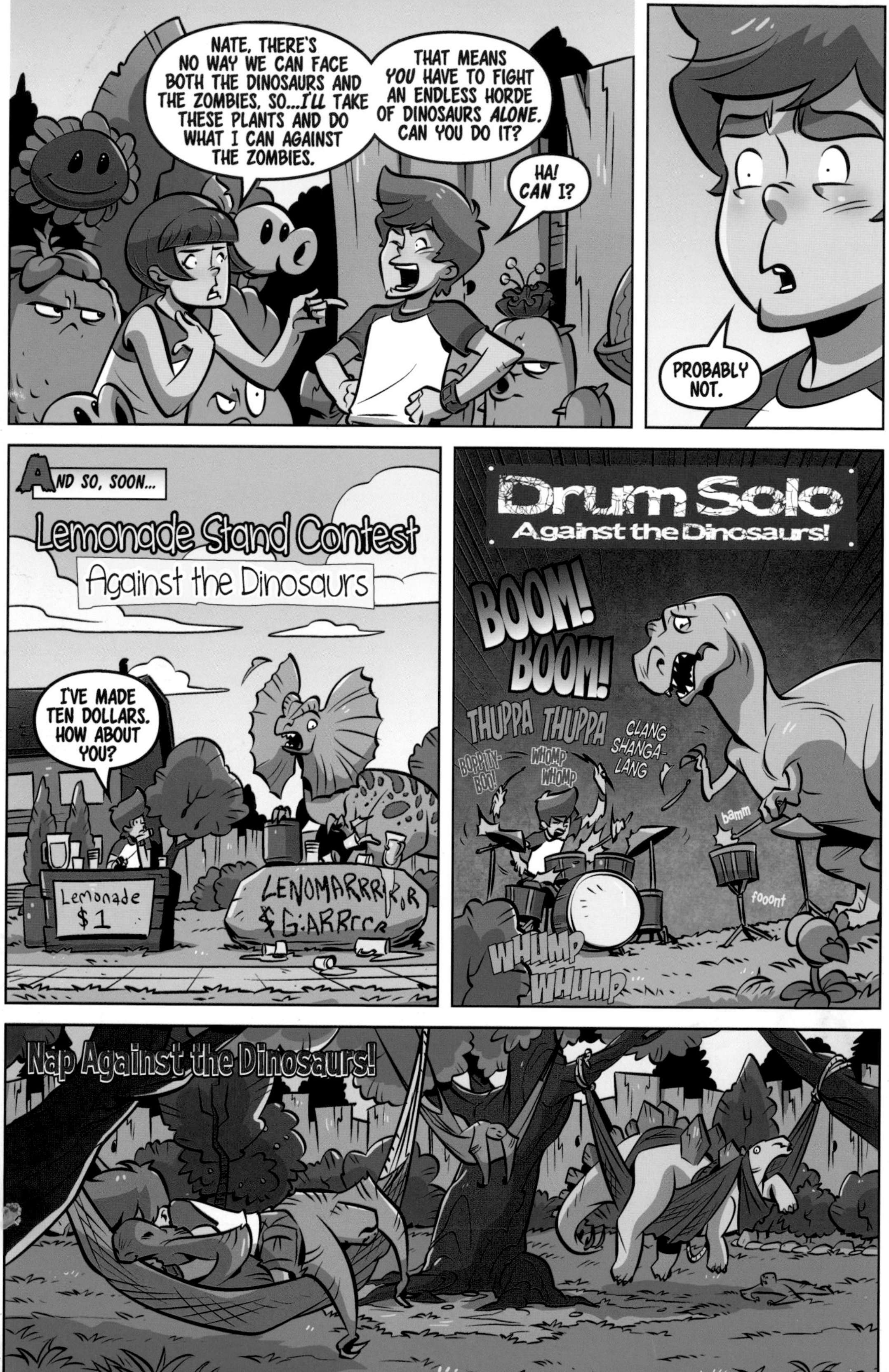

NATE, THERE'S NO WAY WE CAN FACE BOTH THE DINOSAURS AND THE ZOMBIES, SO...I'LL TAKE THESE PLANTS AND DO WHAT I CAN AGAINST THE ZOMBIES.
THAT MEANS YOU HAVE TO FIGHT AN ENDLESS HORDE OF DINOSAURS ALONE. CAN YOU DO IT?
HA! CAN I?
PROBABLY NOT.
AND SO, SOON...
Lemonade Stand Contest
Against the Dinosaurs
I'VE MADE TEN DOLLARS. HOW ABOUT YOU?
Lemonade $1
Drum Solo
Against the Dinosaurs!
BOOM! BOOM!
THUPPA THUPPA
CLANG SHANGA-LANG
BOPPITY-BOO!
WHOMP WHOMP
bamm
fooont
WHUMP WHUMP
Nap Against the Dinosaurs!

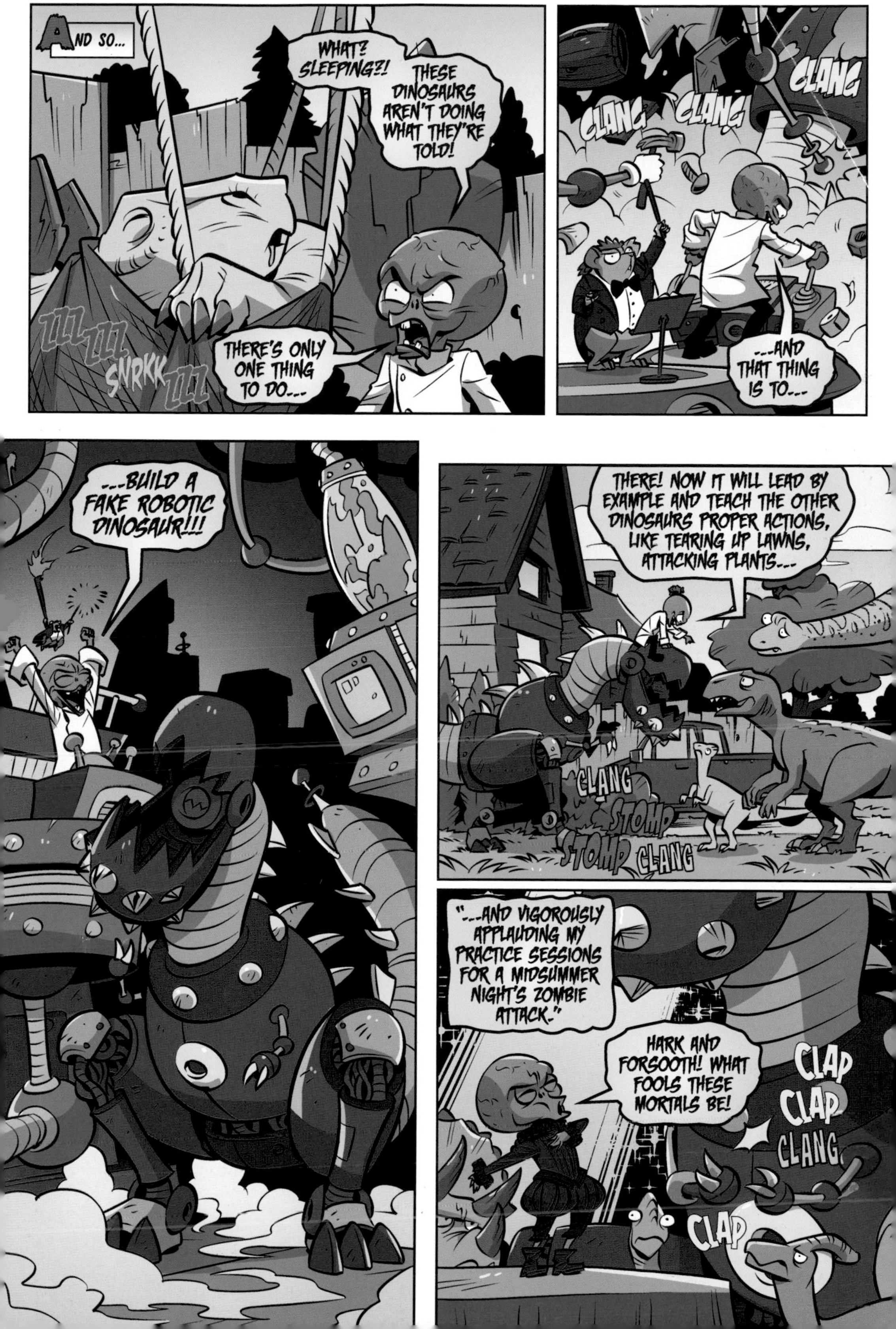
AND SO...
WHAT? SLEEPING?!
THESE DINOSAURS AREN'T DOING WHAT THEY'RE TOLD!
ZZZ ZZZ SNRKK ZZZ
THERE'S ONLY ONE THING TO DO...
CLANG CLANG CLANG
...AND THAT THING IS TO...
...BUILD A FAKE ROBOTIC DINOSAUR!!!
THERE! NOW IT WILL LEAD BY EXAMPLE AND TEACH THE OTHER DINOSAURS PROPER ACTIONS, LIKE TEARING UP LAWNS, ATTACKING PLANTS...
CLANG STOMP STOMP CLANG
"...AND VIGOROUSLY APPLAUDING MY PRACTICE SESSIONS FOR A MIDSUMMER NIGHT'S ZOMBIE ATTACK."
HARK AND FORSOOTH! WHAT FOOLS THESE MORTALS BE!
CLAP CLAP CLANG
CLAP

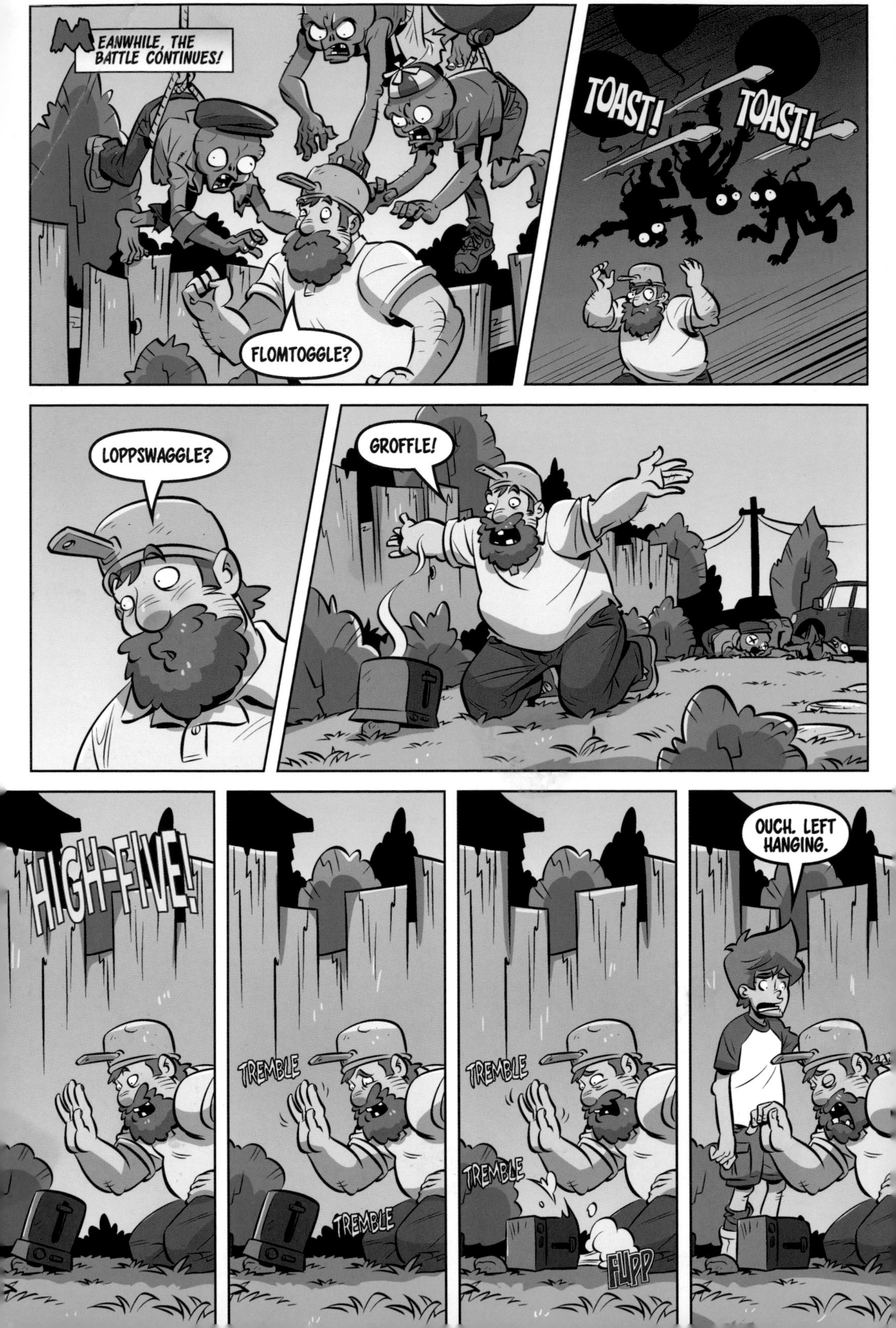
MEANWHILE, THE BATTLE CONTINUES!
FLOMTOGGLE?
TOAST!
TOAST!
LOPPSWAGGLE?
GROFFLE!
HIGH-FIVE!
TREMBLE
TREMBLE
TREMBLE
TREMBLE
FLIPP
OUCH. LEFT HANGING.

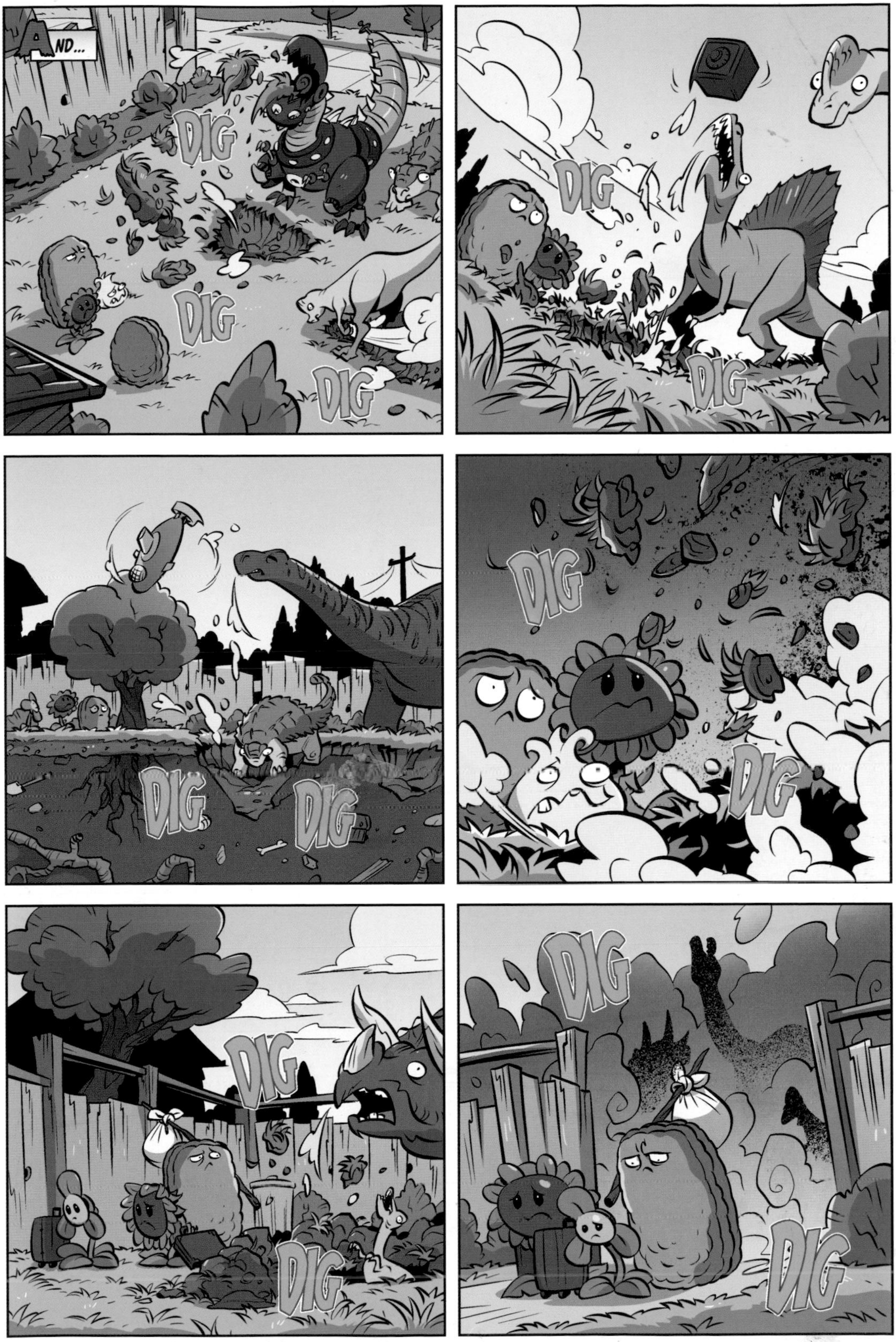
AND...
DIG
DIG
DIG
DIG
DIG
DIG
DIG
DIG
DIG
DIG
DIG
DIG
DIG

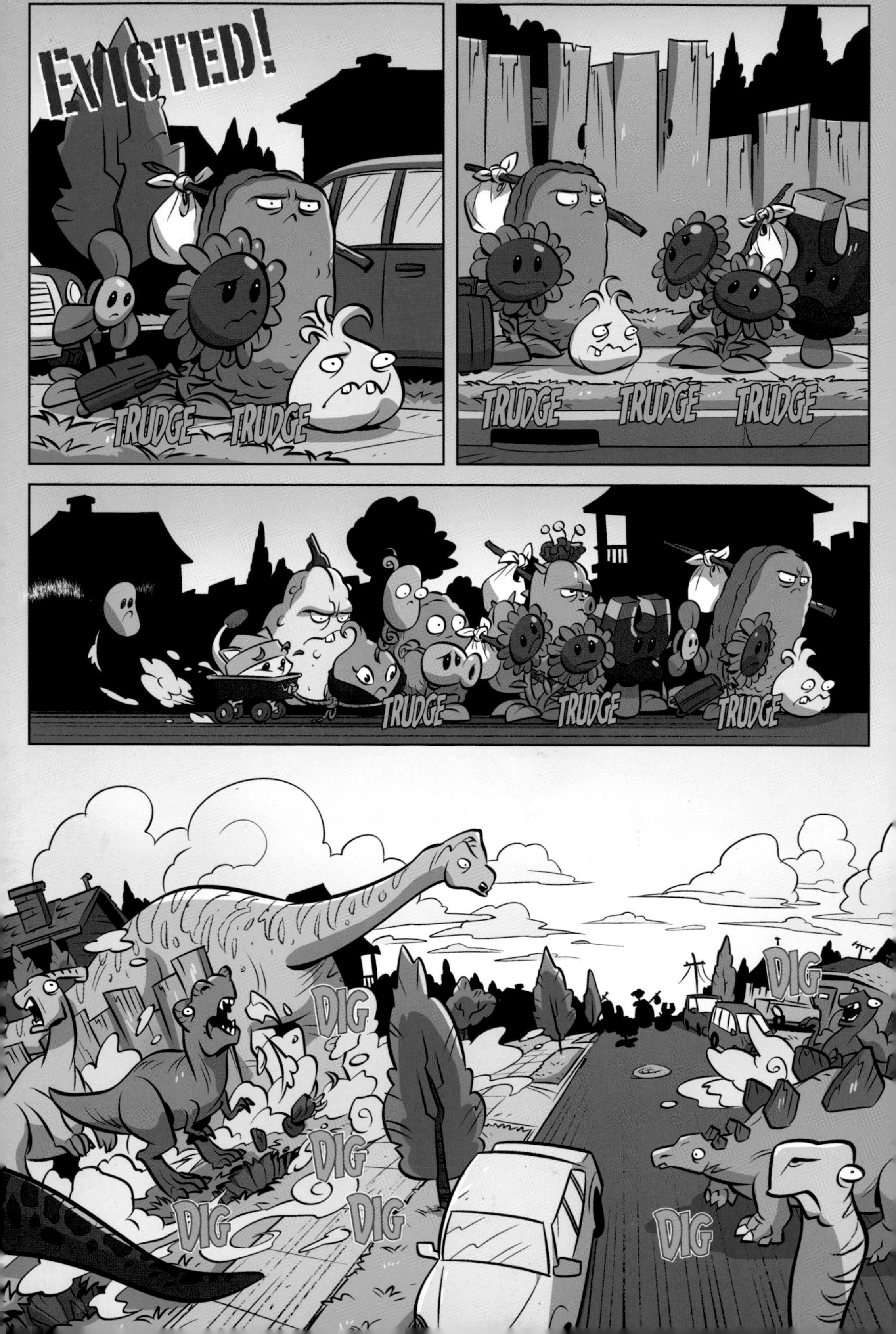
EVICTED!
TRUDGE
TRUDGE
TRUDGE
TRUDGE
TRUDGE
TRUDGE
TRUDGE
TRUDGE
DIG
DIG
DIG
DIG
DIG
DIG

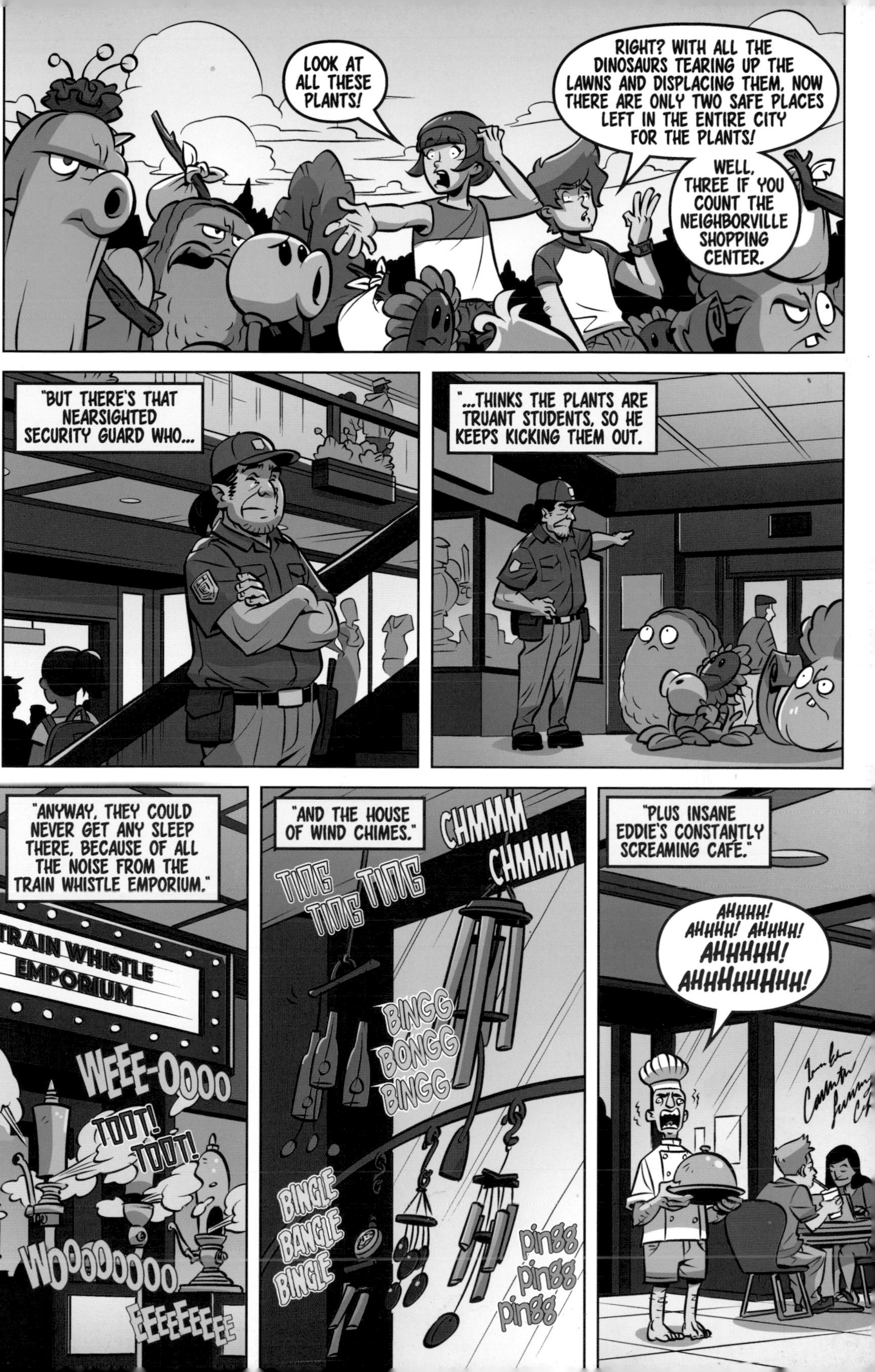
LOOK AT ALL THESE PLANTS!
RIGHT? WITH ALL THE DINOSAURS TEARING UP THE LAWNS AND DISPLACING THEM, NOW THERE ARE ONLY TWO SAFE PLACES LEFT IN THE ENTIRE CITY FOR THE PLANTS!
WELL, THREE IF YOU COUNT THE NEIGHBORVILLE SHOPPING CENTER.
"BUT THERE'S THAT NEARSIGHTED SECURITY GUARD WHO...
"...THINKS THE PLANTS ARE TRUANT STUDENTS, SO HE KEEPS KICKING THEM OUT.
"ANYWAY, THEY COULD NEVER GET ANY SLEEP THERE, BECAUSE OF ALL THE NOISE FROM THE TRAIN WHISTLE EMPORIUM."
TRAIN WHISTLE EMPORIUM
WEEE-OOOO
TOOT! TOOT!
WOOOOOOOO
EEEEEEEEE
"AND THE HOUSE OF WIND CHIMES."
CHMMM CHMMM
TING TING TING
BINGG BONGG BINGG
BINGLE BANGLE BINGLE
pingg pingg pingg
"PLUS INSANE EDDIE'S CONSTANTLY SCREAMING CAFE."
AHHHH! AHHHH! AHHHH! AHHHHH! AHHHHHHH!

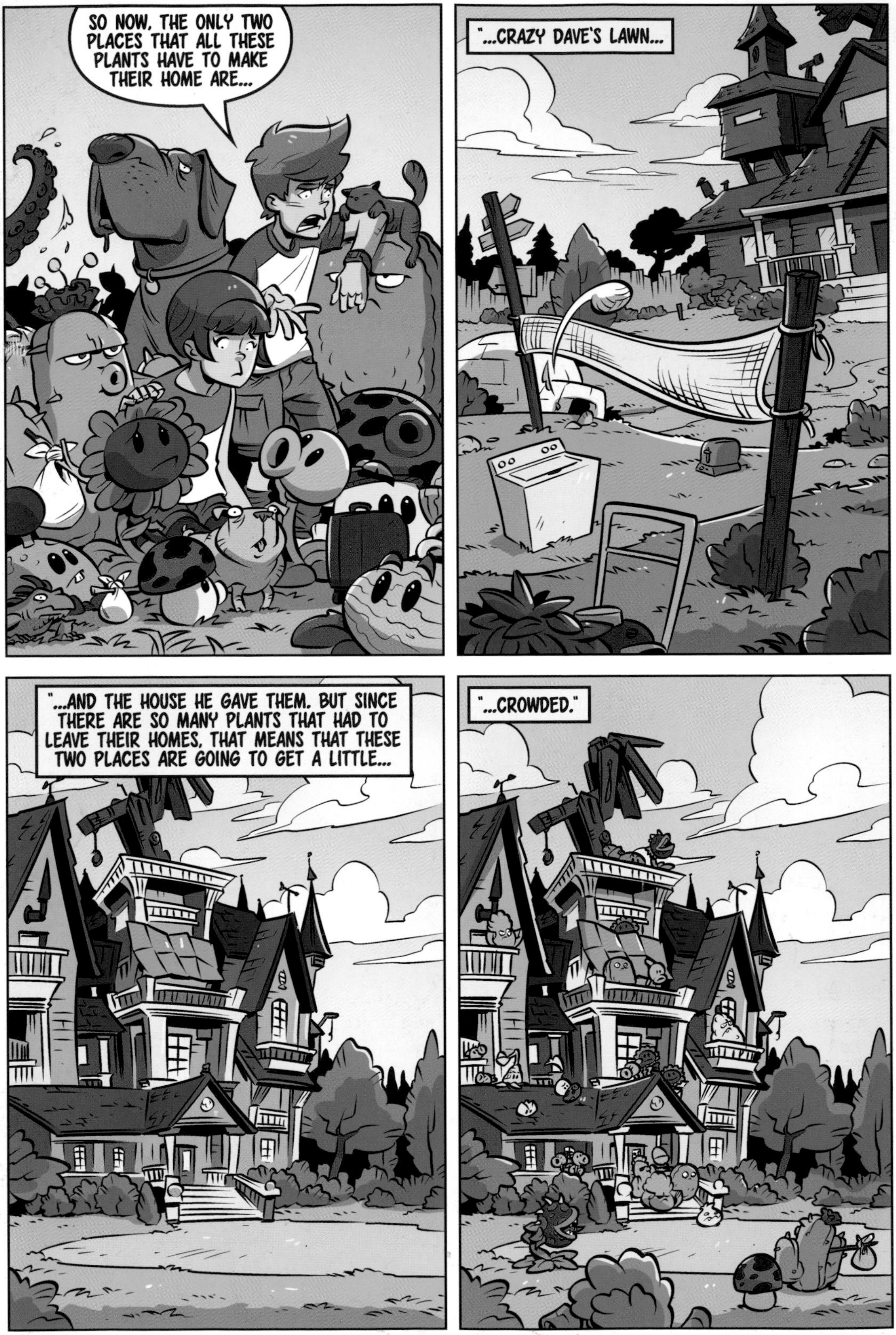

SO NOW, THE ONLY TWO PLACES THAT ALL THESE PLANTS HAVE TO MAKE THEIR HOME ARE...
"...CRAZY DAVE'S LAWN...
"...AND THE HOUSE HE GAVE THEM. BUT SINCE THERE ARE SO MANY PLANTS THAT HAD TO LEAVE THEIR HOMES, THAT MEANS THAT THESE TWO PLACES ARE GOING TO GET A LITTLE...
"...CROWDED."

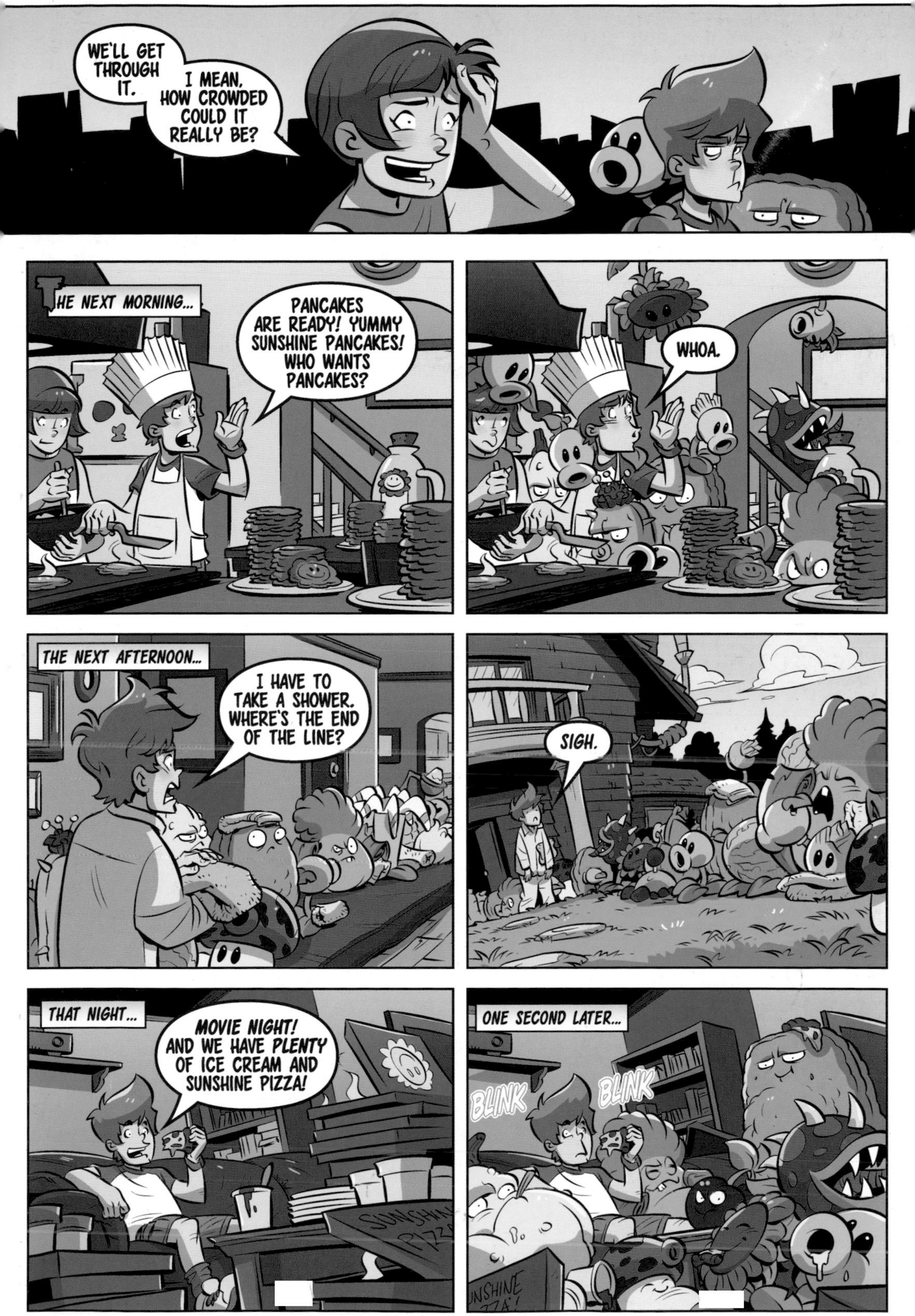
WE'LL GET THROUGH IT.
I MEAN, HOW CROWDED COULD IT REALLY BE?
THE NEXT MORNING...
PANCAKES ARE READY! YUMMY SUNSHINE PANCAKES! WHO WANTS PANCAKES?
WHOA.
THE NEXT AFTERNOON...
I HAVE TO TAKE A SHOWER. WHERE'S THE END OF THE LINE?
SIGH.
THAT NIGHT...
MOVIE NIGHT! AND WE HAVE PLENTY OF ICE CREAM AND SUNSHINE PIZZA!
SUNSHINE PIZZA
ONE SECOND LATER...
BLINK
BLINK

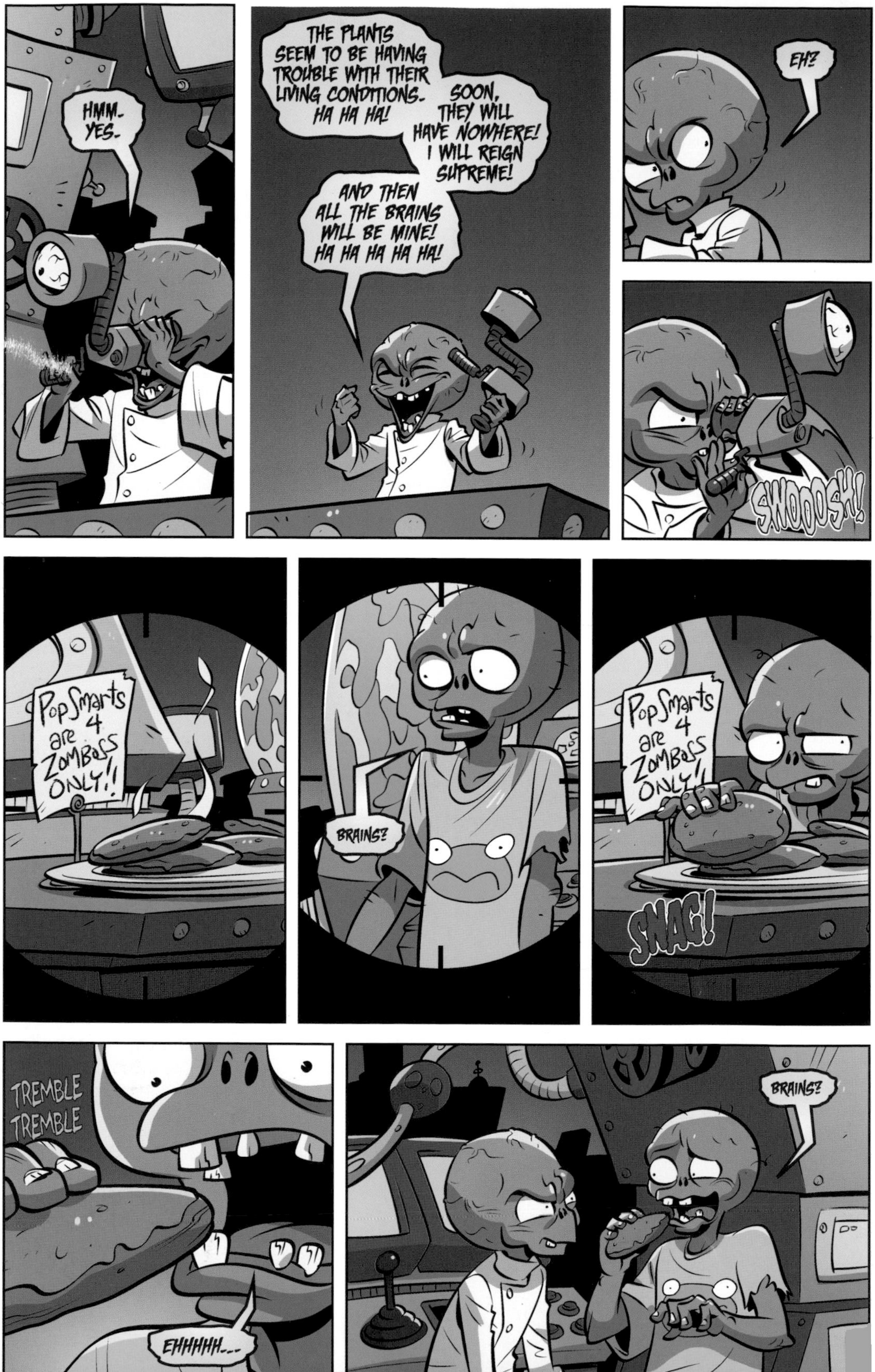
HMM. YES.
THE PLANTS SEEM TO BE HAVING TROUBLE WITH THEIR LIVING CONDITIONS. HA HA HA!
SOON, THEY WILL HAVE NOWHERE! I WILL REIGN SUPREME!
AND THEN ALL THE BRAINS WILL BE MINE! HA HA HA HA HA!
EH?
SWOOOSH!
PopSmarts 4 are ZOMBOSS ONLY!!
BRAINS?
PopSmarts 4 are ZOMBOSS ONLY!!
SNAG!
TREMBLE TREMBLE
EHHHHH...
BRAINS?

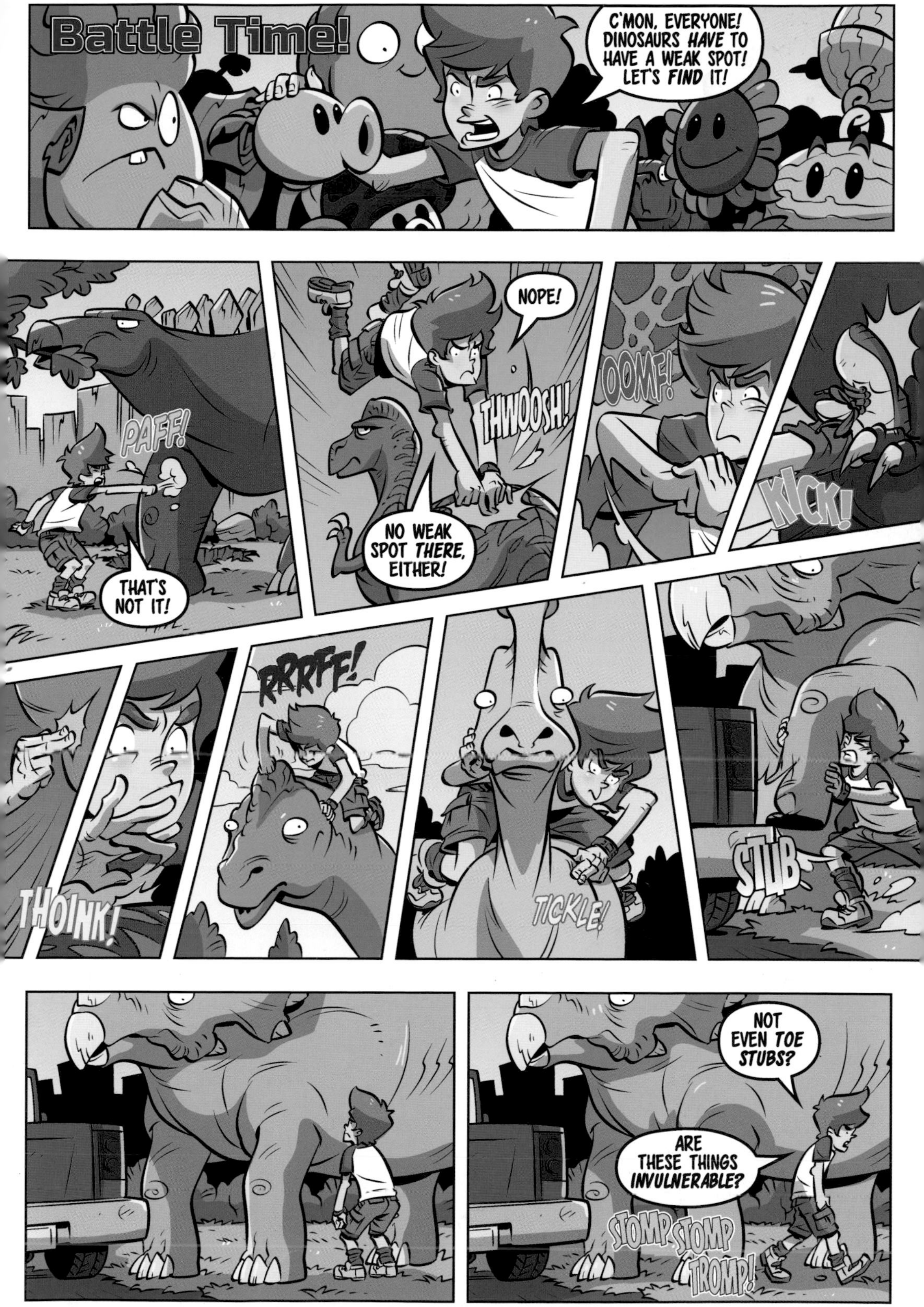
Battle Time!
C'MON, EVERYONE! DINOSAURS HAVE TO HAVE A WEAK SPOT! LET'S FIND IT!
PAFF!
THAT'S NOT IT!
NOPE!
THWOOSH!
NO WEAK SPOT THERE, EITHER!
OOMF!
KICK!
THOINK!
RRRFF!
TICKLE!
STUB
NOT EVEN TOE STUBS?
ARE THESE THINGS INVULNERABLE?
STOMP STOMP
TROMP!

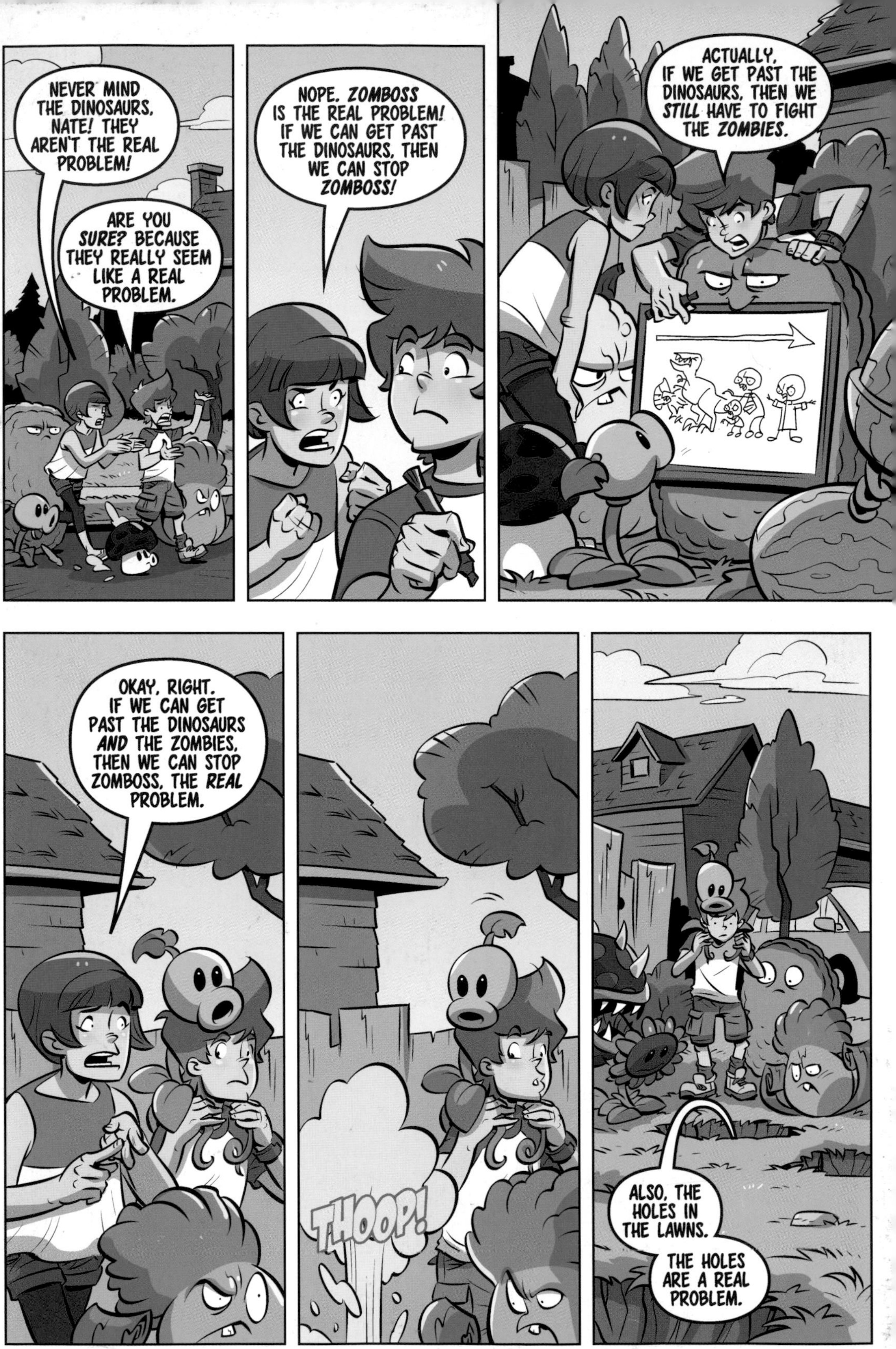
NEVER MIND THE DINOSAURS, NATE! THEY AREN'T THE REAL PROBLEM!
ARE YOU SURE? BECAUSE THEY REALLY SEEM LIKE A REAL PROBLEM.
NOPE. ZOMBOSS IS THE REAL PROBLEM! IF WE CAN GET PAST THE DINOSAURS, THEN WE CAN STOP ZOMBOSS!
ACTUALLY, IF WE GET PAST THE DINOSAURS, THEN WE STILL HAVE TO FIGHT THE ZOMBIES.
OKAY, RIGHT. IF WE CAN GET PAST THE DINOSAURS AND THE ZOMBIES, THEN WE CAN STOP ZOMBOSS, THE REAL PROBLEM.
THOOP!
ALSO, THE HOLES IN THE LAWNS.
THE HOLES ARE A REAL PROBLEM.

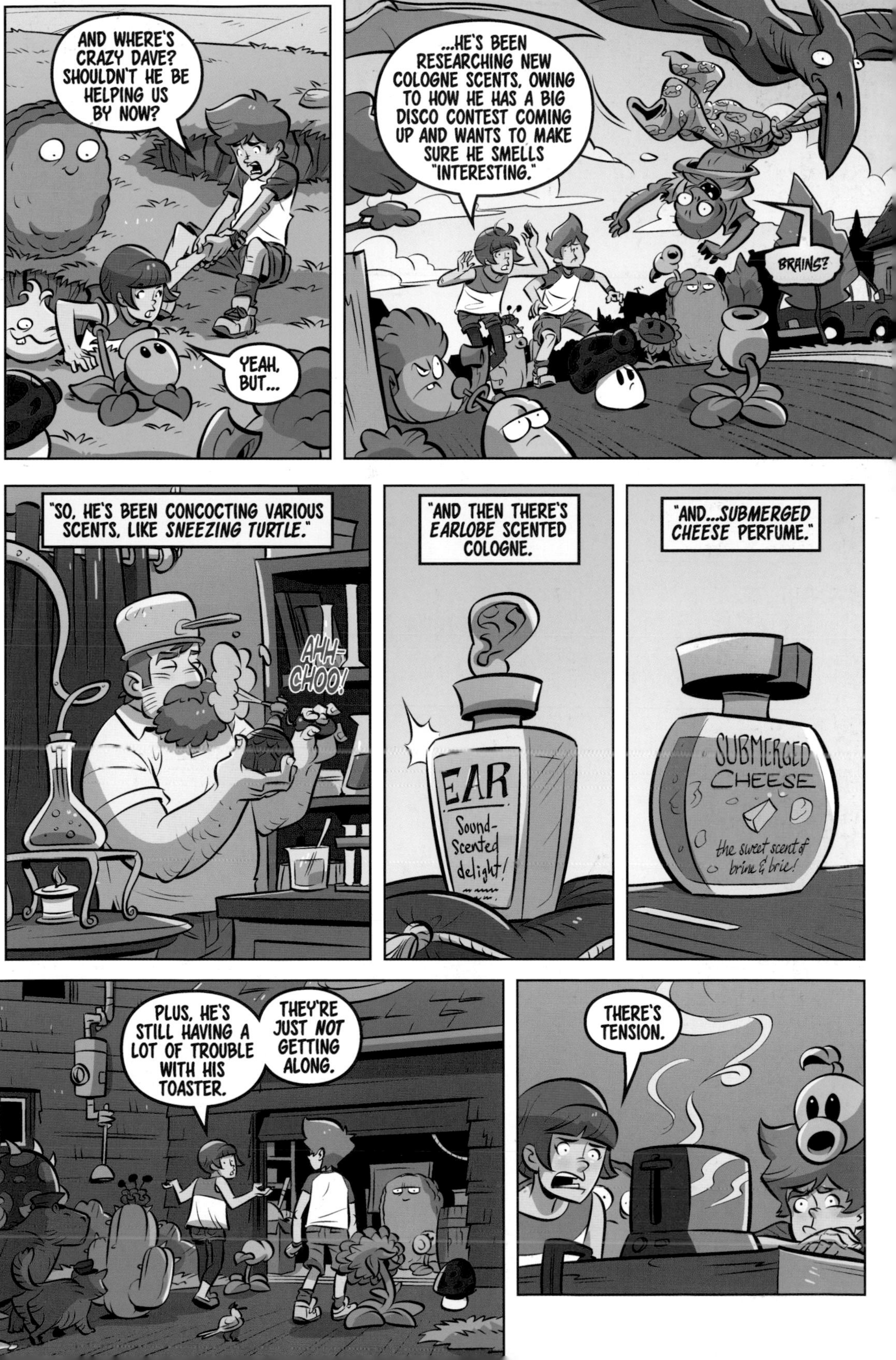
AND WHERE'S CRAZY DAVE? SHOULDN'T HE BE HELPING US BY NOW?
YEAH, BUT...
...HE'S BEEN RESEARCHING NEW COLOGNE SCENTS, OWING TO HOW HE HAS A BIG DISCO CONTEST COMING UP AND WANTS TO MAKE SURE HE SMELLS "INTERESTING."
BRAINS?
"SO, HE'S BEEN CONCOCTING VARIOUS SCENTS, LIKE *SNEEZING TURTLE*."
AHH-CHOO!
"AND THEN THERE'S *EARLOBE* SCENTED COLOGNE.
EAR
Sound-Scented delight!
"AND...*SUBMERGED CHEESE* PERFUME."
SUBMERGED CHEESE
the sweet scent of brine & brie!
PLUS, HE'S STILL HAVING A LOT OF TROUBLE WITH HIS TOASTER.
THEY'RE JUST *NOT* GETTING ALONG.
THERE'S TENSION.

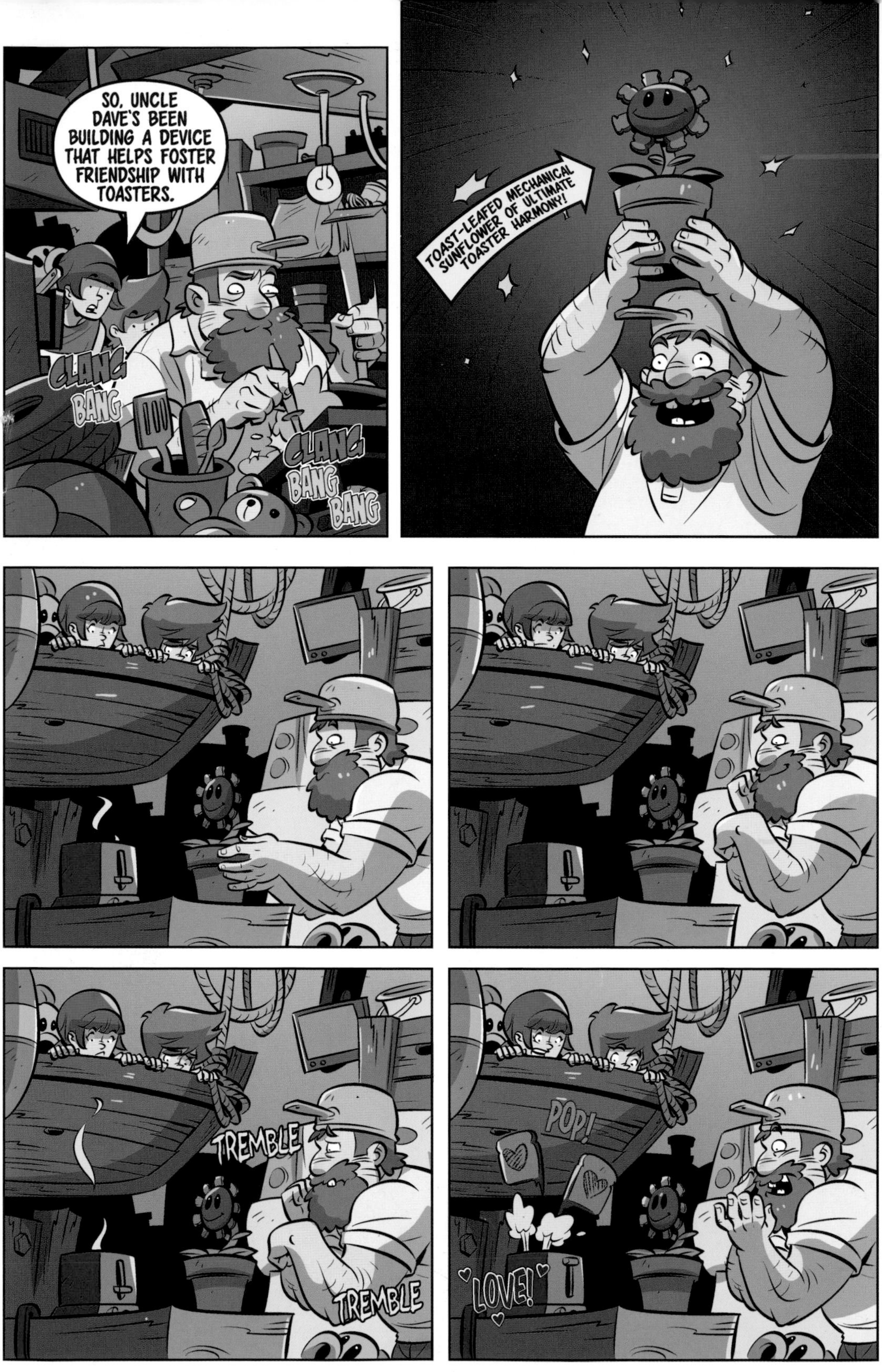
SO, UNCLE DAVE'S BEEN BUILDING A DEVICE THAT HELPS FOSTER FRIENDSHIP WITH TOASTERS.
CLANG
BANG
CLANG
BANG
BANG
TOAST-LEAFED MECHANICAL SUNFLOWER OF ULTIMATE TOASTER HARMONY!
TREMBLE
TREMBLE
POP!
LOVE!

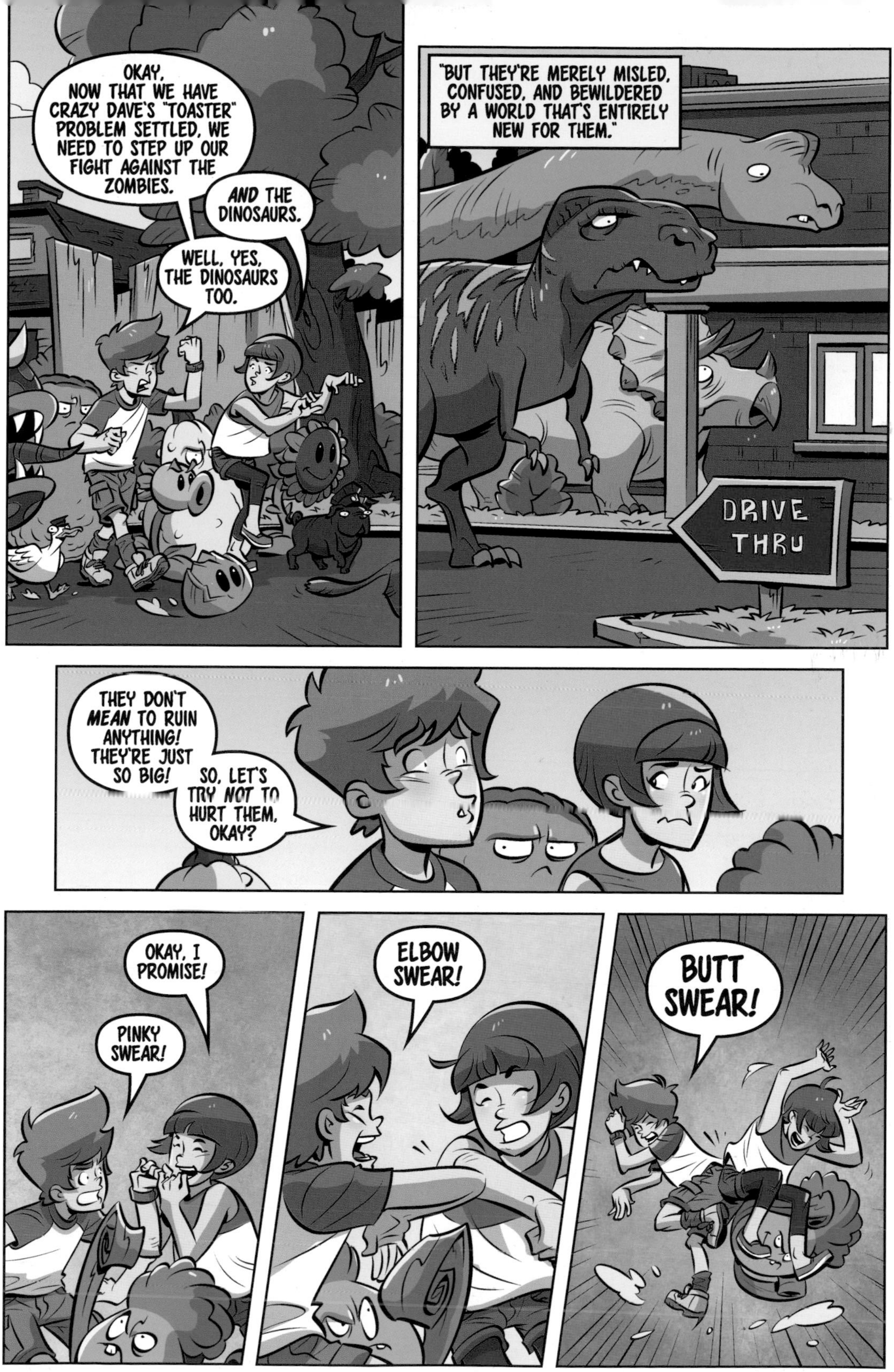
OKAY, NOW THAT WE HAVE CRAZY DAVE'S "TOASTER" PROBLEM SETTLED, WE NEED TO STEP UP OUR FIGHT AGAINST THE ZOMBIES.
AND THE DINOSAURS.
WELL, YES, THE DINOSAURS TOO.
"BUT THEY'RE MERELY MISLED, CONFUSED, AND BEWILDERED BY A WORLD THAT'S ENTIRELY NEW FOR THEM."
DRIVE THRU
THEY DON'T MEAN TO RUIN ANYTHING! THEY'RE JUST SO BIG!
SO, LET'S TRY NOT TO HURT THEM, OKAY?
OKAY, I PROMISE!
PINKY SWEAR!
ELBOW SWEAR!
BUTT SWEAR!

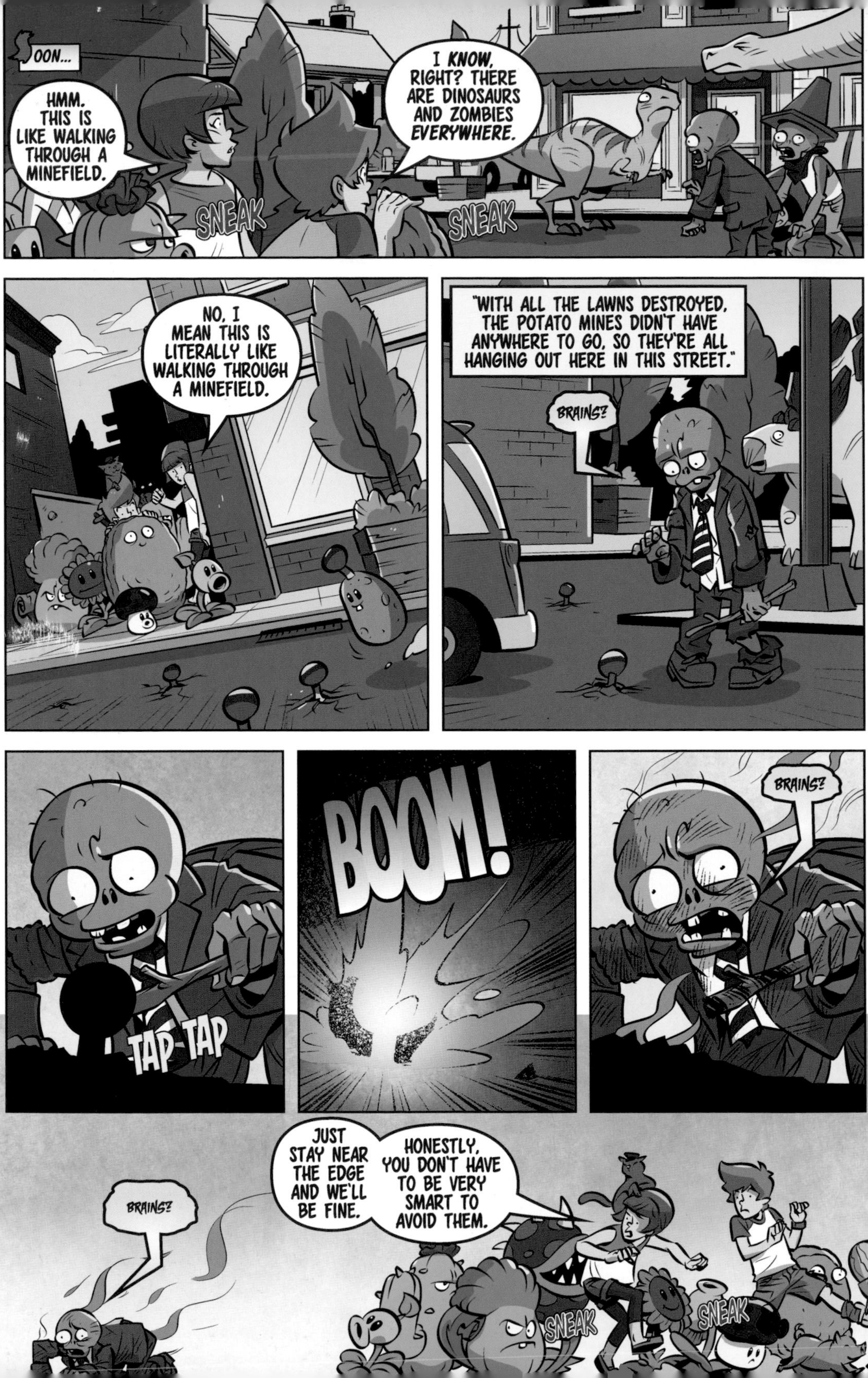
SOON...
HMM. THIS IS LIKE WALKING THROUGH A MINEFIELD.
I KNOW, RIGHT? THERE ARE DINOSAURS AND ZOMBIES EVERYWHERE.
SNEAK
SNEAK
NO, I MEAN THIS IS LITERALLY LIKE WALKING THROUGH A MINEFIELD.
"WITH ALL THE LAWNS DESTROYED, THE POTATO MINES DIDN'T HAVE ANYWHERE TO GO, SO THEY'RE ALL HANGING OUT HERE IN THIS STREET."
BRAINS?
TAP TAP
BOOM!
BRAINS?
BRAINS?
JUST STAY NEAR THE EDGE AND WE'LL BE FINE.
HONESTLY, YOU DON'T HAVE TO BE VERY SMART TO AVOID THEM.
SNEAK
SNEAK

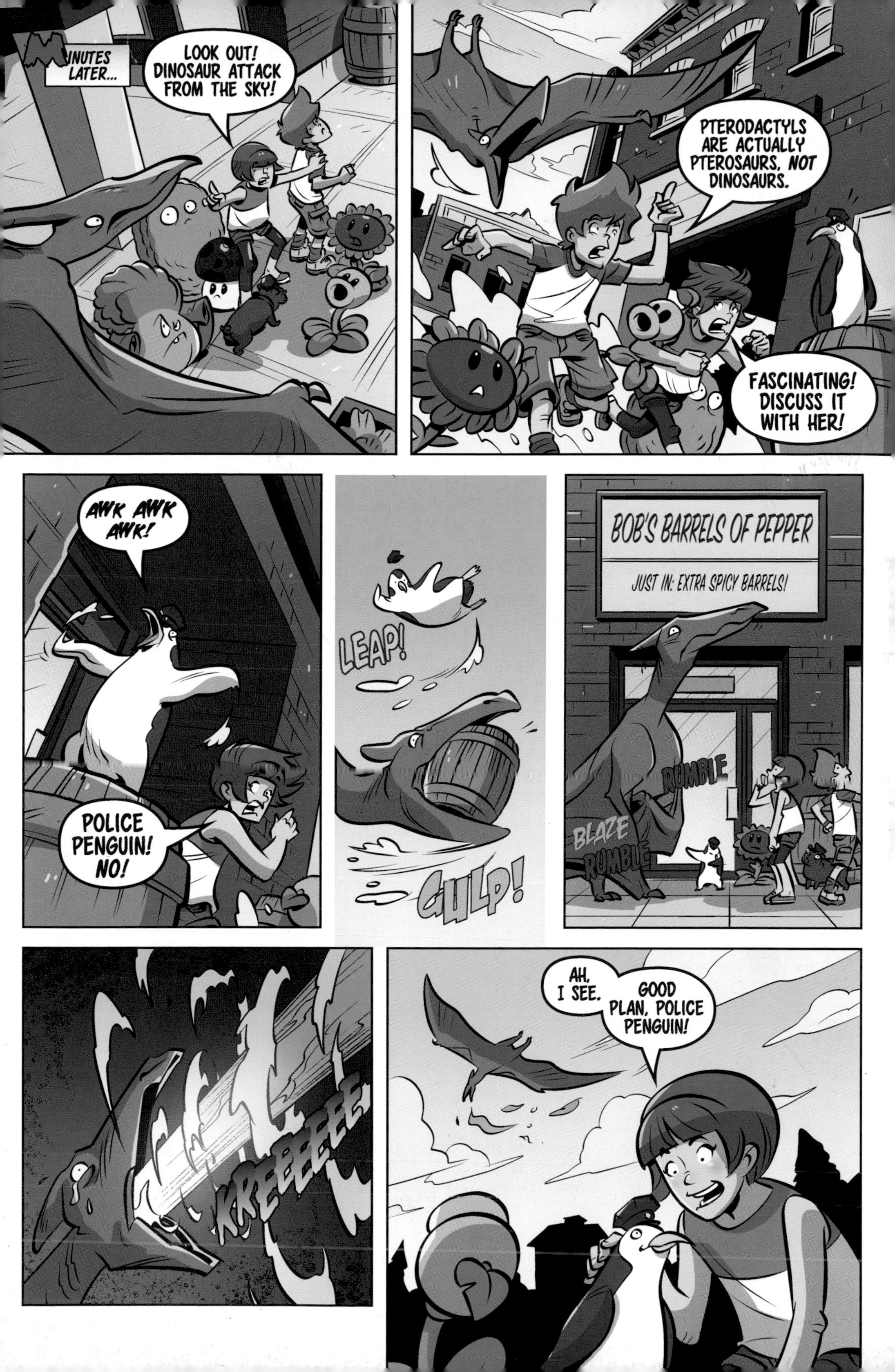
MINUTES LATER...
LOOK OUT! DINOSAUR ATTACK FROM THE SKY!
PTERODACTYLS ARE ACTUALLY PTEROSAURS, NOT DINOSAURS.
FASCINATING! DISCUSS IT WITH HER!
AWK AWK AWK!
POLICE PENGUIN! NO!
LEAP!
GULP!
BOB'S BARRELS OF PEPPER
JUST IN: EXTRA SPICY BARRELS!
RUMBLE
BLAZE
RUMBLE
KREEEEEE
AH, I SEE.
GOOD PLAN, POLICE PENGUIN!

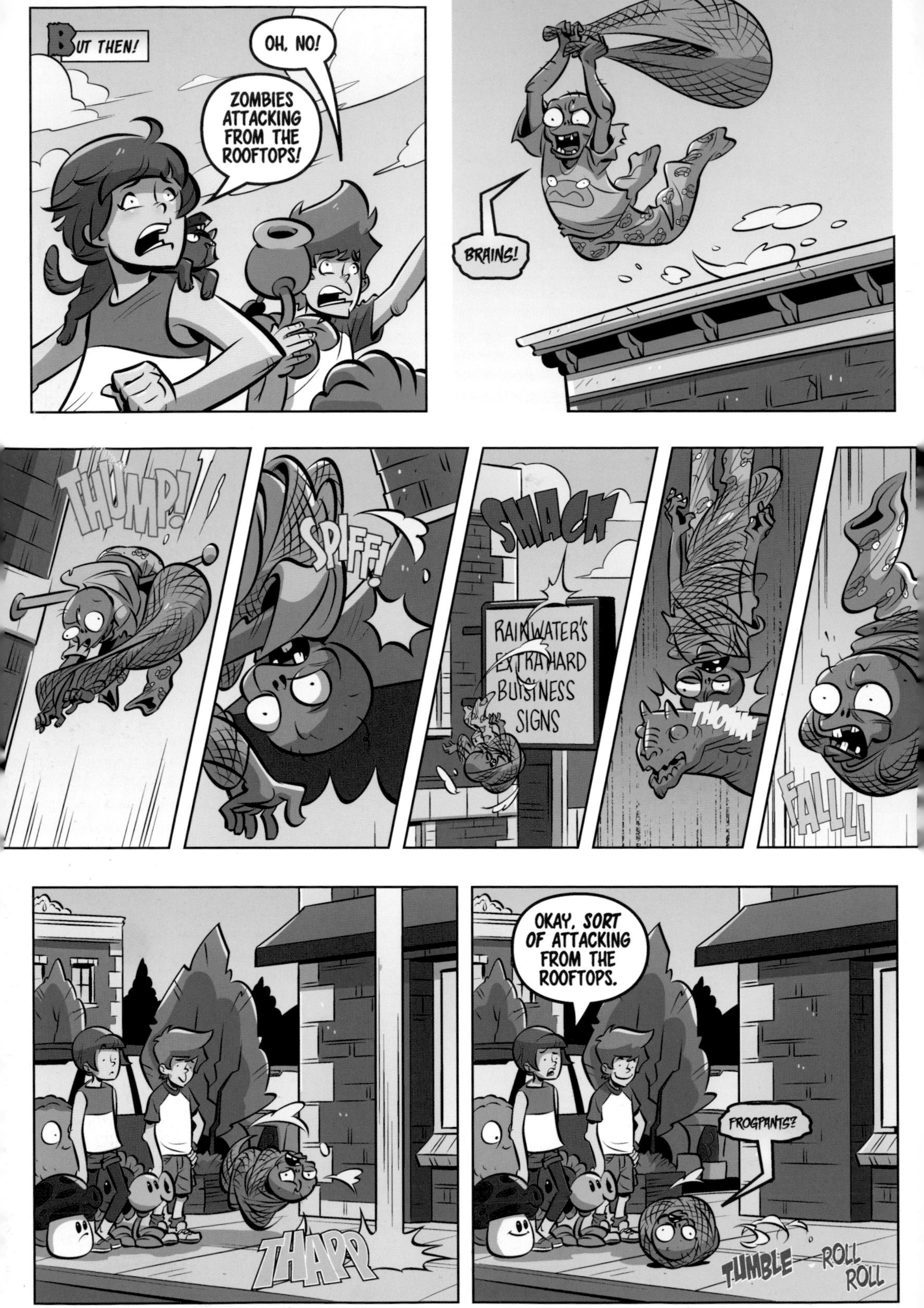
BUT THEN!
OH, NO!
ZOMBIES ATTACKING FROM THE ROOFTOPS!
BRAINS!
THUMP!
SPIFF!
SMACK
RAINWATER'S EXTRAHARD BUISINESS SIGNS
THONK
FALLLLL
THAPP
OKAY, SORT OF ATTACKING FROM THE ROOFTOPS.
FROGPANTS?
TUMBLE
ROLL
ROLL

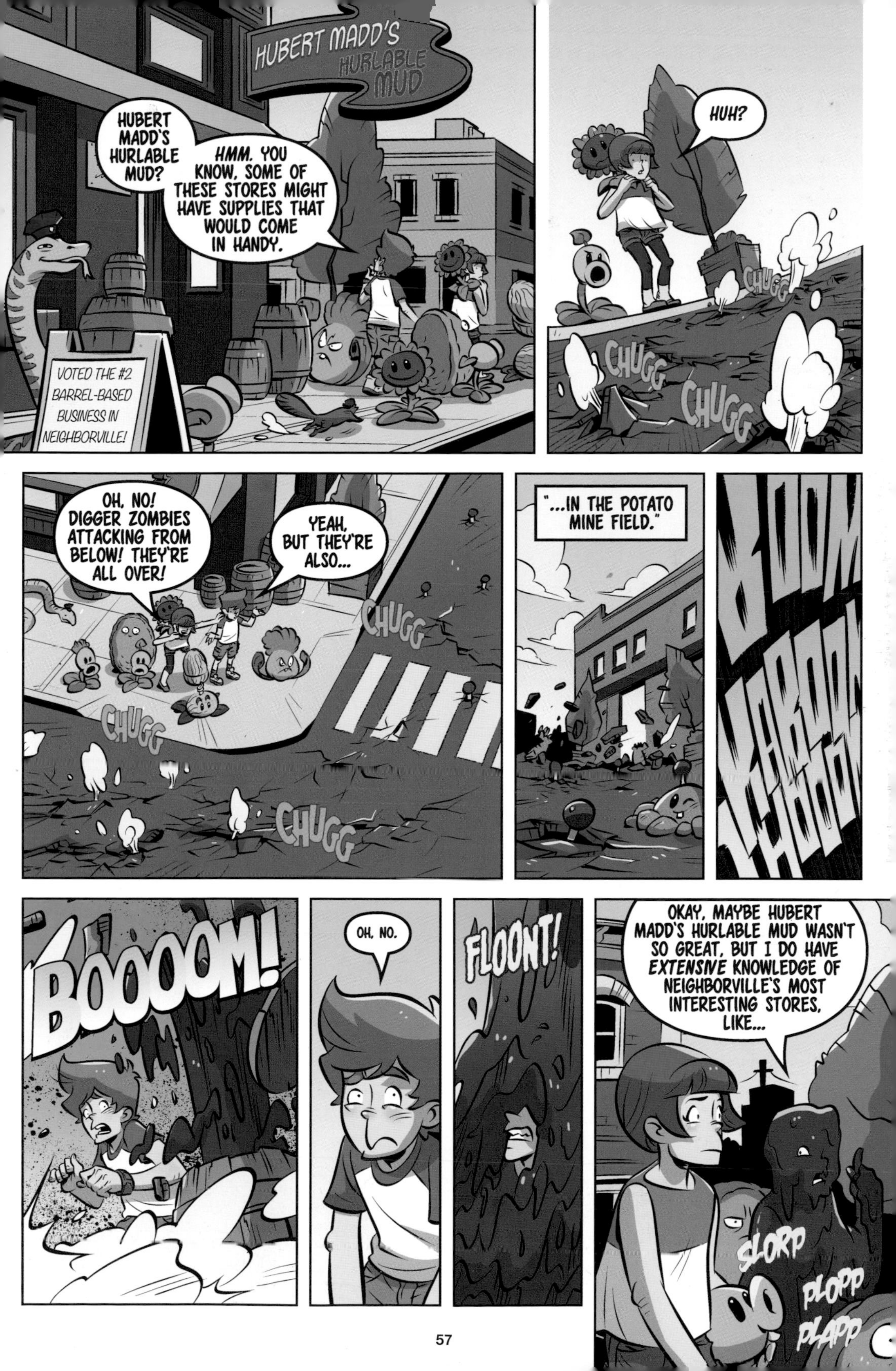

HUBERT MADD'S HURLABLE MUD
HUBERT MADD'S HURLABLE MUD?
HMM. YOU KNOW, SOME OF THESE STORES MIGHT HAVE SUPPLIES THAT WOULD COME IN HANDY.
VOTED THE #2 BARREL-BASED BUSINESS IN NEIGHBORVILLE!
HUH?
CHUGG
CHUGG
CHUGG
OH, NO! DIGGER ZOMBIES ATTACKING FROM BELOW! THEY'RE ALL OVER!
YEAH, BUT THEY'RE ALSO...
CHUGG
CHUGG
CHUGG
"...IN THE POTATO MINE FIELD."
BOOM
KABOOM
BOOOOM!
OH, NO.
FLOONT!
OKAY, MAYBE HUBERT MADD'S HURLABLE MUD WASN'T SO GREAT, BUT I DO HAVE EXTENSIVE KNOWLEDGE OF NEIGHBORVILLE'S MOST INTERESTING STORES, LIKE...
SLORP
PLOPP
PLAPP

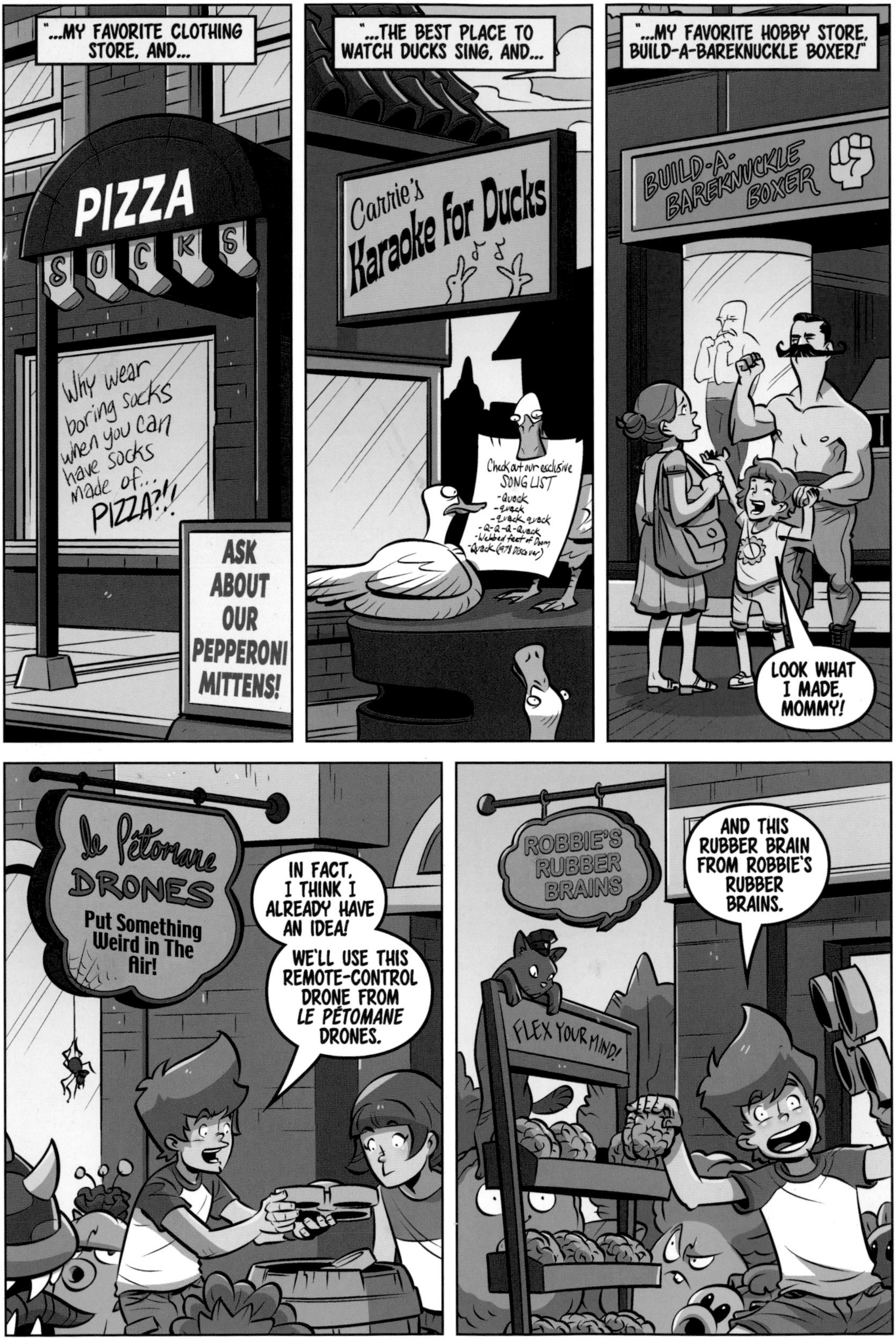
"...MY FAVORITE CLOTHING STORE, AND...
PIZZA
SOCKS
Why wear boring socks when you can have socks made of... PIZZA?!!
ASK ABOUT OUR PEPPERONI MITTENS!
"...THE BEST PLACE TO WATCH DUCKS SING, AND...
Carrie's Karaoke for Ducks
Check out our exclusive SONG LIST
-Quack
-quack
-quack quack
-Q-Q-Q-Quack
-Webbed feet of Doom
-Quack (1978 Disco ver)
"...MY FAVORITE HOBBY STORE, BUILD-A-BAREKNUCKLE BOXER!"
BUILD-A-BAREKNUCKLE BOXER
LOOK WHAT I MADE, MOMMY!
le Pétomane DRONES
Put Something Weird in The Air!
IN FACT, I THINK I ALREADY HAVE AN IDEA!
WE'LL USE THIS REMOTE-CONTROL DRONE FROM LE PÉTOMANE DRONES.
ROBBIE'S RUBBER BRAINS
AND THIS RUBBER BRAIN FROM ROBBIE'S RUBBER BRAINS.
FLEX YOUR MIND!

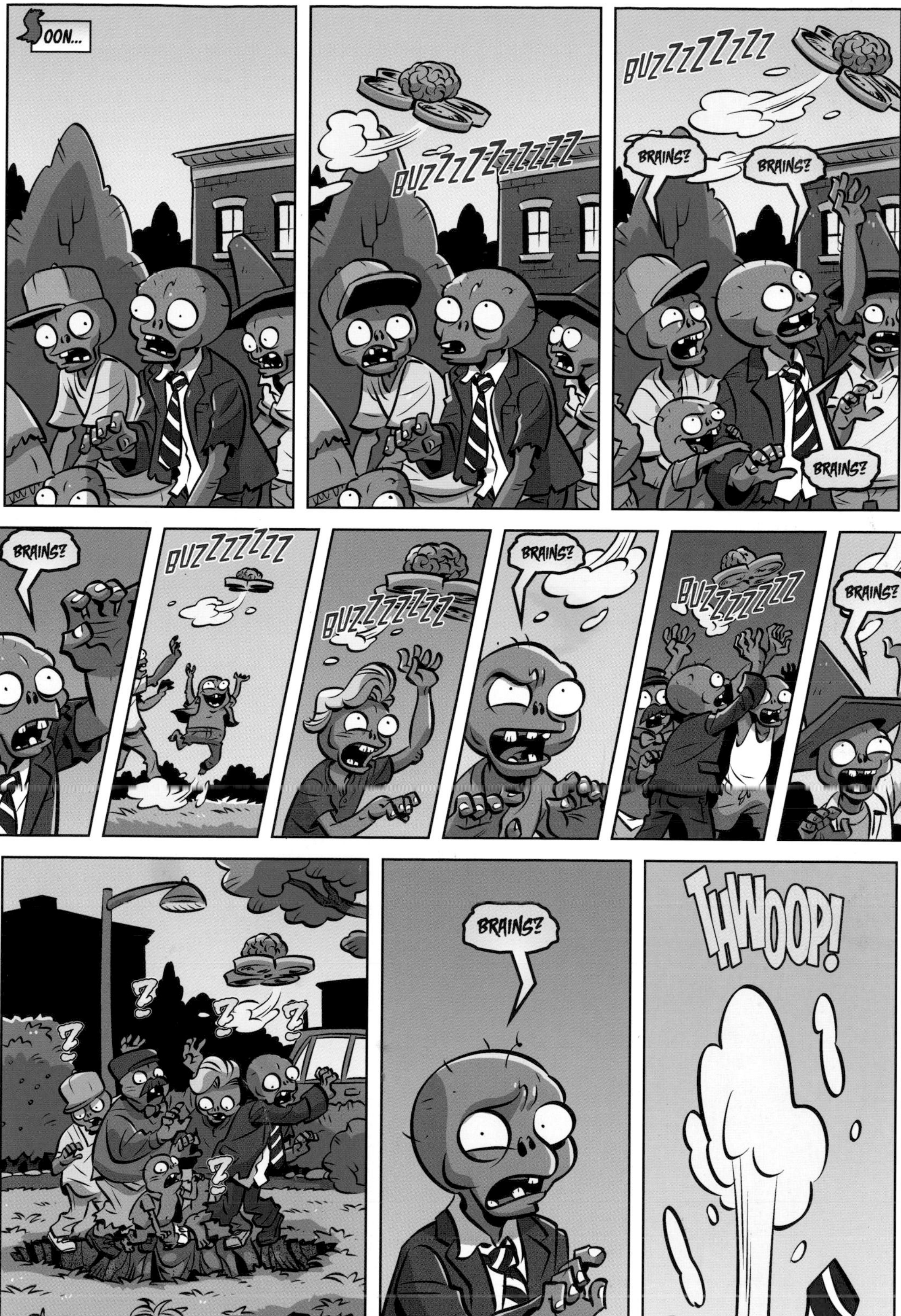
SOON...
BUZZZZZZZZZZZ
BUZZZZZZZZ
BRAINS?
BRAINS?
BRAINS?
BRAINS?
BUZZZZZZZ
BUZZZZZZZZ
BRAINS?
BUZZZZZZZZZ
BRAINS?
Z
Z
Z
Z
Z
BRAINS?
THWOOP!

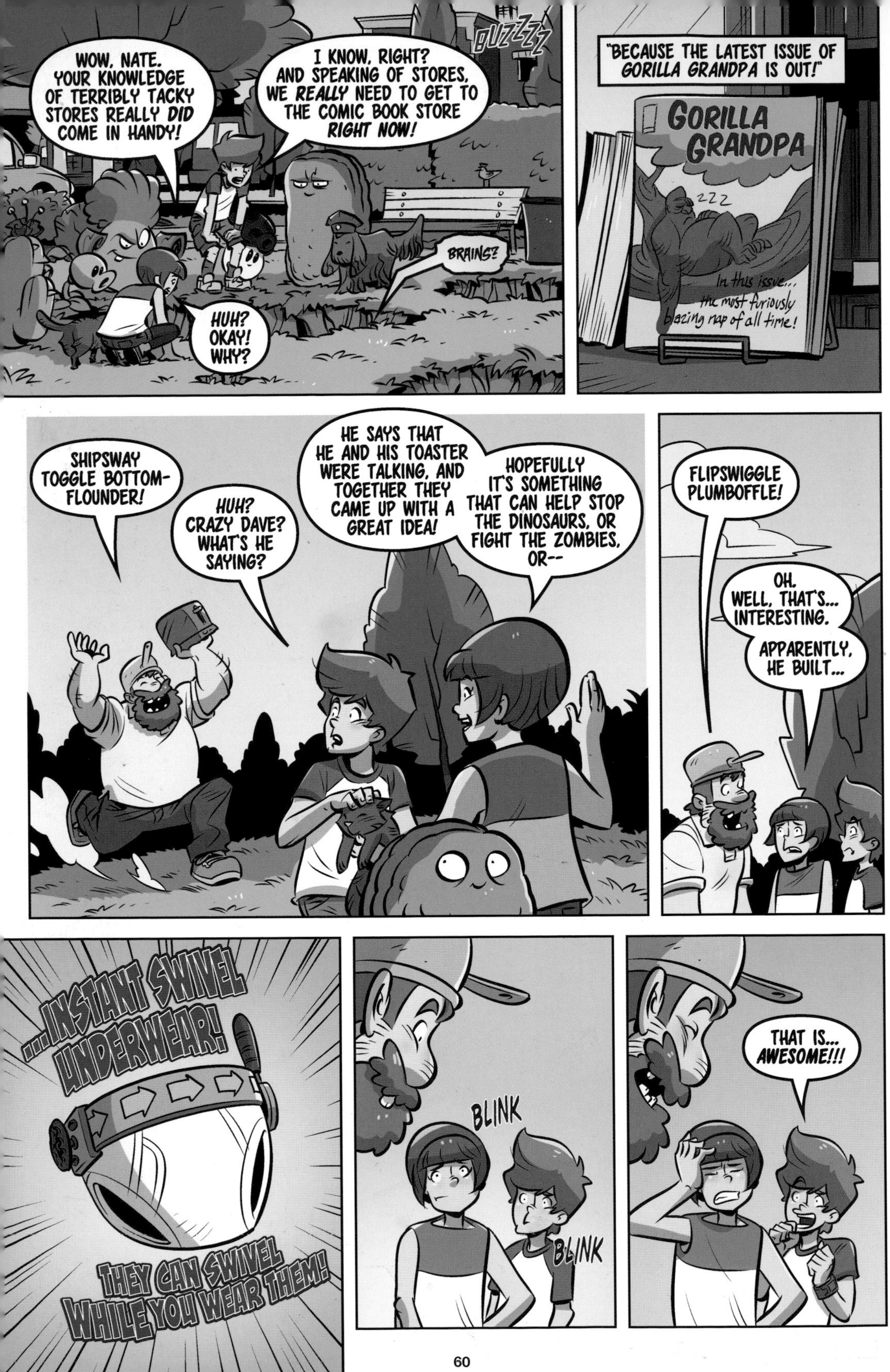
WOW, NATE. YOUR KNOWLEDGE OF TERRIBLY TACKY STORES REALLY DID COME IN HANDY!
I KNOW, RIGHT? AND SPEAKING OF STORES, WE REALLY NEED TO GET TO THE COMIC BOOK STORE RIGHT NOW!
BUZZZZ
BRAINS?
HUH? OKAY! WHY?
"BECAUSE THE LATEST ISSUE OF GORILLA GRANDPA IS OUT!"
GORILLA GRANDPA
ZZZ
In this issue... the most furiously blazing nap of all time!
SHIPSWAY TOGGLE BOTTOM-FLOUNDER!
HUH? CRAZY DAVE? WHAT'S HE SAYING?
HE SAYS THAT HE AND HIS TOASTER WERE TALKING, AND TOGETHER THEY CAME UP WITH A GREAT IDEA!
HOPEFULLY IT'S SOMETHING THAT CAN HELP STOP THE DINOSAURS, OR FIGHT THE ZOMBIES, OR--
FLIPSWIGGLE PLUMBOFFLE!
OH. WELL, THAT'S... INTERESTING.
APPARENTLY, HE BUILT...
...INSTANT SWIVEL UNDERWEAR!
THEY CAN SWIVEL WHILE YOU WEAR THEM!
BLINK
BLINK
THAT IS... AWESOME!!!

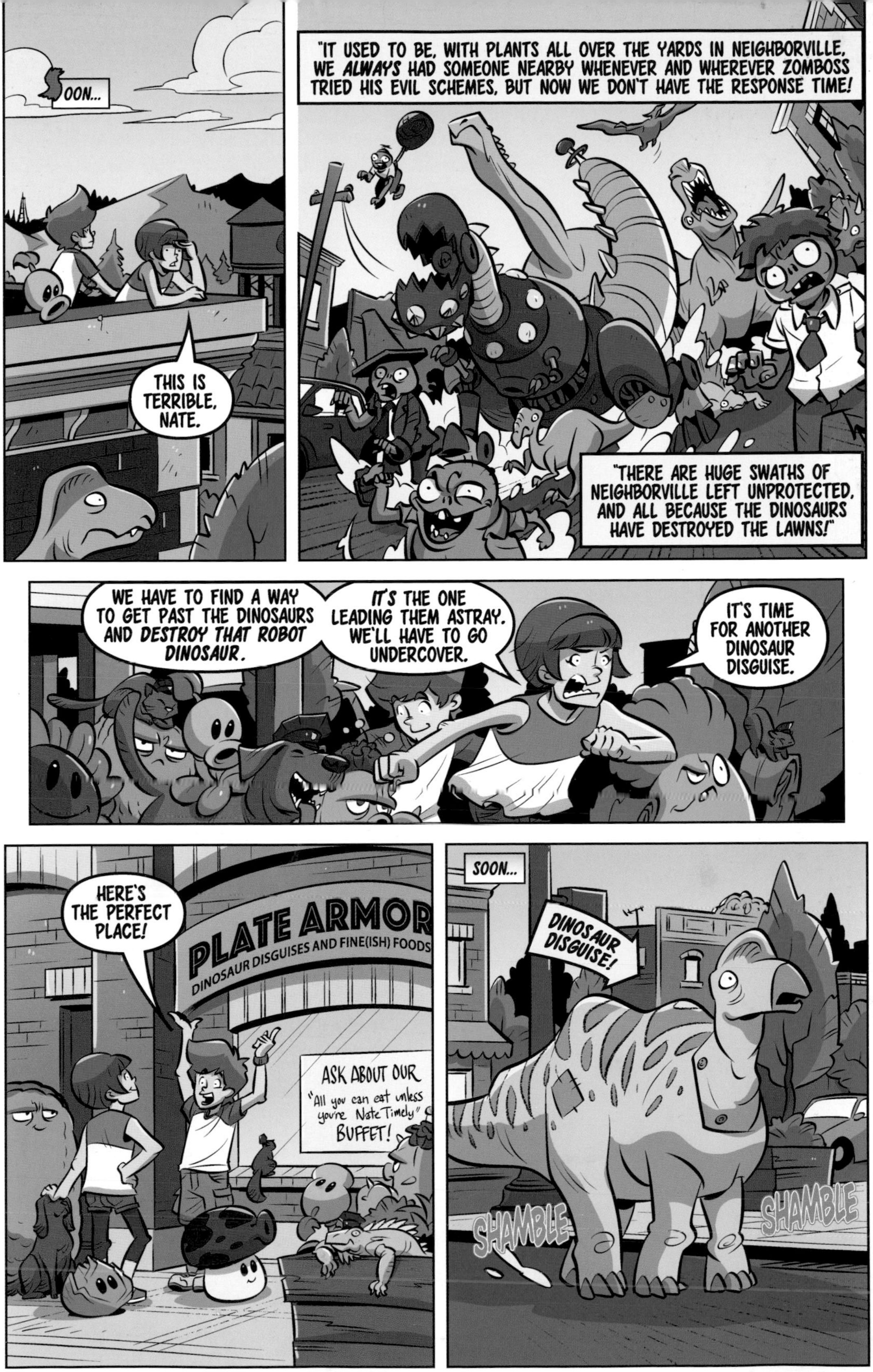
SOON...
THIS IS TERRIBLE, NATE.
"IT USED TO BE, WITH PLANTS ALL OVER THE YARDS IN NEIGHBORVILLE, WE ALWAYS HAD SOMEONE NEARBY WHENEVER AND WHEREVER ZOMBOSS TRIED HIS EVIL SCHEMES, BUT NOW WE DON'T HAVE THE RESPONSE TIME!
"THERE ARE HUGE SWATHS OF NEIGHBORVILLE LEFT UNPROTECTED, AND ALL BECAUSE THE DINOSAURS HAVE DESTROYED THE LAWNS!"
WE HAVE TO FIND A WAY TO GET PAST THE DINOSAURS AND DESTROY THAT ROBOT DINOSAUR.
IT'S THE ONE LEADING THEM ASTRAY. WE'LL HAVE TO GO UNDERCOVER.
IT'S TIME FOR ANOTHER DINOSAUR DISGUISE.
HERE'S THE PERFECT PLACE!
PLATE ARMOR
DINOSAUR DISGUISES AND FINE(ISH) FOODS
ASK ABOUT OUR "All you can eat unless you're Nate Timely" BUFFET!
SOON...
DINOSAUR DISGUISE!
SHAMBLE
SHAMBLE

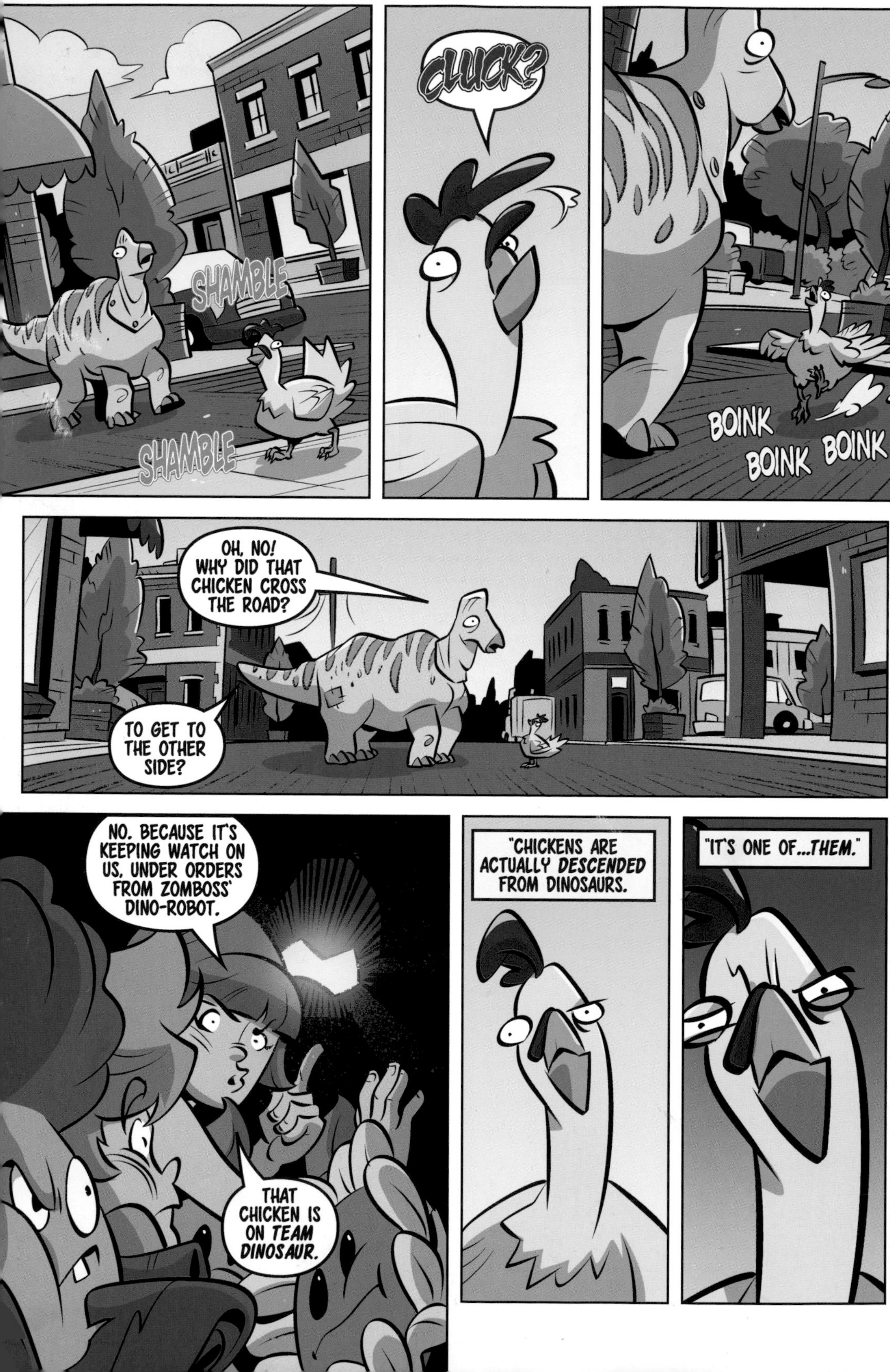

SHAMBLE
SHAMBLE
CLUCK?
BOINK
BOINK BOINK
OH, NO! WHY DID THAT CHICKEN CROSS THE ROAD?
TO GET TO THE OTHER SIDE?
NO. BECAUSE IT'S KEEPING WATCH ON US, UNDER ORDERS FROM ZOMBOSS' DINO-ROBOT.
THAT CHICKEN IS ON *TEAM DINOSAUR.*
"CHICKENS ARE ACTUALLY *DESCENDED* FROM DINOSAURS.
"IT'S ONE OF...*THEM.*"

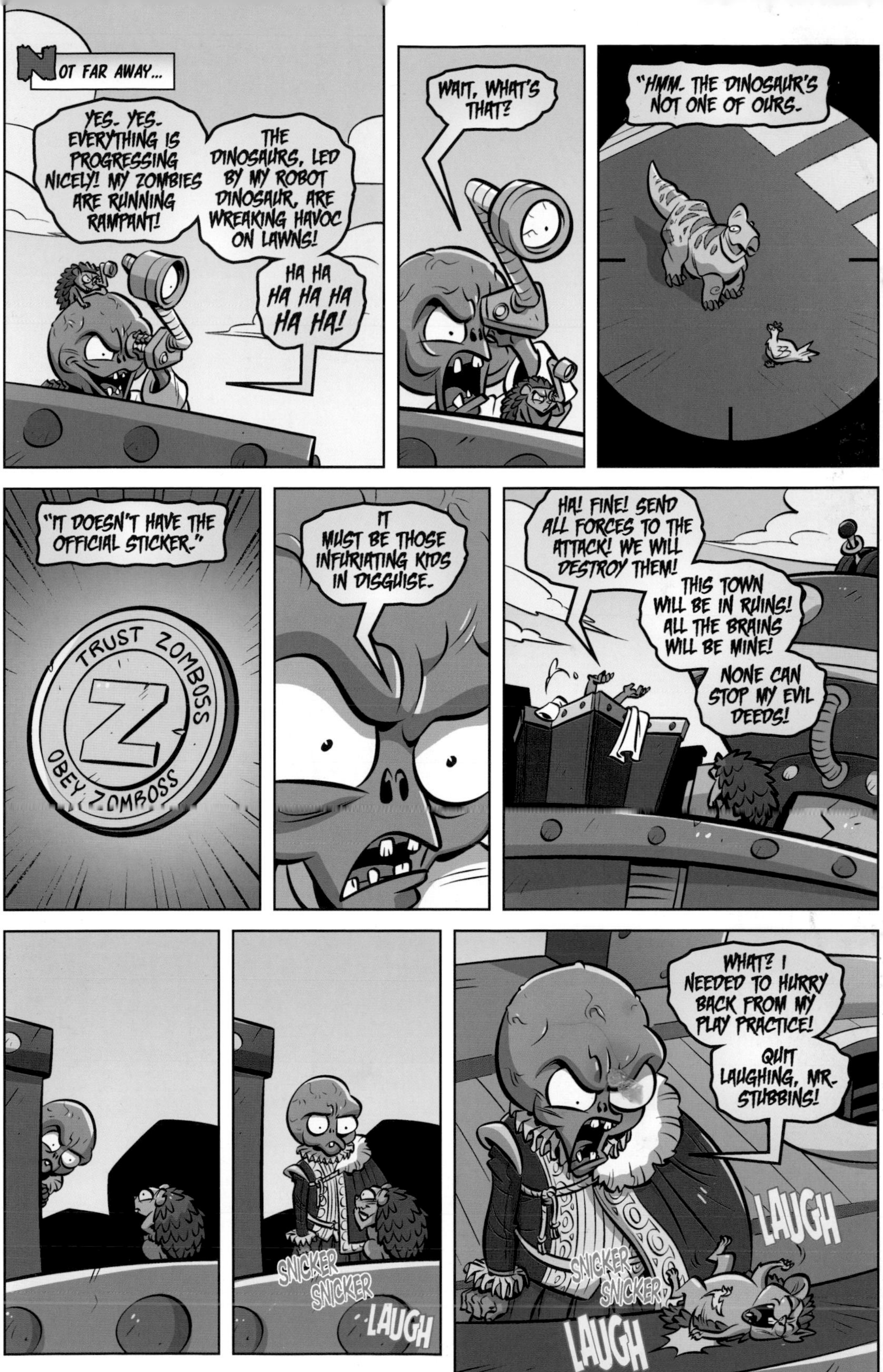
NOT FAR AWAY...
YES. YES. EVERYTHING IS PROGRESSING NICELY! MY ZOMBIES ARE RUNNING RAMPANT!
THE DINOSAURS, LED BY MY ROBOT DINOSAUR, ARE WREAKING HAVOC ON LAWNS!
HA HA HA HA HA HA HA!
WAIT, WHAT'S THAT?
"HMM. THE DINOSAUR'S NOT ONE OF OURS.
"IT DOESN'T HAVE THE OFFICIAL STICKER."
TRUST ZOMBOSS
Z
OBEY ZOMBOSS
IT MUST BE THOSE INFURIATING KIDS IN DISGUISE.
HA! FINE! SEND ALL FORCES TO THE ATTACK! WE WILL DESTROY THEM!
THIS TOWN WILL BE IN RUINS! ALL THE BRAINS WILL BE MINE!
NONE CAN STOP MY EVIL DEEDS!
SNICKER
SNICKER
LAUGH
WHAT? I NEEDED TO HURRY BACK FROM MY PLAY PRACTICE!
QUIT LAUGHING, MR. STUBBINS!
LAUGH
SNICKER
SNICKER
LAUGH

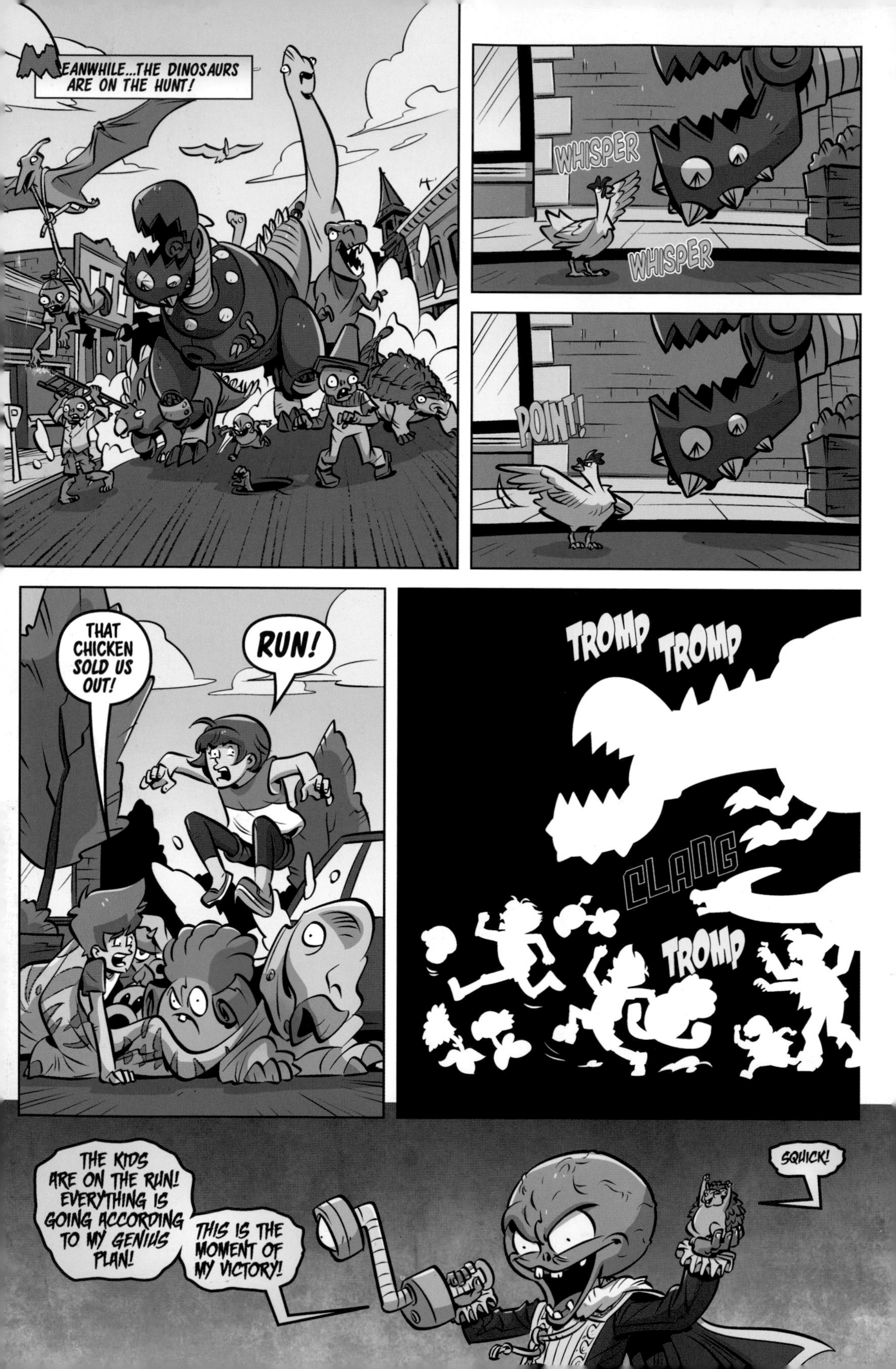
MEANWHILE...THE DINOSAURS ARE ON THE HUNT!
WHISPER
WHISPER
POINT!
THAT CHICKEN SOLD US OUT!
RUN!
TROMP
TROMP
CLANG
TROMP
THE KIDS ARE ON THE RUN! EVERYTHING IS GOING ACCORDING TO MY GENIUS PLAN!
THIS IS THE MOMENT OF MY VICTORY!
SQUICK!

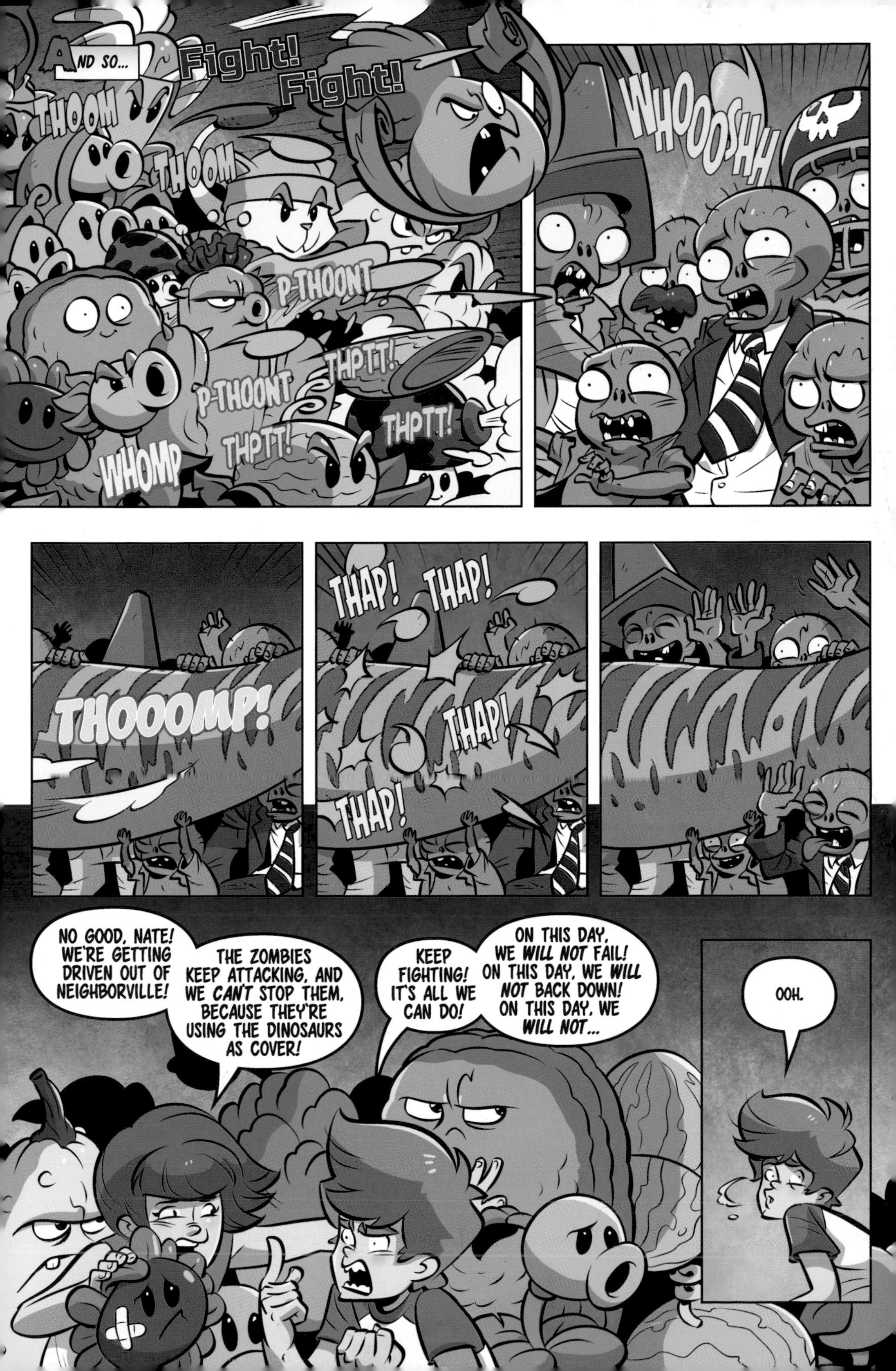

AND SO...
Fight! Fight!
THOOM
THOOM
P-THOONT
P-THOONT
THPTT!
THPTT!
THPTT!
WHOMP
WHOOOSHH
THOOOMP!
THAP! THAP!
THAP!
THAP!
NO GOOD, NATE! WE'RE GETTING DRIVEN OUT OF NEIGHBORVILLE!
THE ZOMBIES KEEP ATTACKING, AND WE CAN'T STOP THEM, BECAUSE THEY'RE USING THE DINOSAURS AS COVER!
KEEP FIGHTING! IT'S ALL WE CAN DO!
ON THIS DAY, WE WILL NOT FAIL! ON THIS DAY, WE WILL NOT BACK DOWN! ON THIS DAY, WE WILL NOT...
OOH.

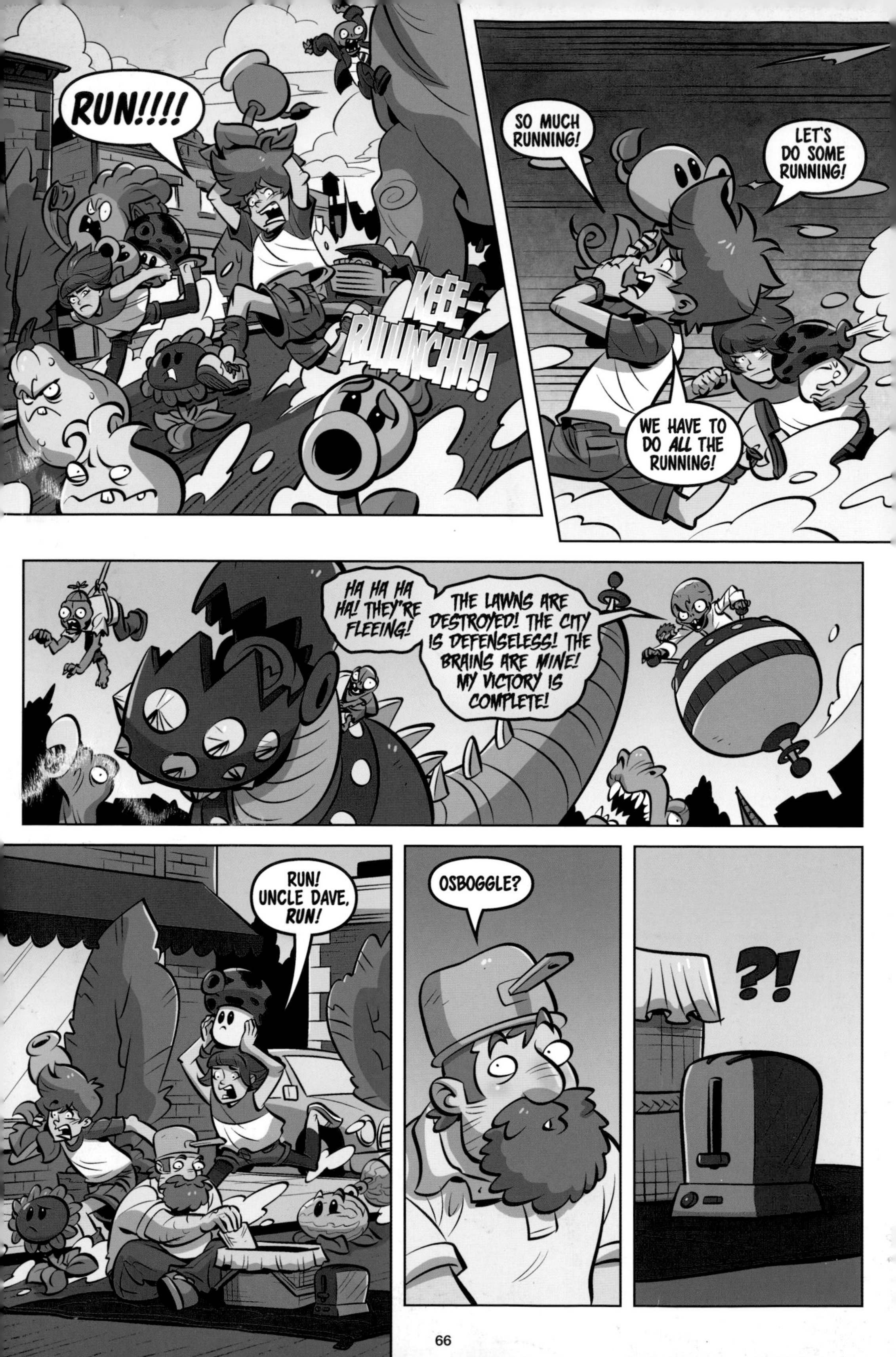
RUN!!!!
KEEE-RUUUNCHH!!
SO MUCH RUNNING!
LET'S DO SOME RUNNING!
WE HAVE TO DO *ALL* THE RUNNING!
HA HA HA HA! THEY'RE FLEEING!
THE LAWNS ARE DESTROYED! THE CITY IS DEFENSELESS! THE BRAINS ARE MINE! MY VICTORY IS COMPLETE!
RUN! UNCLE DAVE, RUN!
OSBOGGLE?
?!

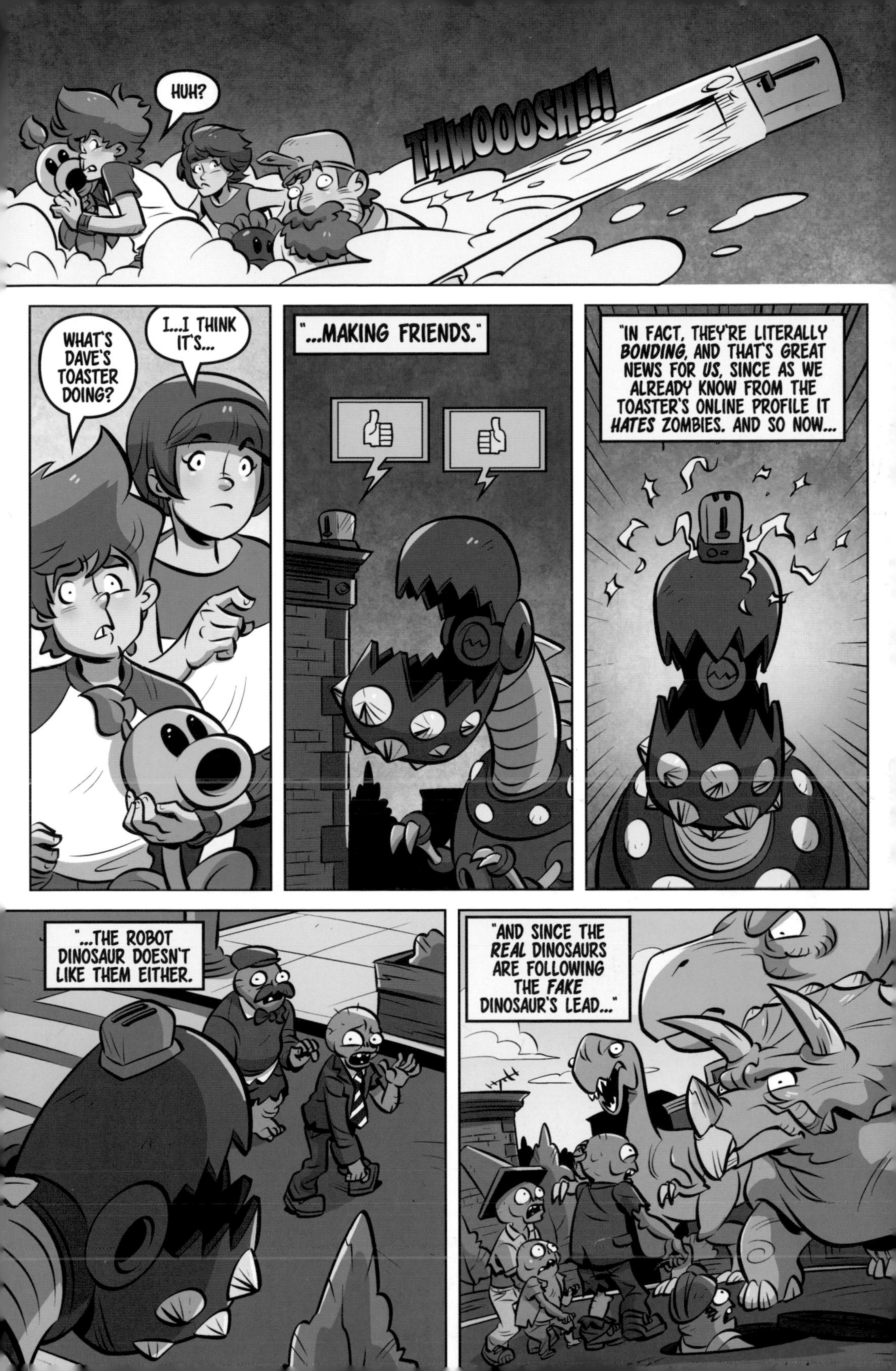
HUH?
THWOOOSH!!!
WHAT'S DAVE'S TOASTER DOING?
I...I THINK IT'S...
"...MAKING FRIENDS."
"IN FACT, THEY'RE LITERALLY BONDING, AND THAT'S GREAT NEWS FOR US, SINCE AS WE ALREADY KNOW FROM THE TOASTER'S ONLINE PROFILE IT HATES ZOMBIES. AND SO NOW...
"...THE ROBOT DINOSAUR DOESN'T LIKE THEM EITHER.
"AND SINCE THE REAL DINOSAURS ARE FOLLOWING THE FAKE DINOSAUR'S LEAD..."

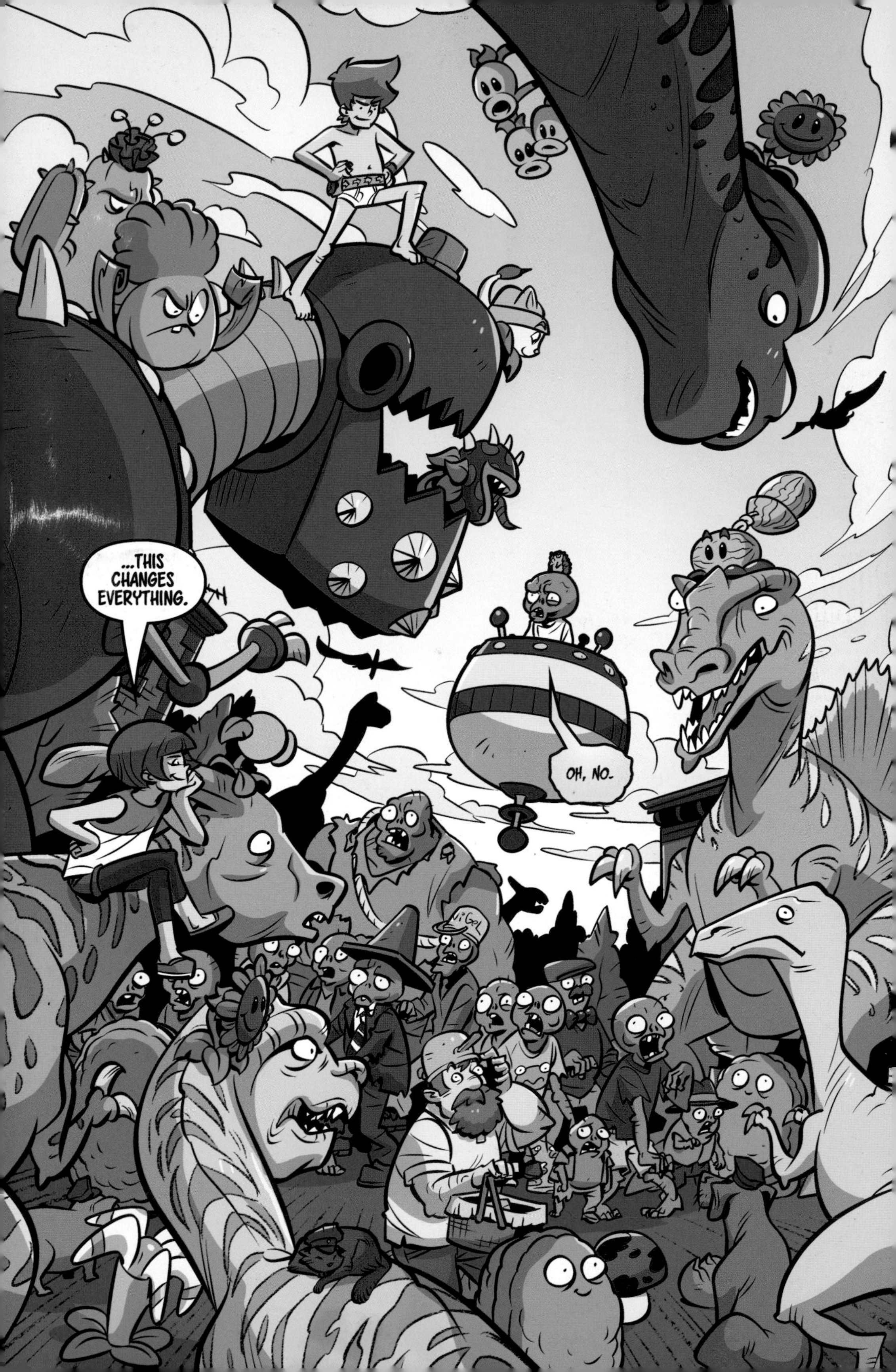
...THIS CHANGES EVERYTHING.
OH, NO.

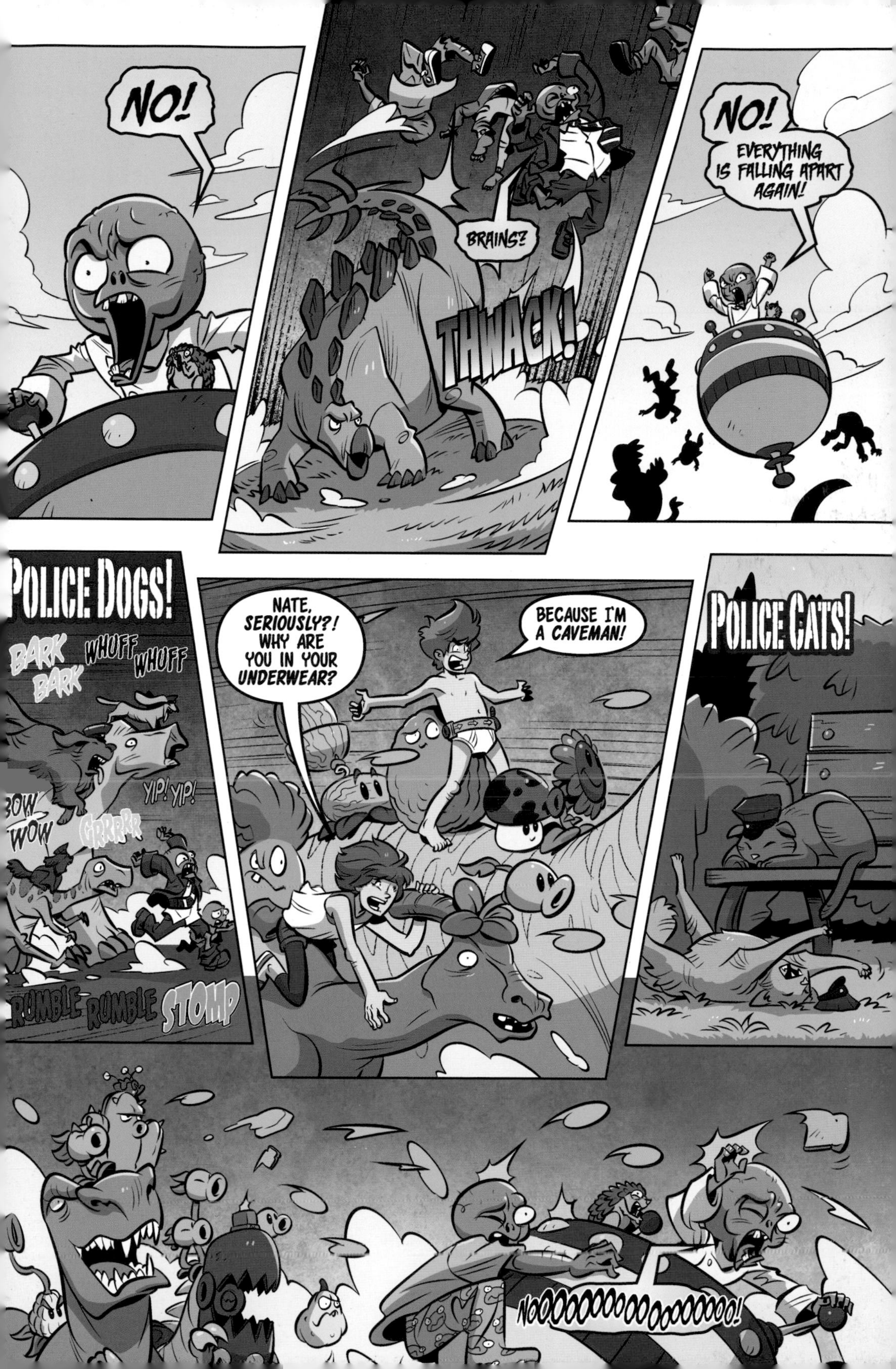

NO!
BRAINS?
THWACK!
NO! EVERYTHING IS FALLING APART AGAIN!
POLICE DOGS!
BARK BARK
WHUFF WHUFF
YIP! YIP!
BOW WOW
GRRRRR
RUMBLE RUMBLE STOMP
NATE, SERIOUSLY?! WHY ARE YOU IN YOUR UNDERWEAR?
BECAUSE I'M A CAVEMAN!
POLICE CATS!
NOOOOOOOOOOOOOOOOOO!

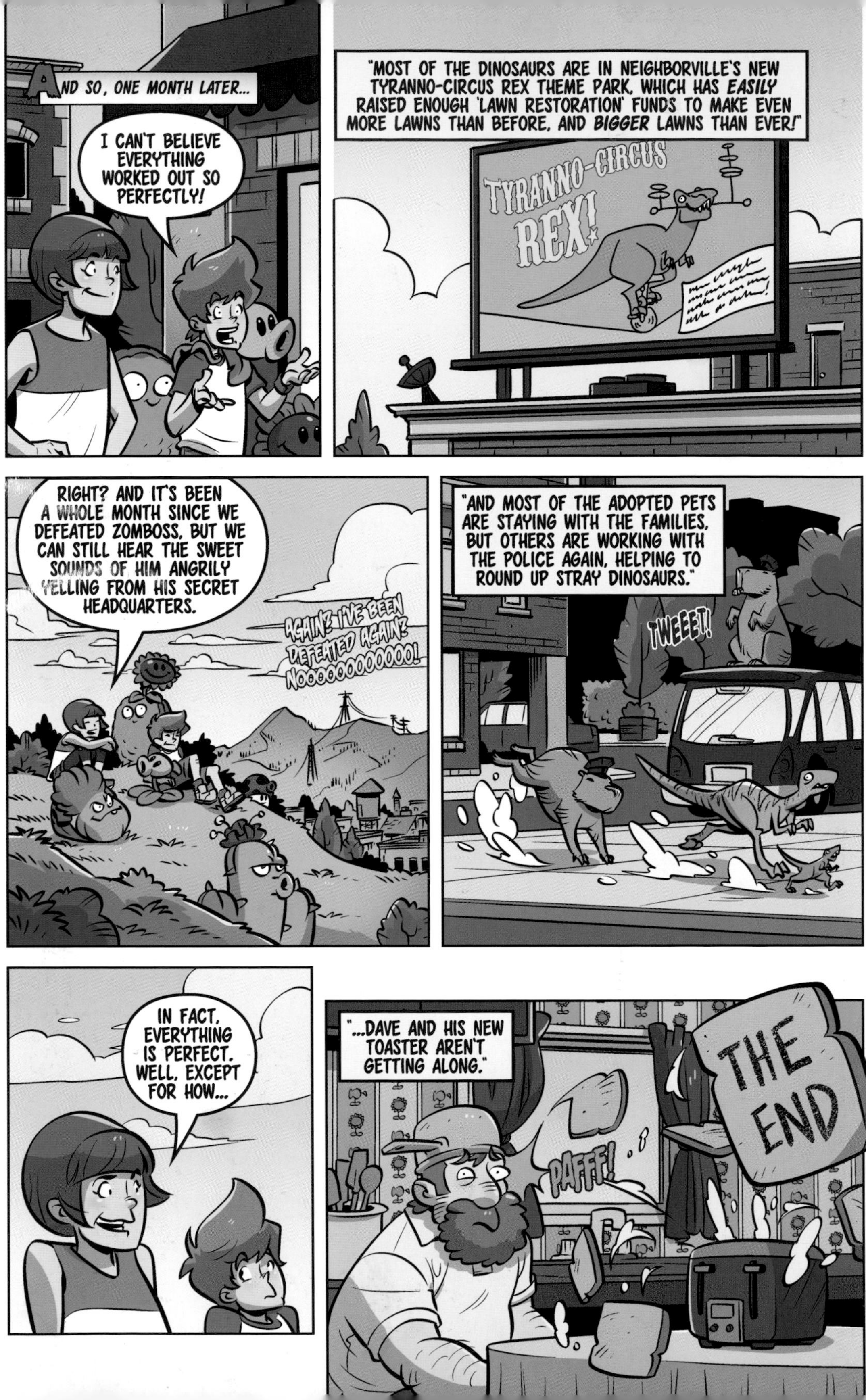
AND SO, ONE MONTH LATER...
I CAN'T BELIEVE EVERYTHING WORKED OUT SO PERFECTLY!
"MOST OF THE DINOSAURS ARE IN NEIGHBORVILLE'S NEW TYRANNO-CIRCUS REX THEME PARK, WHICH HAS EASILY RAISED ENOUGH 'LAWN RESTORATION' FUNDS TO MAKE EVEN MORE LAWNS THAN BEFORE, AND BIGGER LAWNS THAN EVER!"
TYRANNO-CIRCUS REX!
RIGHT? AND IT'S BEEN A WHOLE MONTH SINCE WE DEFEATED ZOMBOSS, BUT WE CAN STILL HEAR THE SWEET SOUNDS OF HIM ANGRILY YELLING FROM HIS SECRET HEADQUARTERS.
AGAIN? I'VE BEEN DEFEATED AGAIN? NOOOOOOOOOOOO!
"AND MOST OF THE ADOPTED PETS ARE STAYING WITH THE FAMILIES, BUT OTHERS ARE WORKING WITH THE POLICE AGAIN, HELPING TO ROUND UP STRAY DINOSAURS."
TWEEET!
IN FACT, EVERYTHING IS PERFECT. WELL, EXCEPT FOR HOW...
"...DAVE AND HIS NEW TOASTER AREN'T GETTING ALONG."
PAFFF!
THE END

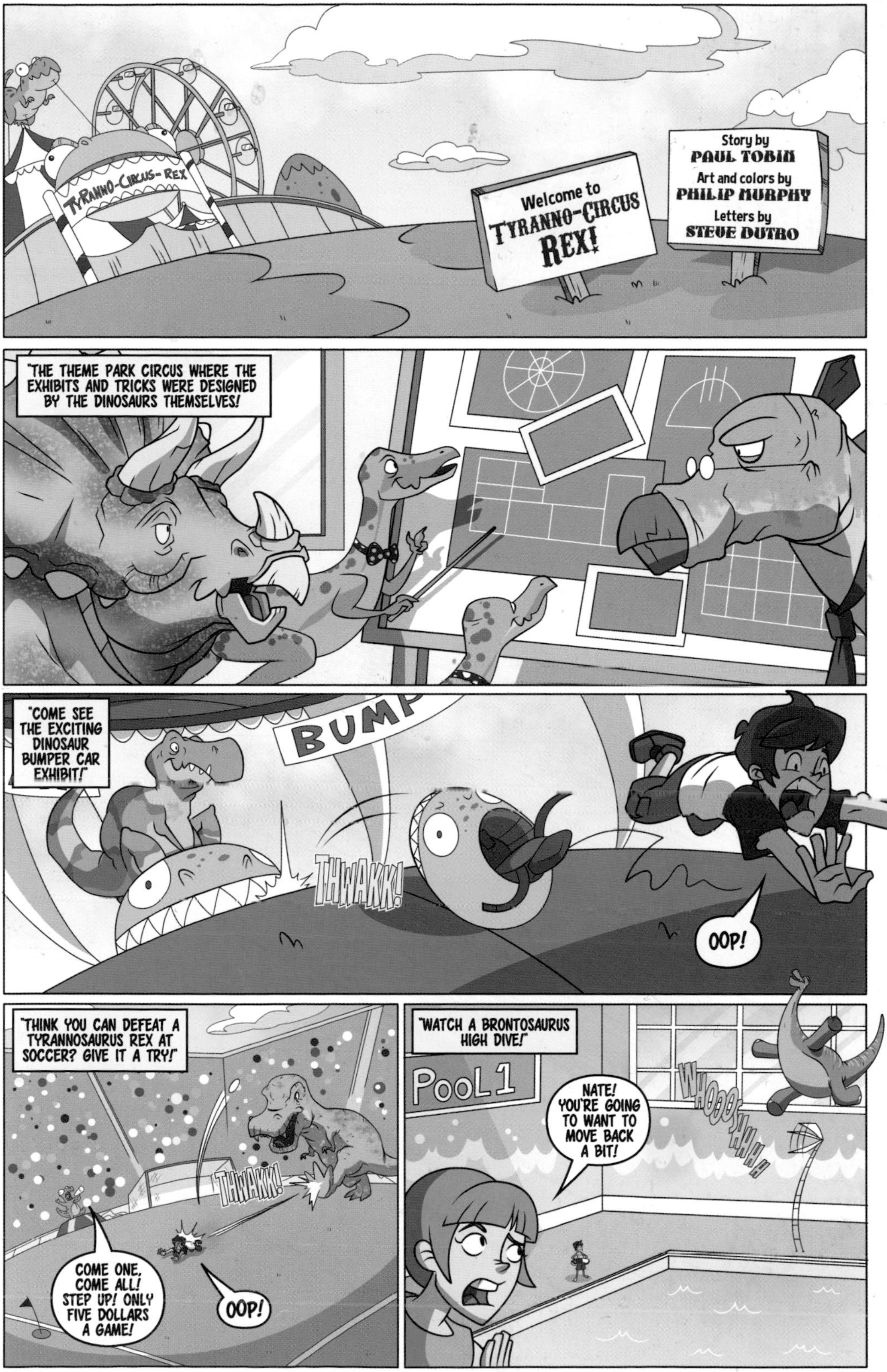
TYRANNO-CIRCUS-REX
Welcome to TYRANNO-CIRCUS REX!
Story by PAUL TOBIN
Art and colors by PHILIP MURPHY
Letters by STEVE DUTRO
"THE THEME PARK CIRCUS WHERE THE EXHIBITS AND TRICKS WERE DESIGNED BY THE DINOSAURS THEMSELVES!
"COME SEE THE EXCITING DINOSAUR BUMPER CAR EXHIBIT!"
BUMP
THWAKK!
OOP!
"THINK YOU CAN DEFEAT A TYRANNOSAURUS REX AT SOCCER? GIVE IT A TRY!"
THWAKK!
COME ONE, COME ALL! STEP UP! ONLY FIVE DOLLARS A GAME!
OOP!
"WATCH A BRONTOSAURUS HIGH DIVE!"
POOL 1
NATE! YOU'RE GOING TO WANT TO MOVE BACK A BIT!
WHOOOSHHHH

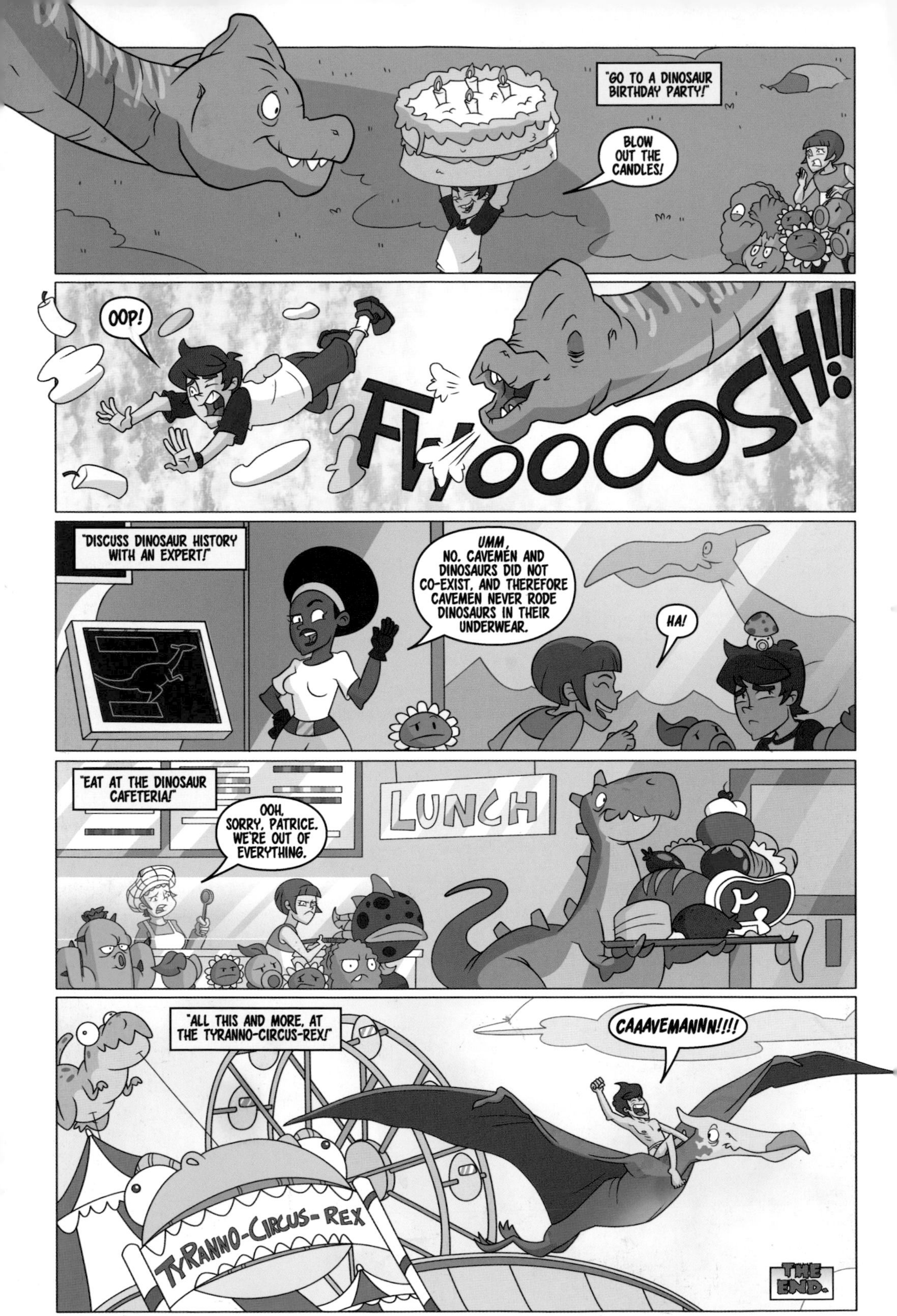
"GO TO A DINOSAUR BIRTHDAY PARTY!"
BLOW OUT THE CANDLES!
OOP!
FWOOOOSH!!
"DISCUSS DINOSAUR HISTORY WITH AN EXPERT!"
UMM, NO. CAVEMEN AND DINOSAURS DID NOT CO-EXIST, AND THEREFORE CAVEMEN NEVER RODE DINOSAURS IN THEIR UNDERWEAR.
HA!
"EAT AT THE DINOSAUR CAFETERIA!"
LUNCH
OOH, SORRY, PATRICE. WE'RE OUT OF EVERYTHING.
"ALL THIS AND MORE, AT THE TYRANNO-CIRCUS-REX!"
CAAAVEMANNN!!!!
TYRANNO-CIRCUS-REX
THE END.

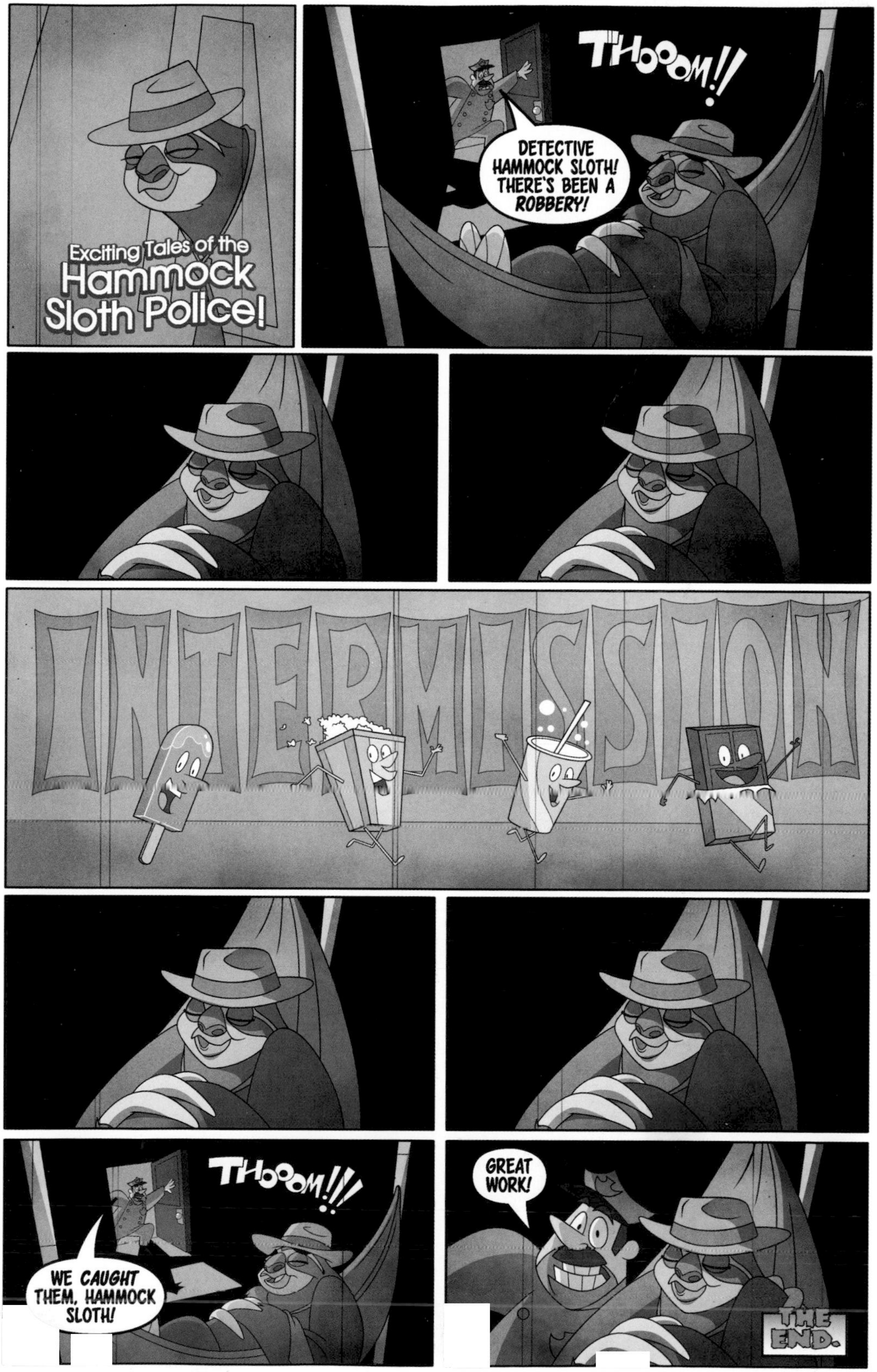
Exciting Tales of the
Hammock Sloth Police!
THOOOM!!
DETECTIVE HAMMOCK SLOTH! THERE'S BEEN A ROBBERY!
INTERMISSION
THOOOM!!!
WE CAUGHT THEM, HAMMOCK SLOTH!
GREAT WORK!
THE END.

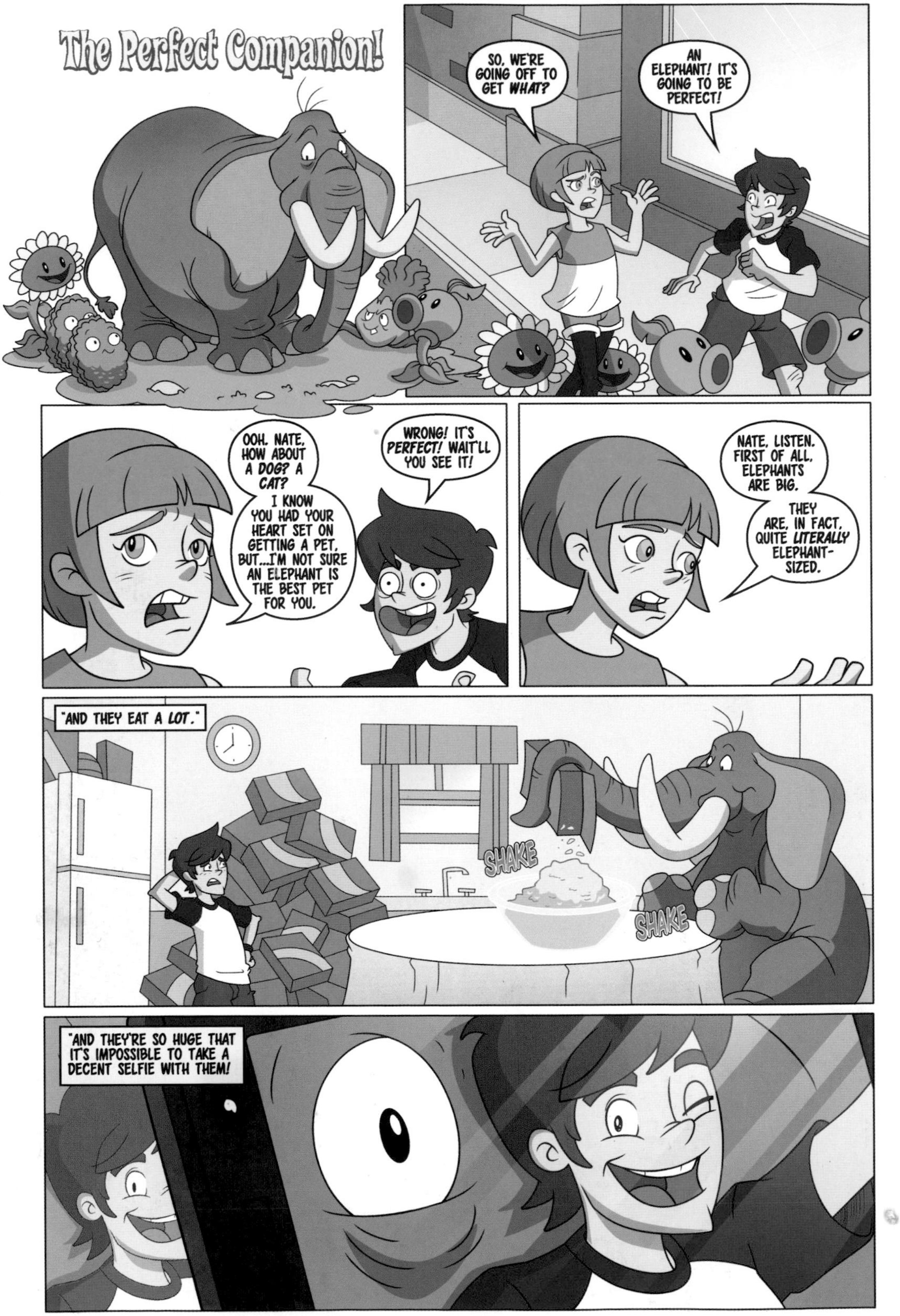
The Perfect Companion!
SO, WE'RE GOING OFF TO GET WHAT?
AN ELEPHANT! IT'S GOING TO BE PERFECT!
OOH. NATE, HOW ABOUT A DOG? A CAT?
I KNOW YOU HAD YOUR HEART SET ON GETTING A PET, BUT...I'M NOT SURE AN ELEPHANT IS THE BEST PET FOR YOU.
WRONG! IT'S PERFECT! WAIT'LL YOU SEE IT!
NATE, LISTEN. FIRST OF ALL, ELEPHANTS ARE BIG.
THEY ARE, IN FACT, QUITE LITERALLY ELEPHANT-SIZED.
"AND THEY EAT A LOT."
SHAKE
SHAKE
"AND THEY'RE SO HUGE THAT IT'S IMPOSSIBLE TO TAKE A DECENT SELFIE WITH THEM!

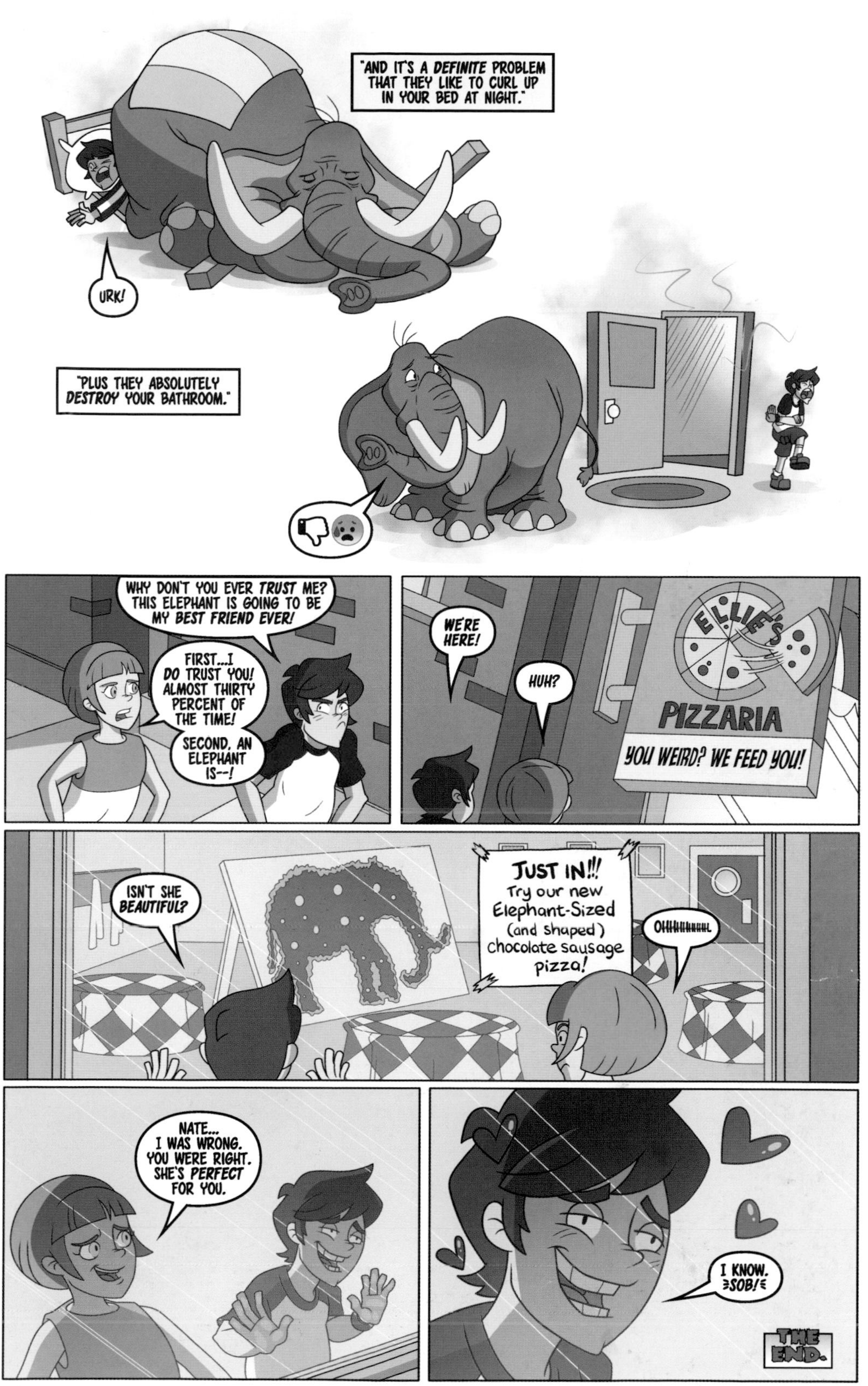
"AND IT'S A DEFINITE PROBLEM THAT THEY LIKE TO CURL UP IN YOUR BED AT NIGHT."
URK!
"PLUS THEY ABSOLUTELY DESTROY YOUR BATHROOM."
WHY DON'T YOU EVER TRUST ME? THIS ELEPHANT IS GOING TO BE MY BEST FRIEND EVER!
FIRST...I DO TRUST YOU! ALMOST THIRTY PERCENT OF THE TIME!
SECOND, AN ELEPHANT IS--!
WE'RE HERE!
HUH?
ELLIE'S
PIZZARIA
YOU WEIRD? WE FEED YOU!
ISN'T SHE BEAUTIFUL?
JUST IN!!! Try our new Elephant-Sized (and shaped) chocolate sausage pizza!
OHHHHHHHH
NATE... I WAS WRONG. YOU WERE RIGHT. SHE'S PERFECT FOR YOU.
I KNOW. SOB!
THE END.

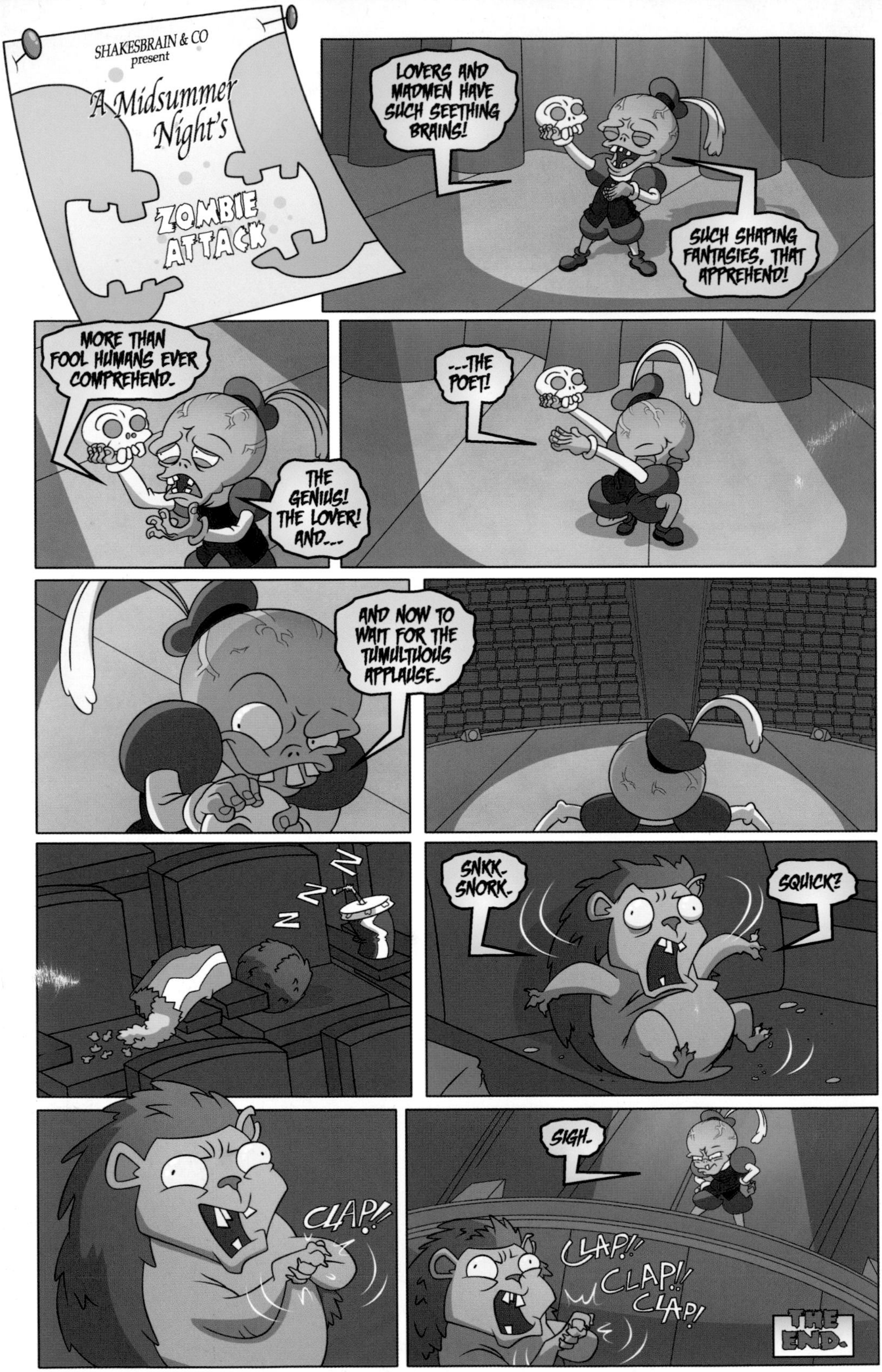
SHAKESBRAIN & CO
present
A Midsummer Night's
ZOMBIE ATTACK
LOVERS AND MADMEN HAVE SUCH SEETHING BRAINS!
SUCH SHAPING FANTASIES, THAT APPREHEND!
MORE THAN FOOL HUMANS EVER COMPREHEND.
THE GENIUS! THE LOVER! AND...
...THE POET!
AND NOW TO WAIT FOR THE TUMULTUOUS APPLAUSE.
Z
Z
Z
SNKK. SNORK.
SQUICK?
CLAP!!
SIGH.
CLAP!!
CLAP!!
CLAP!
THE END.

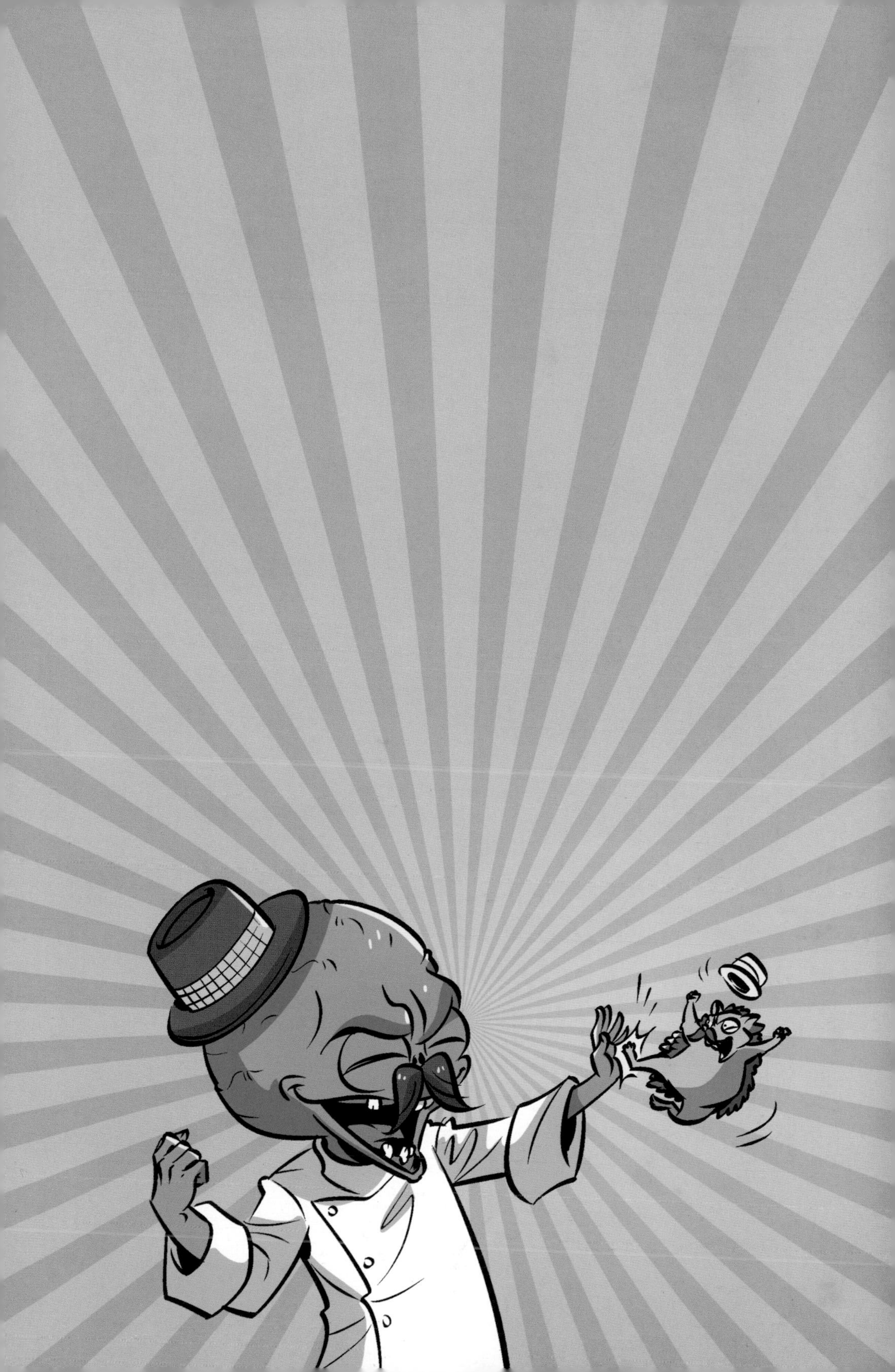

PLANTS VS. ZOMBIES: DINO-MIGHT
cover sketch by RON CHAN

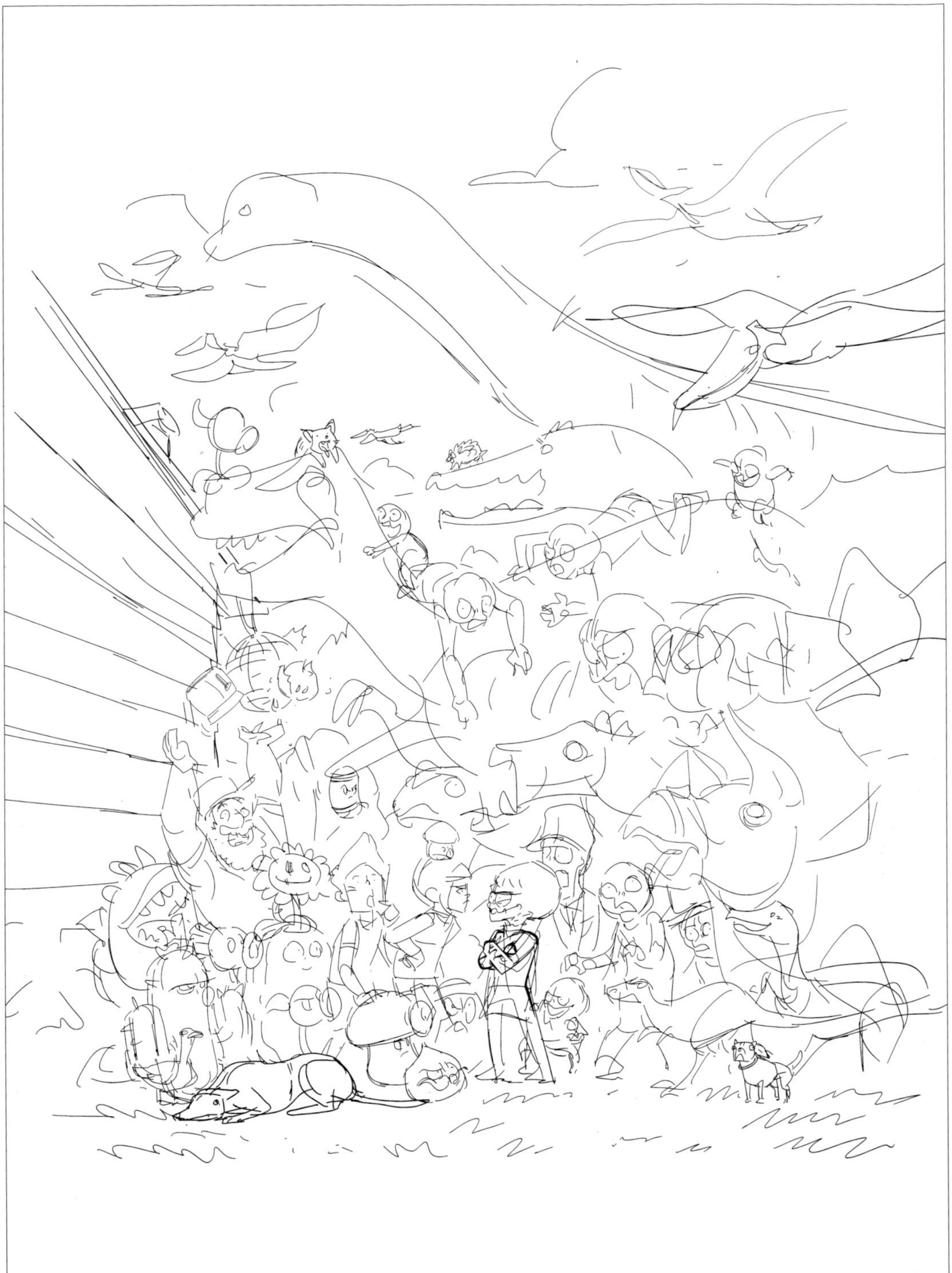

PLANTS VS. ZOMBIES:
DINO-MIGHT
cover inks by RON CHAN

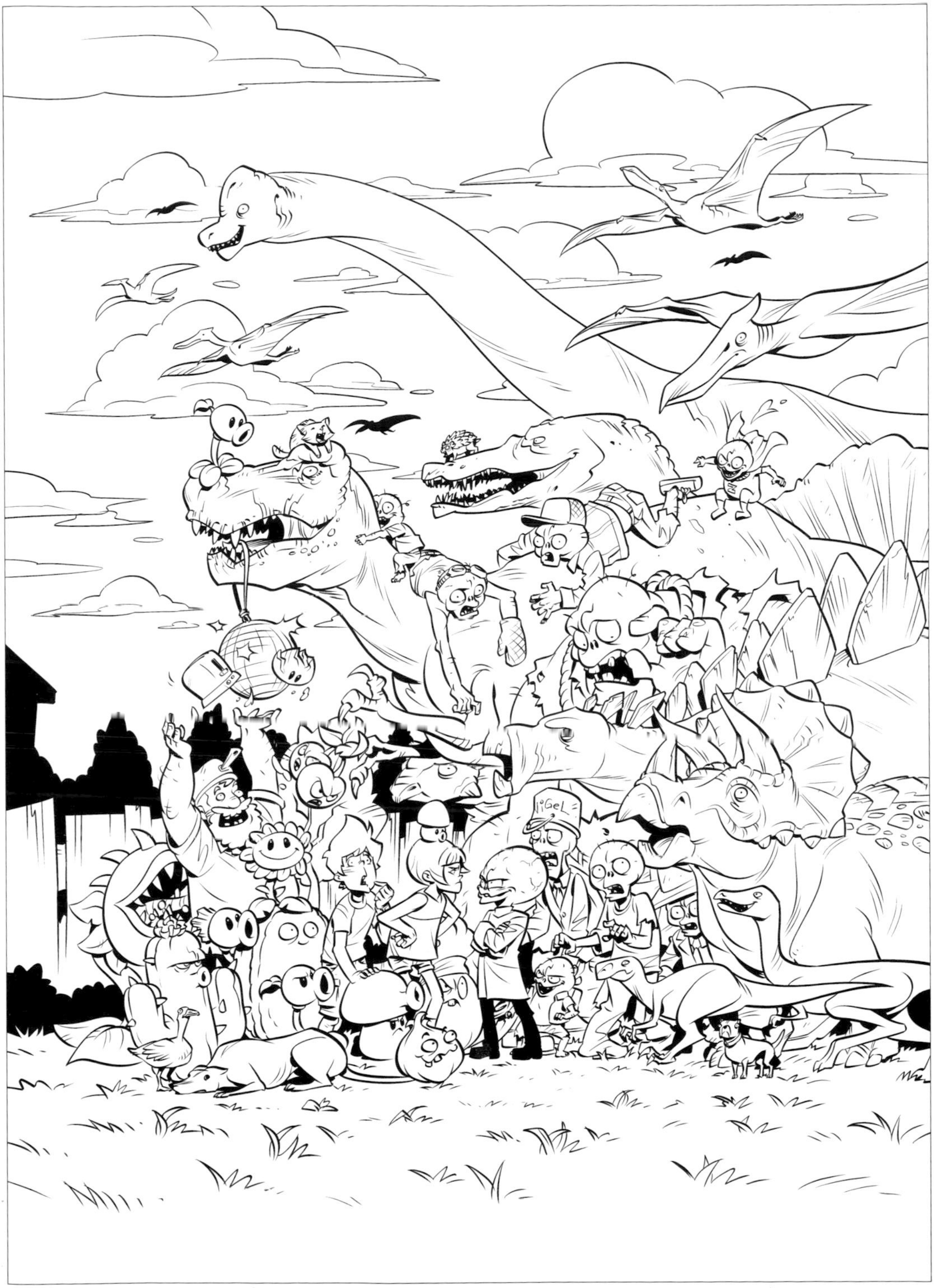
NiGEL

PENCIL ART FROM *DINO-MIGHT* PAGES 28–31 BY ARTIST RON CHAN!

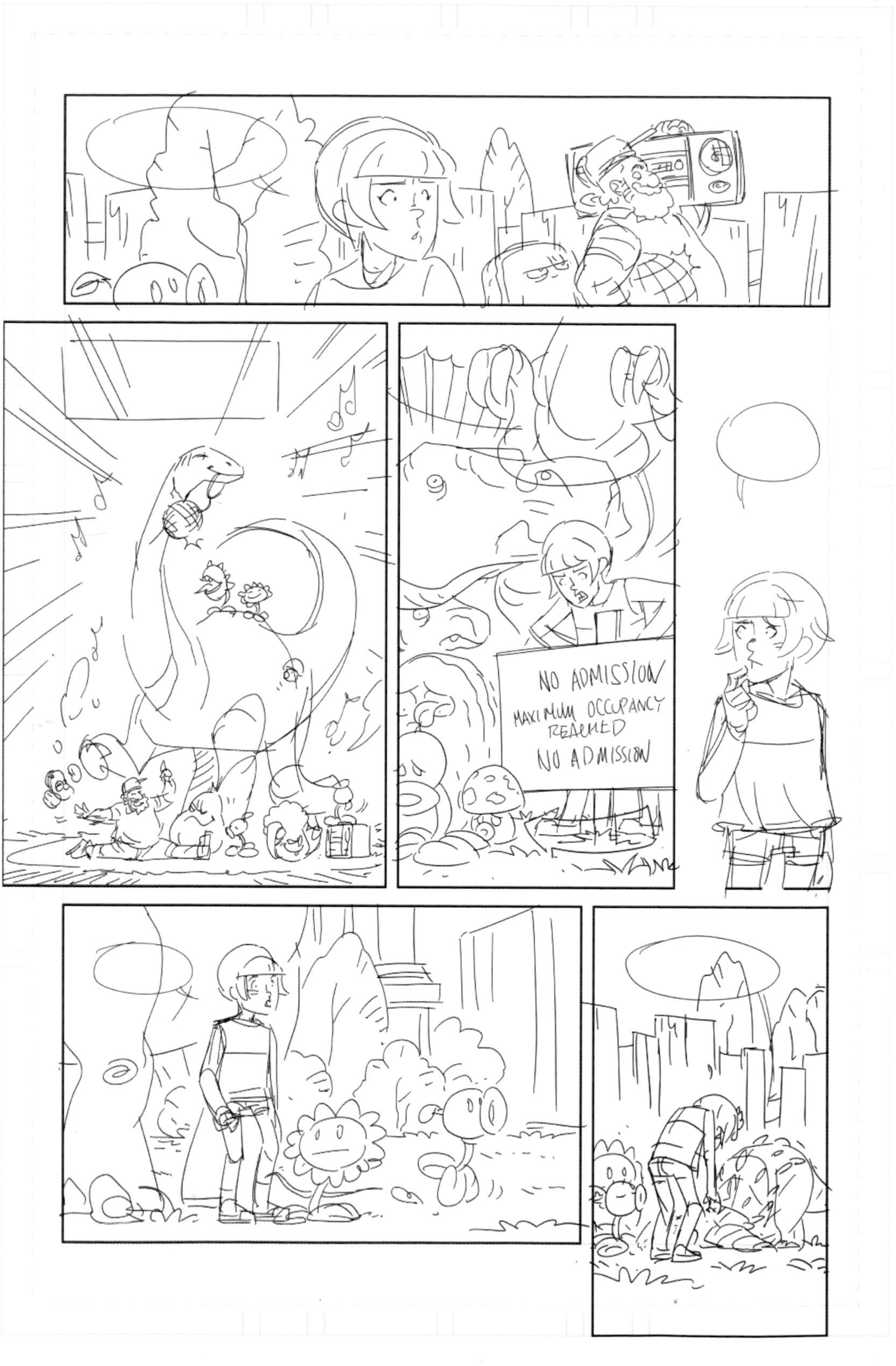
NO ADMISSION
MAXIMUM OCCUPANCY REACHED
NO ADMISSION

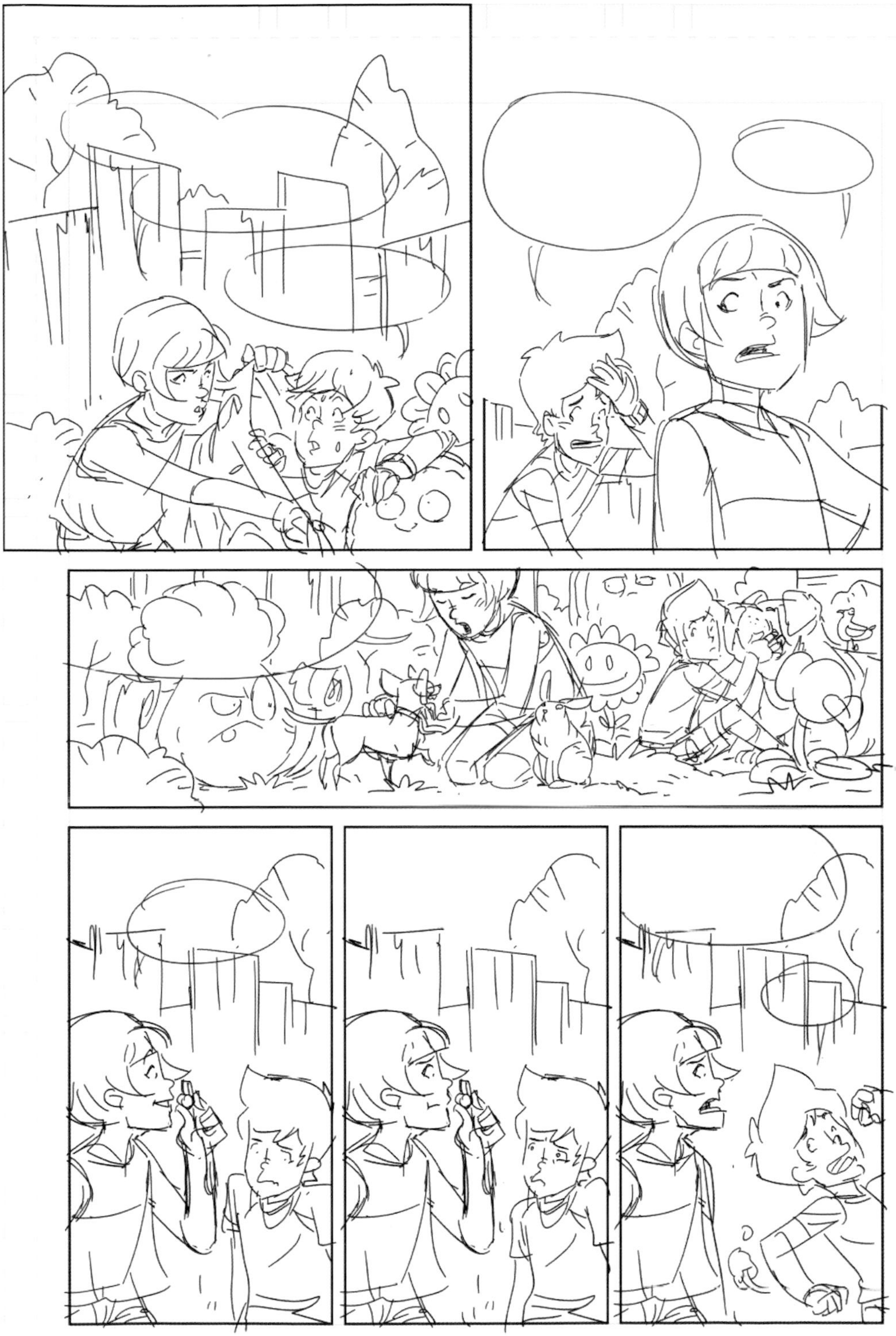

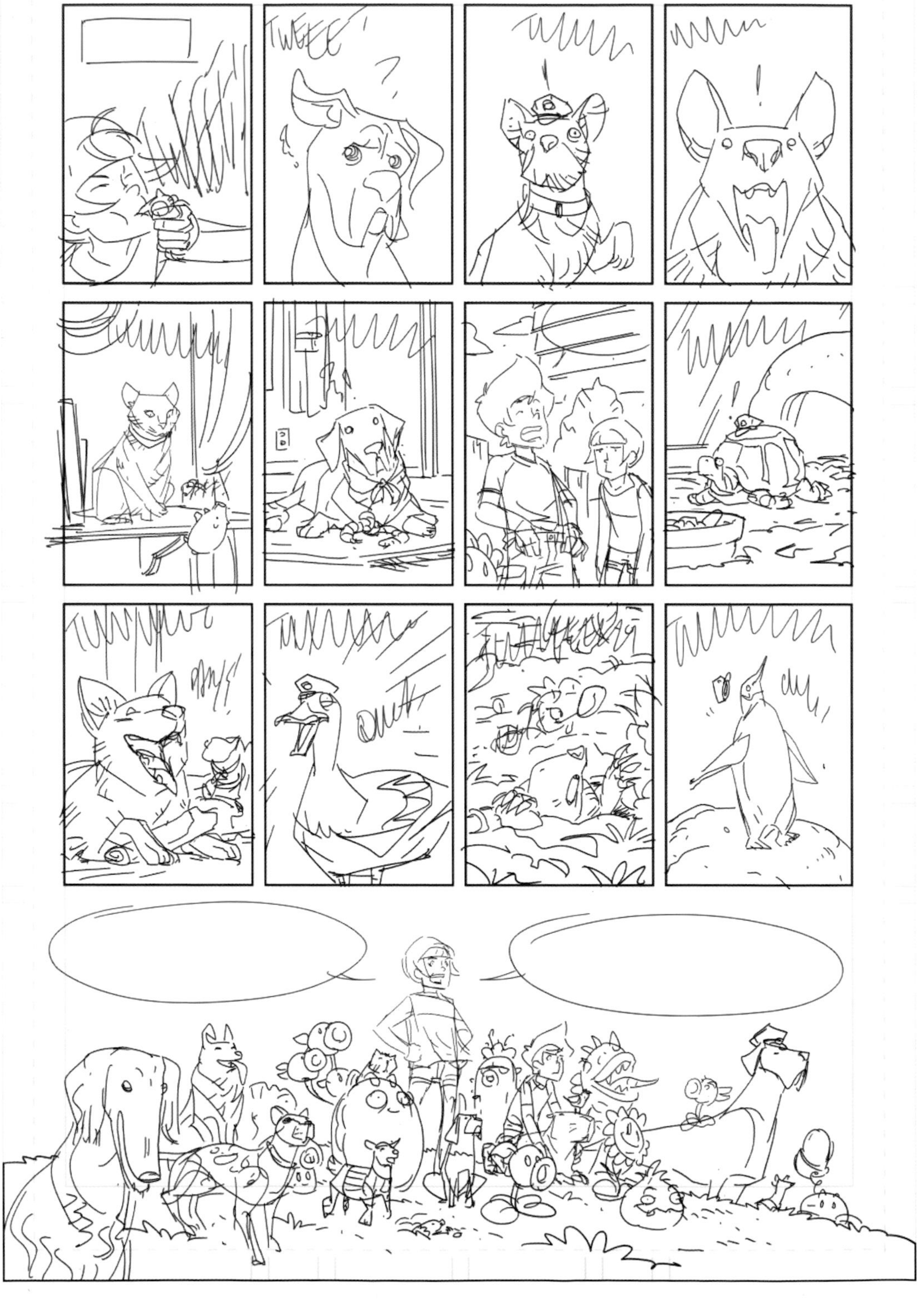

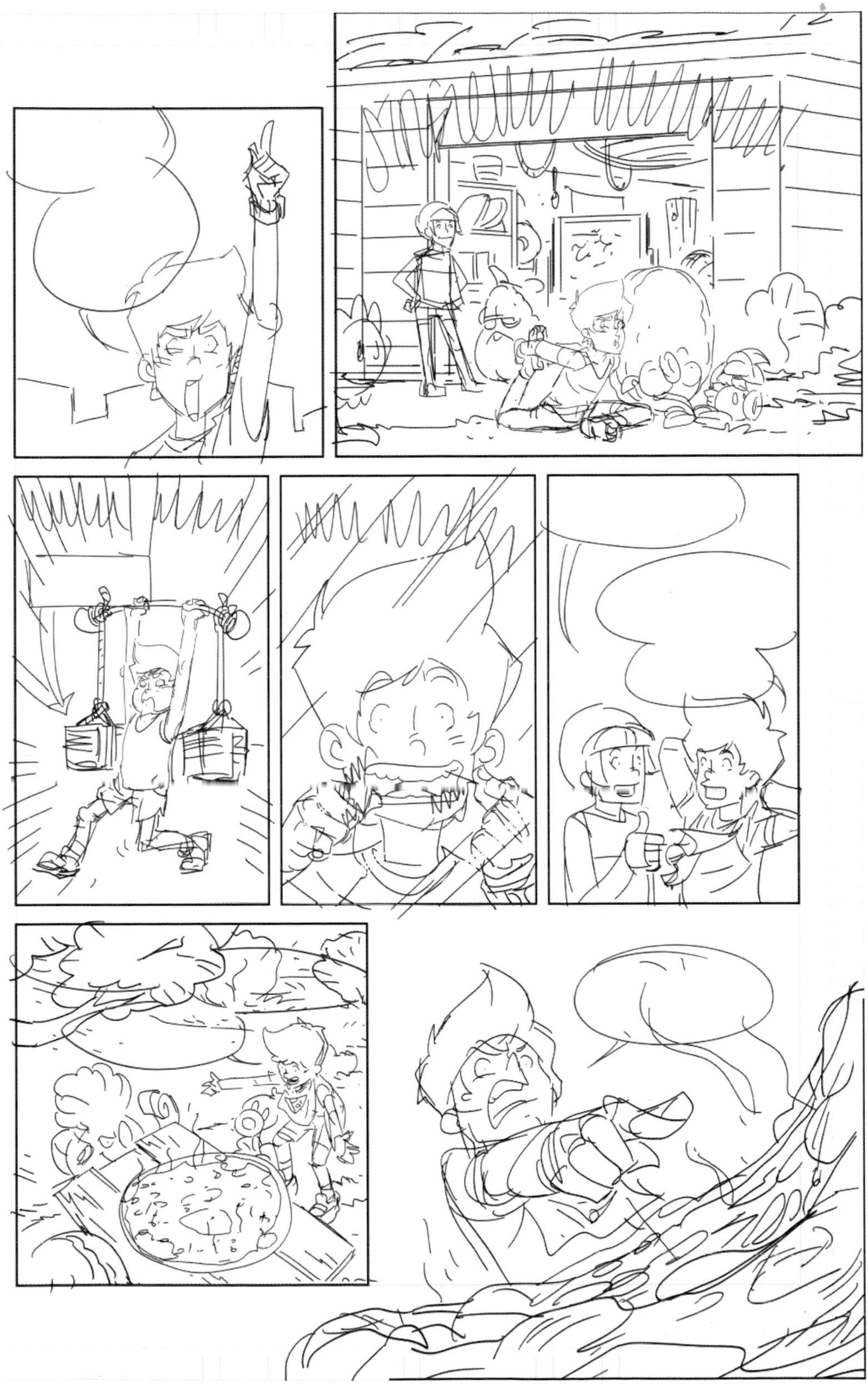

CREATOR BIOS

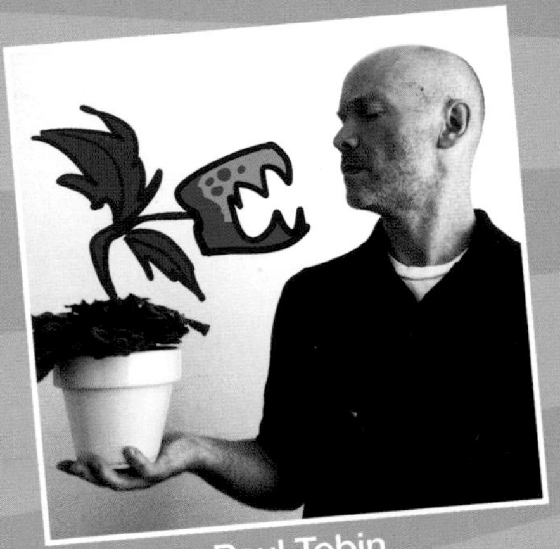

Paul Tobin

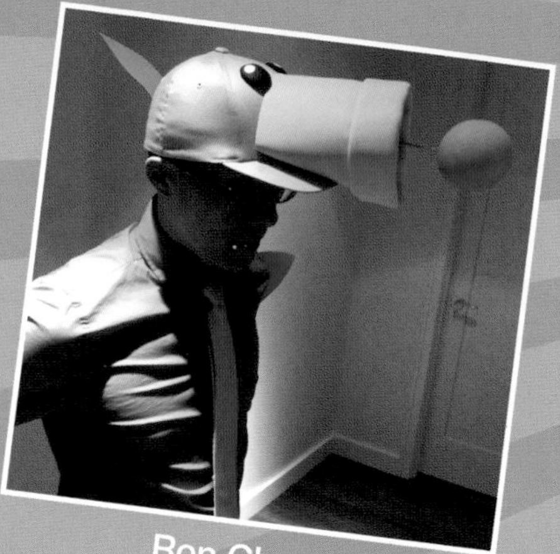

Ron Chan

PAUL TOBIN enjoys that his author photo makes him look insane, and he once accidentally cut his ear with a potato chip. He doesn't know how it happened, either. Life is so full of mystery. If you ask him about the Potato Chip Incident, he'll just make up a story. That's what he does. He's written hundreds of stories for Marvel, DC, Dark Horse, and many others, including such creator-owned titles as *Colder* and *Bandette*, as well as *Prepare to Die!*—his debut novel. His *Genius Factor* series of novels about a fifth-grade genius and his war against the Red Death Tea Society debuted in March 2016 with *How to Capture an Invisible Cat*, from Bloomsbury Publishing, and continued in early 2017 with *How to Outsmart a Billion Robot Bees*. Paul has won some Very Important Awards for his writing but so far none for his karaoke skills.

RON CHAN is a comic book and storyboard artist, video game fan, and occasional jujitsu practitioner. He was born and raised in Portland, Oregon, where he still lives and works as a member of the local artist collective Helioscope Studio. His comics work has been published by Dark Horse, Marvel, and Image Comics, and his storyboarding work includes boards for 3D animation, gaming, user-experience design, and advertising for clients such as Microsoft, Amazon Kindle, Nike, and Sega. He really likes drawing Bonk Choys. (He also enjoys eating actual bok choy in real life.)

Heather Breckel

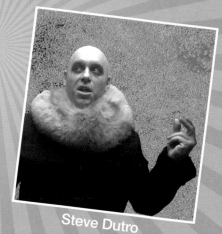

Steve Dutro

HEATHER BRECKEL went to the Columbus College of Art and Design for animation. She decided animation wasn't for her so she switched to comics. She's been working as a colorist for nearly ten years and has worked for nearly every major comics publisher out there. When she's not burning the midnight oil in a deadline crunch, she's either dying in a bunch in videogames or telling her cats to stop running around at two in the morning.

STEVE DUTRO is an Eisner Award-nominated comic-book letterer from Redding, California, who can also drive a tractor. He graduated from the Kubert School and has been lettering comics since the days when foil-embossed covers were cool, working for Dark Horse (*The Fifth Beatle*, *I Am a Hero*, *Planet of the Apes*, *Star Wars*), Viz, Marvel, and DC. He has submitted a request to the Department of Homeland Security that in the event of a zombie apocalypse he be put in charge of all digital freeway signs so citizens can be alerted to avoid nearby brain-eatings and the like. He finds the *Plants vs. Zombies* game to be a real stress-fest, but highly recommends the *Plants vs. Zombies* table on *Pinball FX2* for game-room hipsters.

ALSO AVAILABLE FROM DARK HORSE!

THE HIT VIDEO GAME CONTINUES ITS COMIC BOOK INVASION!

PLANTS VS. ZOMBIES: LAWNMAGEDDON
Crazy Dave—the babbling-yet-brilliant inventor and top-notch neighborhood defender—helps young adventurer Nate fend off a zombie invasion that threatens to overrun the peaceful town of Neighborville in *Plants vs. Zombies: Lawnmageddon*! Their only hope is a brave army of chomping, squashing, and pea-shooting plants! A wacky adventure for zombie zappers young and old!
ISBN 978-1-61655-192-6 | $9.99

THE ART OF PLANTS VS. ZOMBIES
Part zombie memoir, part celebration of zombie triumphs, and part anti-plant screed, *The Art of Plants vs. Zombies* is a treasure trove of never-before-seen concept art, character sketches, and surprises from PopCap's popular *Plants vs. Zombies* games!
ISBN 978-1-61655-331-9 | $9.99

PLANTS VS. ZOMBIES: TIMEPOCALYPSE
Crazy Dave helps Patrice and Nate Timely fend off Zomboss' latest attack in *Plants vs. Zombies: Timepocalypse*! This new standalone tale will tickle your funny bones and thrill your brains through any timeline!
ISBN 978-1-61655-621-1 | $9.99

PLANTS VS. ZOMBIES: BULLY FOR YOU
Patrice and Nate are ready to investigate a strange college campus to keep the streets safe from zombies!
ISBN 978-1-61655-889-5 | $9.99

PLANTS VS. ZOMBIES: GARDEN WARFARE VOLUME 1
Based on the hit video game, this comic tells the story leading up to the events in *Plants vs. Zombies: Garden Warfare 2*!
ISBN 978-1-61655-946-5 | $9.99

VOLUME 2
ISBN 978-1-50670-548-4 | $9.99

PLANTS VS. ZOMBIES: GROWN SWEET HOME
With newfound knowledge of humanity, Dr. Zomboss strikes at the heart of Neighborville . . . sparking a series of plant-versus-zombie brawls!
ISBN 978-1-61655-971-7 | $9.99

PLANTS VS. ZOMBIES: PETAL TO THE METAL
Crazy Dave takes on the tough *Don't Blink* video game—and challenges Dr. Zomboss to a race to determine the future of Neighborville!
ISBN 978-1-61655-999-1 | $9.99

PLANTS VS. ZOMBIES: BOOM BOOM MUSHROOM
The gang discover Zomboss' secret plan for swallowing the city of Neighborville whole! A rare mushroom must be found in order to save the humans aboveground!
ISBN 978-1-50670-037-3 | $9.99

PLANTS VS. ZOMBIES: BATTLE EXTRAVAGONZO
Zomboss is back, hoping to buy the same factory that Crazy Dave is eyeing! Will Crazy Dave and his intelligent plants beat Zomboss and his zombie army to the punch?
ISBN 978-1-50670-189-9 | $9.99

PLANTS VS. ZOMBIES: LAWN OF DOOM
With Zomboss filling everyone's yards with traps and special soldiers, will he and his zombie army turn Halloween into their zanier Lawn of Doom celebration?!
ISBN 978-1-50670-204-9 | $9.99

PLANTS VS. ZOMBIES: THE GREATEST SHOW UNEARTHED
Dr. Zomboss believes that all humans hold a secret desire to run away and join the circus, so he aims to use his "Big Z's Adequately Amazing Flytrap Circus" to lure Neighborville's citizens to their doom!
ISBN 978-1-50670-298-8 | $9.99

PLANTS VS. ZOMBIES: RUMBLE AT LAKE GUMBO
The battle for clean water begins! Nate, Patrice, and Crazy Dave spot trouble and grab all the Tangle Kelp and Party Crabs they can to quell another zombie attack!
ISBN 978-1-50670-497-5 | $9.99

PLANTS VS. ZOMBIES: WAR AND PEAS
When Dr. Zomboss and Crazy Dave find themselves members of the same book club, a literary war is inevitable! The position of leader of the book club opens up and Zomboss and Crazy Dave compete for the top spot in a scholarly scuffle for the ages!
ISBN 978-1-50670-677-1 | $9.99

PLANTS VS. ZOMBIES: DINO-MIGHT
Dr. Zomboss sets his sights on destroying the yards in town and rendering the plants homeless—and his plans include dogs, cats, rabbits, hammock sloths, and, somehow, dinosaurs . . . !
ISBN 978-1-50670-838-6 | $9.99

PLANTS VS. ZOMBIES: SNOW THANKS
Dr. Zomboss invents a Cold Crystal capable of freezing Neighborville, burying the town in snow and ice! It's up to the humans and the fieriest plants to save Neighborville—with the help of pirates!
ISBN 978-1-50670-839-3 | $9.99

PLANTS VS. ZOMBIES: A LITTLE PROBLEM
Will an invasion of teeny-tiny miniature zombies mean the party for Crazy Dave's two-hundred-year-old pants gets canceled?
ISBN 978-1-50670-840-9 | $9.99

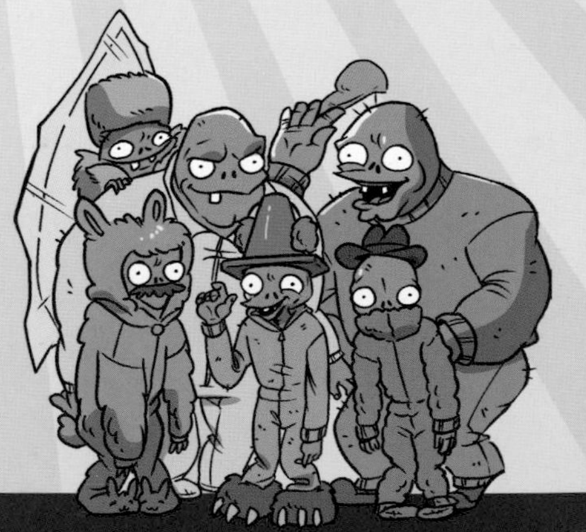

AVAILABLE AT YOUR LOCAL COMICS SHOP OR BOOKSTORE To find a comics shop in your area, visit comicshoplocator.com. For more information or to order direct visit **DarkHorse.com** or call 1-800-862-0052

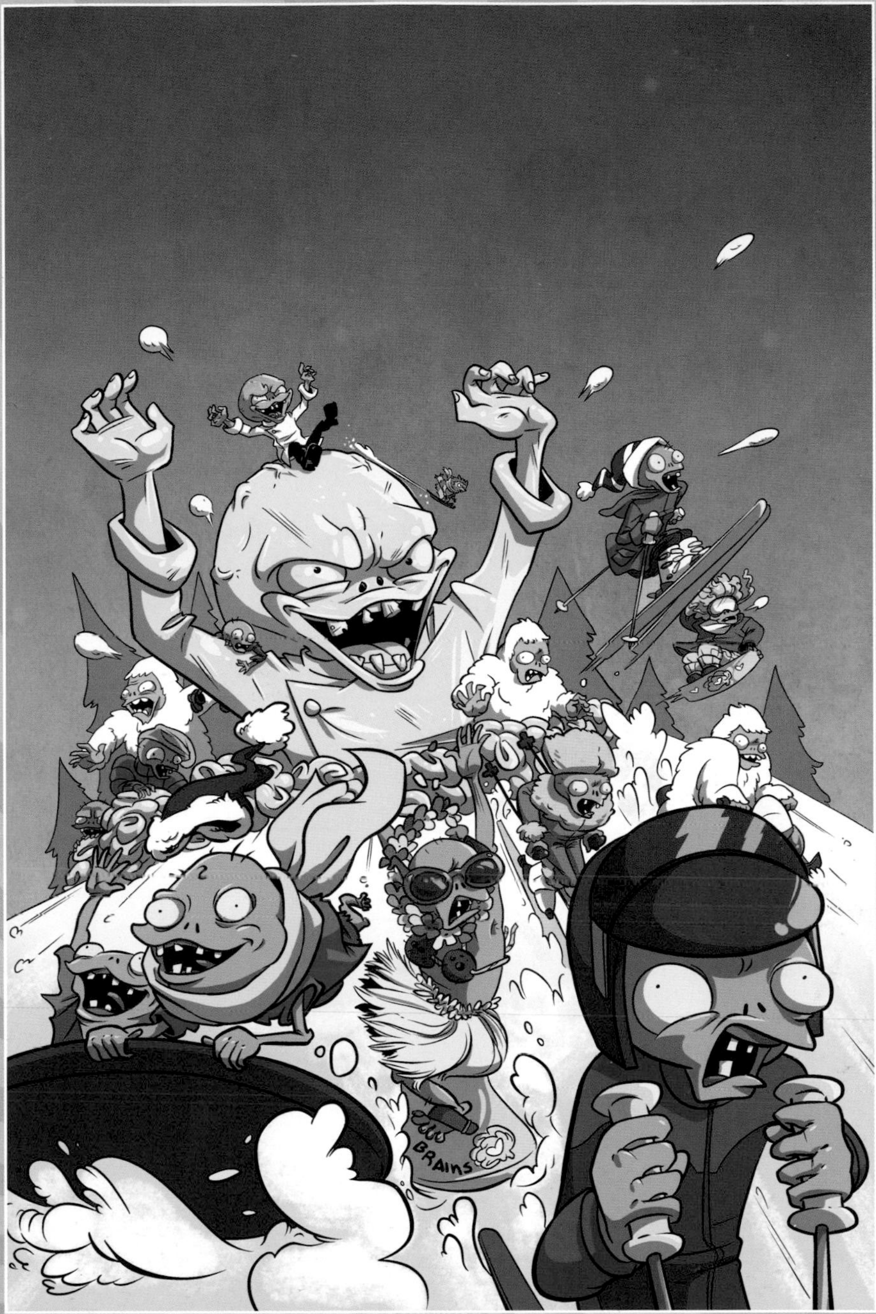
BRAINS

PLANTS VS. ZOMBIES: SNOW THANKS—BLUSTERING IN JUNE 2019!

Dr. Zomboss invents a Cold Crystal, which is capable of freezing Neighborville, creating an eternal winter and burying both plants and humans in snow and ice! With most of the benevolent, zombie-battling plants chilled and immobile, Zomboss hopes to lead his cold-blooded zombie troops on a mission to overrun the city. It's up to Nate, Patrice, Crazy Dave, and the fieriest plants to adapt, fight on, and save Neighborville (with the help of pirates)! This volume features the return of Eisner Award-winning writer Paul Tobin (*Bandette, I Was the Cat*), who collaborates with Cat Farris (*Emily and the Strangers, My Boyfriend Is a Bear*) on this original, standalone graphic novel.

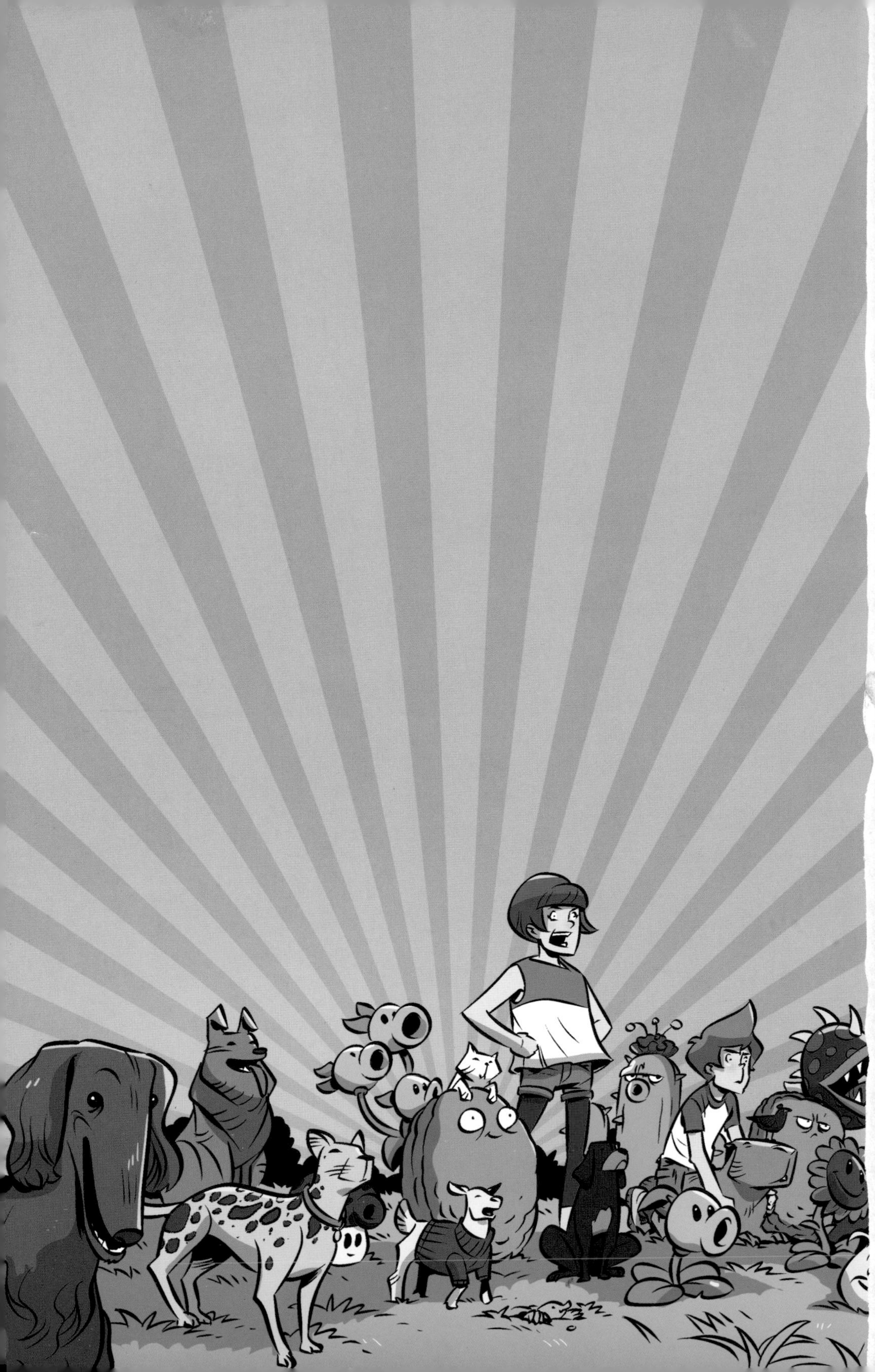

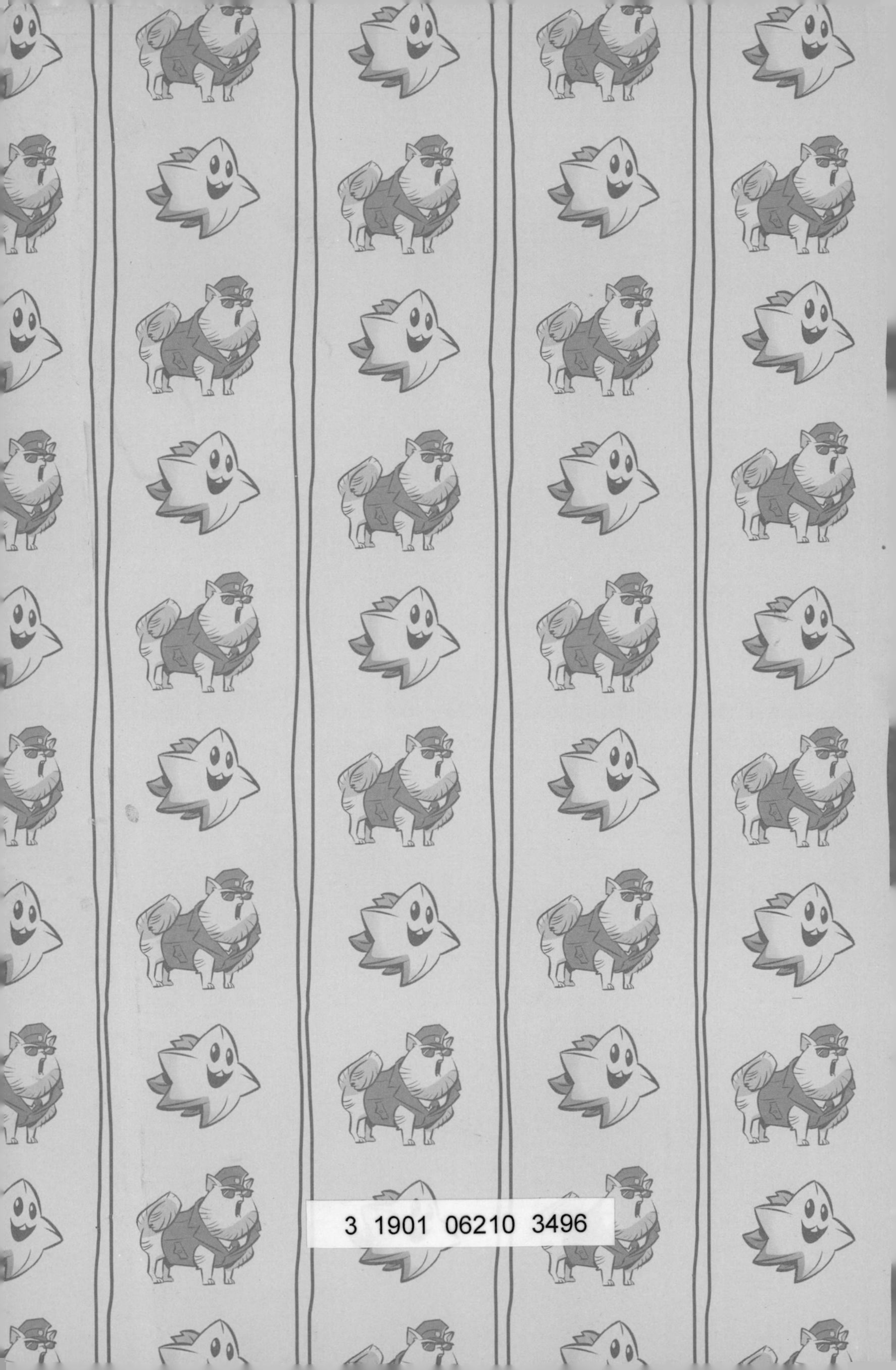